SUICIDE SQUADRON

Bravery and Betrayal in the Bomber Squadrons of World War II

Mack Norton was one of a seasoned bomber crew—and they were scared. Losses were suddenly incredibly high. It seemed the enemy knew their every move in advance. Was it bad luck, bad planning, or had the squadron been infiltrated by German spies? Mack didn't want to play the hero, all he wanted was to stay alive, but the odds against it were looking worse and worse.

Please note: *This book contains a small amount of bad language.*

SUICIDE SQUADRON

SUICIDE SQUADRON

by
Dan Brennan

Magna Large Print Books
Long Preston, North Yorkshire,
England.

British Library Cataloguing in Publication Data.

Brennan, Dan
  Suicide squadron.

A catalogue record for this book is
available from the British Library

ISBN 0-7505-1216-4

Published in Large Print 1998 by arrangement with
Dan Brennan

Magna Large Print is an imprint of
Library Magna Books Ltd.
Printed and bound in Great Britain by
T.J. International Ltd., Cornwall, PL28 8RW.

For Helen Harmsworth Brennan
Subaltern-Radar Predictor Officer
570 Ack-Ack Battery
Royal Artillery
and for
All the Cheerful Lads, Living and Gone
of
No. 10 Halifax Bomber Squadron
Royal Air Force

Chapter 1

I felt dizzy. Now, I thought, now. Then I felt the acute surge come over me, as if my blood were suddenly too hot. I moved faster beneath the trees of Berkeley Square. But the hard, hot ball in my stomach seemed to get bigger and bigger. I started to run. The hard, hot ball was still there. I ran faster, lifting my knees high, running full speed. I began to feel better. But I was sweating. My chest ached. I sat down on a bench under the trees. I heard myself panting.

It was dusk, cool and dim. Then I heard the sound again. Above the sound of taxis passing. I mustn't close my eyes. If I closed my eyes the noise would pound inside my skull. But I was so weary. My eyelids felt so heavy. I lay down on the bench, closed my eyes, and the sound was there in my head, those bloody engines, vroom, vroom, vroom, those bloody engines, saying hurry up, hurry up, hurry up.

The London dusk felt cold. But it was colder up north in Yorkshire. The aircrews would be getting into the Halifax bombers now, their guts hollow with fear. And then

9

that terrible waiting in the dark silence. For a fraction of a second the earth would seem to cease turning. That feeling would be there now with the silence rising all around in the stillness of the fields. That terrible moment between sunset and dark would be there, with all the world dead still; the pilots and gunners would be watching the dying green light of the land being sucked up into the darkening sky in that last, long instant just before the rocket signaling take-off plunged like a dying star across the sky. And they would know the mission was on in the roar and explosions of engines starting up, then the slow rolling death-march of the machines taxiing out of the revetments. Oh, Christ, thank God I was here in Berkeley Square.

I stared up through the leafy branches at the soft, indigo sky. So peaceful here beneath the green leaves stirring faintly in the breeze.

I sat dreaming about my hotel room. Flemming's Hotel. Ah, the wonderful hot water in the white clean tub. It would be so good. No more ice cold showers in a Nissen hut washroom with swinging doors and farm geese walking under the swinging doors into the shower. No more icy Yorkshire winds through the shower stalls. At least not for a few days. How

10

could just plain old hot water soaking flesh be so blissful? How could it be so close to the most wonderful feeling in life? Oh, God, those lovely cool clean hotel sheets. And delicious hot tea and fresh eggs and toast. How long had it been since I'd tasted an egg in the morning? More than two years. There was only soggy powdered egg on the squadron before a mission. It would be heaven waking up tomorrow morning in the hotel bed.

I closed my eyes. I didn't want to look up at the sky. It was darker now. The sun was gone. It didn't help to close my eyes. I could feel the stars up there, millions of miles away, cold and remote, icy cold in the darkness. My flesh shuddered, I felt dizzy again. I opened my eyes to keep the whirling feeling from starting. It was always the same and it came when I closed my eyes. It was like a nightmare; my body rolled in a ball, my knees against my chest as in embryo, and my body was whirling away from the earth, outward, into space, higher and higher, whirling then spinning, faster and faster toward the cold, remote stars.

I blinked my eyes and shook my head a couple of times. I stood up. The moon was out, round and orange. The dizzy feeling slowly dissolved. I forced myself to whistle and walk slowly. Sometimes it helped, but I couldn't keep my eyes from looking up at the moon. It looked as if it were on fire. A big round ball of orange fire. My soul whirling alone in space.

Far below me the North Sea was black, blacker than the sky. The moon shining down on all the black, coldness of the sea. The night fighters were cruising like sharks smelling for blood. The North Sea, a gigantic cold monster, was waiting, patient and merciless.

I turned into Shepherd Market. The whores with their white powdered faces moved like ghosts against the dark shop windows. I went quickly into Shepherd's Bar and squeezed between two Royal Artillery majors and ordered a gin and Dubonnet. The room was jammed.

A sudden fear gripped me. Where was Joan? Maybe a bomb had hit her train. Loneliness swept over me among all these people. The din of their voices rose around me. Their voices seemed to touch my skin. Only last week a Dornier had dropped a bomb through the glass roof of the train station at York. I began to murmur her name. Joan, Joan. Like a litany, a prayer. The major next to me glared, cleared his throat and turned away. I looked at my drink. The glass was empty.

I couldn't recall drinking it. I ordered another quickly.

Suddenly her voice was there. I thought I was dreaming. Where was she? I turned. Faces blurred in the din of voices.

'Mack,' I heard her voice through the din of voices. 'Mack.'

But I could not see her. Her voice sounded like an echo. Was she really here? I felt suddenly empty, futile. I turned again, to the bar. Was I drunk or dreaming? And then suddenly she was there, her face a few inches in front of my eyes, as if she had popped magically out of the floor.

'Where were you?'

'I'm sorry I'm late,' she said. Her eyes were sapphires. She was beautiful, tall; jet-black hair, swept smoothly over her skull and coiled at the base of her neck, the coil pinioned by a small Spanish comb. She was Irish Gypsy on her father's side and Norman on her mother's side. Joan DeMarney, her WAAF Section Officer's cap raked a little, a little swanky, slanted on the side of her head. Her smile was wonderful. I longed to kiss her.

Her fingers touched my fingers. I drew her hand down and pressed it against my hip. She smiled. My heart kicked over. I felt alive again.

'There was a bomb on the tracks,' she said.

'Come on now,' I said. She must be kidding. It was an old story. Phone the Mess when you're going to return late from leave: 'Bomb on the tracks, sir. Train delayed, sir.'

'Truth,' she said. 'How long do you have?'

'Forty-eight,' I said quickly because the numbers sunk me in guilt. I should be with them. Yorkshire. I should be taking off with them. They would be going out alone to die. I should be with them. I turned quickly to the bar to kill the guilt. Forty-eight hours reprieve. It wasn't enough.

'Two gin and Dubonnet,' I called to the bartender.

She stood there with a cigarette between her lips. My hand, touching the lighter in my pocket, trembled. I didn't want her to see my hands.

She stooped her head toward me. I handed her the lighter. She did not take it. My hand was shaking.

For a fraction of a second she seemed to glance at my hand, lifting her eyes from the tip of her cigarette, and then her fingers took the lighter, and her long dark lashes blinked, concealing her gaze.

She handed me the lighter. I took it quickly.

'How's everything?' she said in that

bright, cheery, innocent voice the British are so fond of using when they're sinking slowly face-to-face into quicksand.

'Fine,' I said. I felt numb, dead. Be cheerful, I thought, don't spoil her leave. A plume of smoke swirled across her face. I stared at her. Suddenly she stepped past me, fetched our drinks from the bartender.

'Here,' I heard myself say. 'I'll get it.' I felt for my wallet.

I found a glass in my hand.

She was standing in front of me again, saying, 'Cheers,' smiling, lifting her glass, touching the rim of my glass. 'Cheers,' I heard my voice say mechanically.

I don't know how long we stood there without speaking. I wanted to speak. There was nothing to say. My brain was frozen. I knew only I was going to die. There was no escape. I couldn't even put these words into my mind. But I could feel it. There was only the terrible dead feeling inside me. No happiness ever again. Dead. Oh, God, what would happen if I quit, if I told the Wing Commander I could not fly anymore? It was the most terrible thing in the world. I couldn't admit I was afraid. Nobody would admit that. You went on and on and on and you died. Maybe it was better than saying you were afraid. No, maybe I wouldn't die, but they were all dead or missing in action, all my air gunnery class from Canada. I had seen all their names in the casualty lists.

I felt her squeezing my arm.

'Mack,' she said. 'Mack.'

'Fine weather,' I heard my voice say, feeling my lips curve in a practiced cheery British smile. 'But rather shaky lately.' I heard my voice, cheery, very blithe. 'Decent drink.' I knew all the cliché dialogue of the British after two years as an American volunteer in the RAF. It came naturally and normally to my lips.

'Mack, what is it? What's happened?'

I glanced over my shoulder for the waiter. I looked back at her.

'What?' I said absent-mindedly.

'Stop it!' she hissed.

'Shut up,' I said. 'Please, I'm okay.'

'Okay!' she said, imitating an American nasal accent, then tossing her head, slipped her voice back to a fine, cheery artificial lilt. 'Well, what would you like to do?'

'Dinner?'

'Right.'

'*Doctor's Dilemma?* Olivier and Leigh?'

'Wizard.'

'Mirabelle's?'

'Whizzo!' she said, with exaggerated enthusiasm, mocking the RAF slang.

16

'Let's get out of here.'

Then as it had happened before, the numbness, the feeling of deadness in all my limbs, suddenly passed. Immense relief swept over me. What the hell was I worrying about? I had done one tour of operations. Thirty missions. The terrible lassitude was gone from my legs. I would survive this second tour. Piece of cake. Crazy exhilaration shot into me. I caught her arm.

'Come on,' I said, filled with happiness, wanting to celebrate the lifting of the numb dead feeling. Hell, let somebody else die. I mustn't die. Why must I feel bad about others dying? I must think of my own life.

Curzon Street was black. The sky strewn with stars. I grabbed Joan's arm, made her skip down the street with me. Searchlights sabred darkness over Hyde Park. I looked at the long white beams and laughed. Somebody was getting shot up tonight over the Ruhr Valley. But not Mack Norton. He was alive. With the most wonderful girl in the world. I wanted to laugh. T.S Ten Squadron. Tough Shit, lads. Mack Norton was alive.

'God,' I said, feeling so wonderfully happy, stepping under the canopy of Mirabelle's restaurant, 'I could dance all night.'

Chapter 2

The band sounded far away. All the distances in the room seemed strange. I was drunk. Fine. Drunk. Drunk. Drunk. Fine. I lifted Joan's shoulder with my right hand. Just to make sure it was there. I felt like giggling. It was a wonderful night. Wonderful!

Somebody bumped my shoulder. The band thudded, remote.

'Who was that sod?' I said.

'Let's sit down,' Joan said. I didn't want to sit down. This was fun. Just sashaying around the floor, bumping a few British red-tabbed officers in the fanny, saying, 'Ah, beg pahdon, suh,' very formal and correct, 'Beg pahdon, suh,' then bumping him again the next time around.

'You're a beast,' Joan giggled.

'Bloody beast.'

'Please don't bump him again.'

'Where did he buy that mustache?'

'Your mother's mustache,' she said.

'Where did you hear that?'

'Bloody Yanks.'

'Ruddy, bloody Yanks,' I said.

The thudding of the band came again. It

was all in my head. Then I saw Stanhope. Hadn't seen him in ages. He was dancing with a beautiful blonde Wren officer. Good old Stanhope. Screened after two tours of ops. Training sprog pilots at Abingdon. Probably get himself pranged by some sprog pilot on operational training. Safe on ops. That was the ticket. Ops. Safer than circuits and bumps with sprog pilots. Stay on ops. Go for a bloody Burton at operational training units. Shakier than combat. Good old ops. Stay on ops. That's the ticket, Norton.

'Hoy!' I yelled. 'Stanhope!'

But Stanhope wasn't there. He'd gone behind another couple. 'Hoy!' I yelled again. 'Stanhope!'

Somebody bumped me again. I felt myself falling. I fell against a pillar and pushed away from it. I was alone. Joan was gone.

'Joan,' I said. I didn't know why but I was suddenly frightened again. Then I saw Stanhope and I was suddenly happy again. I remember pushing a couple away who were dancing between me and Stanhope.

'Sir,' a voice said behind me suddenly. 'Sir.' The voice was pleasant and friendly.

Then I saw the waiter holding my arm.

'Sir, your table is over here.'

It made me sore. What the hell was he doing holding my arm? I wasn't that

19

drunk. Leading me like a child, the bloody sod. I wasn't that drunk. I jerked my arm away. The dance floor and the people spun around.

Christ, I thought, you're for the bloody tiles, you're smashed, Norton.

I felt rotten. It would embarrass Joan. I must find her. I reached for the waiter's arm. 'I'm okay,' I said.

'Yes, sir. Fine now. Come along now, sir. Just fine.'

I saw her face. She was at the table. Damn it, I was tottering. I leaned over the table. I felt glassy. My hands and arms and legs and head felt glassy and shiney. Even my lips felt glassy.

'Saw Stanhope,' I told her.

'Sit down, darling.'

'Come on,' I said. 'Get Stanhope. Go to Chelsea. Murderer's Arms. Have a party.'

'Sit down,' she said. I couldn't quite see her, but her voice was nice. I sat down slowly. It was okay. I didn't fall.

'How is he?'

I didn't like the way she was watching me.

'Listen,' I said. 'I know I'm tight. But I'm okay.'

'How is Stanhope?'

'Where is he?' I turned, trying to see him and the room spun again. 'He's going

20

to prang,' I said, 'if he keeps dancing out there.'

'Do you care for some coffee?'

'Poison the Ameddicans. Where's Stanhope?'

I saw her lean across the table. Her face was white. She put her hand on my wrist. Her face was lowered. She was looking up at me.

'Stanhope's dead,' she said. 'And you're drunk.'

'Just saw Stanhope. You don't know what you're talking about.'

'You were here three months ago. Please, Mack. Let's go. We'll go to Chelsea and have a party.'

'Little left rudder,' I heard my voice saying. I sounded foolish, but my voice was saying it. 'Easy does it, lad.'

The waiter came over to the table. Joan said something to him. He nodded.

'Drink,' I said.

She stood up. 'I'm going,' she said. 'Are you coming?'

'Don't be so serious, Joan. Fun night.'

'Mack,' she said and came around the table and stood beside me and I turned my head and looked at her. 'I'm leaving.' She was pulling my leg. I knew she was pulling my leg. Who did she think she was fooling?

I couldn't see her face very well. The

21

light shone on her face. So I really couldn't tell. But when I thought about it I thought maybe she wasn't kidding because her voice sounded different. Not very funny.

'Old stern puss,' I said. Then I saw her face and felt lousy suddenly. It was her eyes. So sad. And her lips. Tight and thin. It frightened me.

'Joan,' I said. 'I'm sorry. Waiter! Check, please.'

She was turning away. I felt more frightened. I mustn't lose her. I must be drunk. She was right. I was drunk. I mustn't fall down. I tried to keep up with her. The room was spinning. I bumped against a table.

She was kidding me. Old Stanhope wasn't dead. I must be drunk and she wanted to get me out of here before I made a bloody scene. I bumped against another table. Somebody shouted at me.

Stanhope was great on parties. At Marston Moor. Was it last New Year's Eve in the Mess or 1940? No matter. Great party. The padre drunk trying to pinch all the little WAAFS' fannies and Stanhope corking on a Hitler mustache with his hair pulled down over one eye while we carried him around the room singing *Deutschland Uber Alles,* with the padre screaming must stop it stop stop it.

Suddenly it was dark. I fell down. Light flashing on cobblestones. Bloody hell, I was drunk. She was right. Drunk. But it all seemed so funny.

I sat on the cobblestones laughing. Then the dark rain on my face. Didn't people know there was a war on? Turn off the bloody rain. Here sits the Ameddican savior of the British Empire. Not a single sod to turn off the rain.

'Turn off the rain, you sods!' I shouted. Stanhope out on the lawn at Bournemouth. Blue afternoon. Everybody drinking ale. Eastman had the phonograph. Bunny Berrigan. Was it August or September? All that blue sky for the contrails like streaks of flour criss-crossing the sky. Eastman was dead. But that was years ago. Maybe his wife was dead too. Where was his wife? I couldn't remember.

The wind was blowing the rain all over the streets. Slashing the cobblestones.

'Come on, Mack.' I heard Joan's voice. Suddenly I wanted to sleep. Just sleep. An immense lassitude came over me. I lay down.

'Come along now, lad,' a voice said. Then my eyeballs jumped. Bloody copper. He was shining a light right on my eyelids.

Somebody hoisted me up and I got my legs under me. Then the cold hit me and something else. I started to shake

23

all over. I could feel my bones shaking inside my skin.

'Come along, mate. 'Ere we go. That's a lad.'

Then I passed out. But just as suddenly it seemed a hand roused me. I felt my flesh shudder and my body came bolt upright. God, it was time for ops. I had been asleep. I was in the barracks. I had dreamed London. It was time for briefing. My guts jumped.

'Murderer's Arms,' a voice said. It was Joan. We were in a taxi. She was right. I must have been terribly drunk. Stanhope was dead. He'd been dead almost a year, conned in searchlights over Essen, smashed by flak. Or was it Essen? Was it Rostock? I could not remember the target.

'Mack,' she said. 'Let's go to the hotel. There's a raid on.'

'Flemmings,' I said. I thought of the Murderer's Arms pub. There was always a good gang in there when I was on leave. Especially Terry Manston and his girl friend Betty Barnes, a couple of West End actors. Sometimes they would have a taxi driver stay with them two days during raids so they could always get a taxi.

'Let's go see Terry and Betty,' I said.

'Flemmings,' Joan told the driver.

I wondered if it were raining over Germany. God, two hundred Halifax bombers stooging around in the dark and rain, like huge schools of fish, bumping and falling in each other's slip streams.

I put my arms around her and kissed her. I was so happy to be here with her. The fields of Yorkshire, the flare path lights seemed centuries away. There would be soft pillows and cool, clean sheets here and love in a warm bed. I longed to stay here forever. Christ, one more day of leave.

Chapter 3

The sergeant's Mess was dark. It was past midnight. The bar was closed, but there was a light in the kitchen. Peter Dickson, a navigator and Monica, the cook, were sitting on the kitchen table drinking bottles of India Pale ale.

'How was leave?' Peter asked. He smiled.

I set my kit bag on the floor.

'Good. Where'd you get the ale?'

Peter winked at Monica.

'Half a mo',' she said and slid off the table and opened the big icebox against the wall and returned with a bottle of ale. I took the bottle and said, 'How's it going?'

Peter shook his head and stopped smiling.

'Bloody awful. We lost half the squadron on Dortmund night before last.'

A terrible gust of fear and sadness struck me. I felt paralyzed.

My throat was dry, my arms weak. Suddenly I felt elated. Maybe they would disband the squadron. Send us to training units.

'Dowman.' He lifted one hand and ticked off the names of the missing air crews on his fingers. 'Carter. MacDaniels. Deckert.'

'Carter!' My voice hissed in shocked astonishment. The most experienced crew on the squadron. On their third tour of operations. Impossible. Carter knew every trick of the trade, all the evasive actions to take against search lights, flak, nightfighers. Carter was invincible. And he had gone for Burton.

I saw Monica staring at me, the bottle lifted in her hand, half way to her lips.

'What happened?' I said.

Dickson shrugged, raising his eyebrows. 'I don't know. Nobody knows.'

'Did you see anybody get hit?' I asked. Silly question. On a moonless night you couldn't see beyond two hundred yards if that far. Unless, of course, the search lights conned a machine. And the aircraft would be so far away, another tortured moth, fluttering in shafts of light.

'There was a kite below us,' Dickson said. 'Two engines on fire. Under control. But I didn't see anybody bail out.'

'What's the gen?'

'Squadron will stand down for a week or two until we get some sprog crews. They might send us to Seventy-Eight squadron over at Linton-on-Ouse. They caught a packet too.'

'Jesus! MacDaniels. Deckert. I can't believe it.'

'The shit was murder over the target. They've got a new flare. Bloody huge chandelier thing. Dripping all kinds of colors. Comes down very slowly. Never saw it before. They're dropping them above the bomber stream. Like high noon. All the bloody fighters come winging in when they've got the sky lit up. Freeze your balls when you see it.'

'Keeerist!'

'Have another ale,' Monica said. 'Those lads won't be drinking it.'

Dead men's ale, I thought; the crews had bought it and put it in the ice box for a little bash at three in the morning after debriefing. It was all paid for. Good ale.

'Cheers,' Dickson handed me a fresh bottle and clinked his bottle against it.

I felt all my nerve sliding away again.

I felt strangely smaller and smaller, dread filling my shrinking skin. There was no way out. Where do you go to quit? I was afraid to admit I was scared. I was too ashamed to admit fear to anybody. Nobody ever said they were scared. You had to be a raving and shaking maniac to be taken off combat by the medical officer. There was a rumor that the more missions you flew the better chance you had of surviving. Bull crap. Maybe after fifteen missions in the first tour the odds started to swing in your favor. But what about the middle of a second tour or a third tour? Hell, there was a whole new set of odds because Jerry had new conditions for you to face, new weapons, new methods of night fighter attack and coordination. Maybe your own intelligence officer wouldn't tell you. Better you didn't know. Make a flier too damn windy if he really knew the odds. Experience apparently hadn't helped any of those veteran crews.

'Did you have the Jerry colors of the days?' I asked.

Dickson nodded. Usually toward the end of each operational briefing the intelligence officer would give us the Luftwaffe colors of the day. Red-red. Green-red-green. If you got conned in a searchlight you could pop off the right colored flares and make the flak and searchlight batteries think they were shooting at one of their kites. I'd never heard of anybody using it successfully. But it was always comforting information to have. Apparently we had an agent with a wireless set in Germany who had the inside track daily on some daily Luftwaffe intelligence. I wondered if the Jerries had somebody in England sending back our colors of the days.

'Were there a lot of searchlights?' As I asked I felt at once thrilled and frightened. In my mind I could still see the vast field of searchlight beams south of Berlin, mile after mile, all in rows, sharp beams of light sticking up like monstrous spears, waiting to move the instant our pathfinder force dropped the first colored sky marker signaling the aiming point of the attack.

'Bags. Bloody bags. All around Dortmund now,' said Dickson. 'As bad as Essen.'

I drank quickly to keep from grinding my teeth. The mention of Essen struck an old sense of fear. We all expected to die when we attacked Essen. Two thousand flak guns. Thousands of searchlights.

Oh, Christ, I'm going to die soon, I thought, filled with anguish. What would those last terrible moments be like? Blown to pieces suddenly? I had been wounded twice, once in the arm, and in the thigh, sudden shocking blows, like being slugged with a hammer, no pain at first. The thought of a gut wound with the machine on fire filled my dreams at night; whirling and spinning down through the flak bursts, down, down, down, through round balls of smoke centered with orange flashes of fire, spinning, the centrifugal force pressing my chin down against my chest, my body weighing a ton, my guts in my lap, unable to move, the parachute chest pack just out of reach. Would there be one last roaring, tearing sensation of terrible pain just as the machine smashed into the earth?

'Oy!' Dickson was saying. 'Drink up!' He was grinning, his eyes bleary. He started humming 'Bless 'Em All.' I took another beer from Monica and picked up my kit bag.

Outside it was dark but the heavens were filled with stars. And moonlight. A beautiful night for JU 88's. I felt futile and empty as I walked along the dark Yorkshire lane to my Nissen hut.

The room was dark and cold. I snapped on the light. In the corner the coke stove was black. No coal yet. Not for another month. My sidcot suit from training school, lined with eiderdown, lay on my cot. It was the best garment to sleep in during the fall and winter when the coke fire would die during the night.

I looked over at Jamison's empty bed.

Carter's mid-upper air gunner. Poor old Jamison, a traveling salesman before the war, with all those beautiful Scandinavian girls waiting for his return. Well, he wouldn't be needing his shoes. I pulled them out from under his bed. Very expensive hand-made shoes. A perfect fit. I slid them under my bed. I wondered who would be trying them on some morning sitting on the edge of my bed saying, 'Did you hear? Norton went for Burton last night.'

I undressed, drew back the two RAF issue blankets. Then I sat on the bed in my long underwear and slid into the sidcot suit and zippered myself in. I walked to the edge of the bed. The floor below was icy cold. I leaned far out and just managed to reach the wall switch and snapped off the light.

I couldn't sleep. I was afraid to sleep. The old nightmare would start again. The oxygen bottles on fire, melting our flesh into the metal walls of the fuselage, turning our bodies into liquid. The dream had gone away for a week, but I was frightened it would return. It was a constantly recurring nightmare.

I slept but I didn't know how long and then the nightmare came again, only it was new. My pilot was dead over the control column and we were falling through the stars over Kiel into the North Sea. I was calling for help but my mouth wouldn't open and I could not get off the floor of the aircraft. My body was glued to the floor and my parachute pack was just out of reach. Coming straight at my head was a big black JU 88 night fighter like a prehistoric monster with the blue flashes of its cannon fire like burning coals for eyes and crazy radar aerials festooning the bulbous black nose like the hair of a lunatic. The machine hung for a long instant in the black sky, firing round balls of fire, while I lay paralyzed and unable to move.

I woke sweating and shaking in a transport of fear.

Chapter 4

In the morning it was raining. Members of the crew I flew with were lounging around my room. Somebody had scrounged some coal. There was a fire going and the air smelled of toasted bread, greyish bread from the Mess.

'Think there'll be a call on tonight?' asked Dickson, speaking to no one in particular.

'You're crackers,' said Stevens, our wireless operator. 'With this bloody Met?'

But you could never tell. The weather that came off the Irish Sea could always be translated into whether we would attack Germany. The Irish probably sent weather reports to Germany so the Jerries knew if we were coming.

'It'll probably clear up and we'll stand by to fly with Seventy-Eight squadron,' Dickson said. He had a moose-like face, a former lumberjack from Ontario. He could drink the crew under the table. He rolled his eyes nonchalantly toward the ceiling. 'Stevens, you know something? I just looked at your horoscope today. You'll never finish a tour.'

'Now you can stop worrying,' Folkes said.

'You might live till spring,' said Dickson gleefully.

Stevens did not answer.

It shouldn't have bothered me to hear this bantering about dying. A year ago it had not, but now I was so damn windy the bantering frightened me. The fear inside was very real again, an empty, lost hollow sensation. My arms and legs felt weak.

'Listen, blokes,' George Robinson said. 'I want to ask all of you something.'

George Robinson was our pilot. He was English from Lancashire, but he didn't have a Lancashire accent. He leaned forward on the edge of the cot, his empty pipe clamped upside down between his lips. He had flown a tour of ops on both Whitley and Halifax bombers, a thin, blonde, serious young man, with white eyelashes on his right eye.

'I'm going to stick my neck out,' he said. 'You can do what you want to do about it, but all of us must be in this together.'

Nobody moved. I had a feeling what he was going to suggest. Or was I dreaming? Was my desire to live so strong I believed he was going to ask what I wanted and was afraid to mention?

Bob Folkes, the Canadian bomb-aimer, suddenly spoke. 'One more trip like Dortmund and we've had it.'

Robinson turned his head, looked straight at Folkes. He pointed the stem of his pipe at Folkes, and as Folke's mouth opened to speak Billy Jaynes interrupted. He was the son of a Cardiff pub owner, and an excellent crap shooter since I had introduced the American game into the Mess.

Jaynes shook his head, guffawed faintly, a little arrogantly, 'It'll never work, George.'

'What?' said George, but he did not look at Jaynes, his voice coming around the stem of his pipe which he had inserted into the corner of his mouth.

'Duff gen,' said George.

Everybody looked at Jaynes. He lay back on the cot with his head on shoulders against the wall.

'Why don't we ever get some mine laying jobs?' Maisen said, but nobody appeared to hear him. They were all looking again at George Robinson.

Mine laying was considered a piece of cake, over the northern tip of Denmark, down into the Kattegat to seal off the Baltic outlet where Germany trained its navy. Piece of cake. No flak. No fighters.

'Our luck's running good,' said Robinson. 'Fifteen more trips and we're out of it. We've probably got more time over the Ruhr than half the crews here have eating breakfast. But—'

'—But squadron losses are fifty percent the last two weeks,' Jaynes interrupted.

Robinson nodded. 'Mostly sprog crews.'

Sure, I thought sprog crews, but who had ever measured our experience against the odds we were running into? Who knew the survival odds anymore? Experience? how meaningful was it anymore? Maybe the science boffins at High Wycombe had it all laid out on statistical charts. I remembered how right in the middle of the Battle of Britain just before I had gone on Whitley's asking a Hurricane pilot what was the best defensive device for a tail gunner. 'Lots of armor plating,' he replied, having become a squadron leader in three weeks because there wasn't anybody left from his flight to promote.

Fifty percent squadron losses, I thought, anything beyond five percent was considered disastrous. Bomber command could not survive with continuous losses beyond four percent.

Robinson nodded in agreement with Jaynes. 'The trouble is,' he said, 'bomber command cannot saturate the defenses. If we make a maximum effort, with four percent losses, bomber command can't operate for a week.'

'Unless bomber command can saturate the defenses,' said Robinson, 'our losses are going to climb. Command is trapped. They can't run saturation raids, and if they run less than a saturation capacity bomber command will shortly become virtually non-operational.'

'I'll drink to that,' said Dickson. 'That's my goal. Non-operational.'

'What the hell are you trying to tell us?' Jaynes asked.

'It's only a matter of time until we get the chop,' said Robinson.

'So what's new?' Maisen laughed.

'Why can't they run more millenium raids?' Folkes said.

'Forty losses out of a thousand bombers?'

Robinson said. 'How long do you think bomber command would last?'

I thought of the millenium raids last summer; every aircraft in England had been called up to put one thousand bombers over Bremen, Blenheims, Hampdens, Whitleys, kites operationally obsolete for more than a year. It had scared the hell out of Jerry, such a show of strength, and their defenses had been saturated, with searchlights wobbling all over the sky, and flak suppressed after the third wave of bombers. It had stunned the hell out of their defenses but bomber command would need nearly 2,000 first line aircraft to maintain such pressure, and right now we were mounting 200 aircraft at the most in a maximum type raid.

'I'm open to suggestions,' said Maisen, smiling.

Robinson held up one hand. 'First, we're all going to take a pledge that whatever we decide in this room doesn't go beyond the room. Right?'

There was a long pause and then everybody nodded slowly.

'All right,' said Robinson. 'Let's look at it this way. Call it cowardice, if you wish. But right now I feel our missions are meaningless.'

'Oh, I don't know,' Jaynes drawled. 'I can't buy that idea completely.'

'How do you figure?' Stevens said.

'Well, let me put it this way. You figure we're whistling in a graveyard. Maybe we are, George. Maybe so. But maybe we might just walk all the way through whistling,' Jaynes smiled.

'Or get buried,' said Maisen.

'May Day!' cried Folkes in a mock serious voice. This was the radio distress call from aircrews in trouble.

'I want to be certain everybody understands,' said Robinson.

'Like what?' I said. 'Stop beating around the bush.'

'Raise your hands,' said Robinson. 'Everybody swear nothing you hear in this room goes beyond this room.'

I put my hand up. Folkes' hand came up immediately. Stevens glanced at Jaynes. They raised their hands together. Eddy Maisen rolled over on his stomach, faced down, lifted his arm. 'Unanimous,' he muttered.

'O.K.' Robinson said. 'Everybody understands. Bomber command is tossing us down the crapper. No end except to make a political show against Germany. There aren't enough bombers for any real strategic or tactical purpose. There won't be for at least two years.'

'Ah, yes,' Jaynes said imitating a very fruity Oxford accent. 'But remember, lads, you're taking the King's shilling.'

'Bloody ignorant Welsh,' said Stevens. He had been a school master and he spoke now in his best school master's voice. 'Her sergeant's we. It's the Queen's shilling.'

Robinson leaned forward and caught Jaynes' wrist and hissed, 'Quit buggering about! How many trips do you think we do to Essen and survive? Not a hope in hell anymore of finishing a tour of ops.'

'Maybe we can have the war called off,' said Jaynes in an innocent, cheery voice without even glancing at Robinson's fingers clenched around his wrist. 'Dear Hitler,' Jaynes smiled at Robinson; 'I am twenty-one, sound of limb and mind. Three lovely girls are mad about me. Would you consider negotiating a separate peace for a Halifax kite W-William? Your obedient servant, Flight Sergeant Jaynes.'

'Knock it off, George,' I said, and struck at George's hand just as George released Jaynes' wrist. 'Listen, you twits,' I heard myself shout. 'On our last three trips we've been conned five times in searchlights and shot up! God only knows how we got out of it. There simply aren't enough kites put over each target. The Krauts can pick us and choose with those searchlights. If all the ME110's ever get released from the Russian front there'll be 2,000 front night fighters over Europe.'

Robinson said, 'Let's vote.'

The room was silent.

'The next trip to a Baltic target,' Robinson said. 'Rostock, Lubeck. Stettin. Or Berlin. We abort and go into Sweden. Vote on it.'

Just then in the silence we heard the sound of engines coughing, bursting into life, faraway, across the field. Christ, I thought, they're testing aircraft for a mission tonight.

That did it. Just the sound of those machines being tested, that faraway thunder reverberating across the field. Nobody moved. Nobody spoke.

I looked at Robinson. His head was slanted faintly, listening, his pupils suddenly pin points. The room was frozen.

It was a sound we would never forget as long as we lived, like the tolling of a bell, and whenever we heard it we knew there was almost no turning back.

We could feel all the action of the mission moving toward us; the lockers opening, our hands taking out the flying suits, our cold fingers snapping on the parachute harnesses, then filing out after briefing, the cold drive around the dark perimeter track in the hooded trucks, sitting with our elbows on our knees, going toward the excitement that wouldn't start until we were in the midst of the shell fire and

40

slithering light beams with our voices calling out the flak and fighters. Then we would be out of the tense part into the excitement. But now hearing the engines warming up, being tested in the afternoon, that's when the tense part started, and then hours later the elation on being alive, walking out in the dark morning after debriefings, and then there was the weary letdown and immense fatigue before you dropped off to sleep.

Now the tense part was there again in the room as it had been so many nights before.

'They're crackers,' Jaynes said. 'There's only three kites. They can't be putting up only three kites.'

'I didn't want to tell you,' said Robinson, 'but we're going to attack with Seventy-Eight squadron. They're short three kites.'

'What's the target?' somebody asked.

Robinson shrugged. 'I don't know.'

'Let's vote,' said Jaynes.

Robinson looked at all of us at once, a single sweeping glance. From his tunic breast pocket he drew a sheet of stationery. Now in my mind I could see that hour of take-off again, all of us out by our machines, sitting or standing on the grass around the cement revetment, waiting for the green rocket from the control tower. The dark earth eating into the rim of the

41

sun. The trees behind us all in shadow, a last ray of sunlight coming through the branches, then fading, the earth swallowing the sun. Then darkness and the green rocket arching across the sky.

I looked at the little white square of paper in my hand. My ballot.

'Don't use script,' Robinson said. 'Just print yes or no. It's got to be unanimous.'

I turned my back and with the slip of paper on my knee I voted 'Yes,' folded the ballot and handed it to Robinson. Each ballot was the same size. Robinson had cut them out with perfect uniformity. As we turned them in, he dropped each one without looking at it into his tunic side pocket.

I don't know what made me think then of a Welsh air gunner named Craig Jones. He'd been dead a year. But for a year before they caught him he lived in the sergeant's Mess and never flew a mission. He'd been transferred from Pocklington, a satellite aerodrome and somebody had forgotten to send his records along, so every payday he went back to Pocklington five miles away and stood in the pay parade and collected his money. The rest of the time he snared pheasants from a nearby Duke's estate or sat in our mess and played shove ha'penny. He got to be a pretty good crap shooter, too, after

I introduced the game to the British. He went for a Burton on Ludwigshaven, owing me three quid trying to toss a four after rolling box cars twice in a row. But he had a hell of a lot of luck for a year, I thought, as I sat there thinking about all the lads who had been shot down while Jones was roasting pheasants. But nobody had ever turned him in. It was a fine joke. Everybody wanted him to sit the war out just to prove how screwed up the ground pounders were who kept track of the office records.

God, I thought, I hope everybody votes for Sweden. Just then Robinson opened the door. He had gone out into the hall to count the votes. He stood there in the open doorway, leaning against the door frame, his hat raked on the side of his head with a swanking air. My heart kicked over with relief. He was smiling. God, we were all so young then.

He shook his head. 'Bad luck,' he said. Still smiling, he put both hands against the sides of the door and pushed. He smiled a little more, dropped his hands.

'How many—?' somebody started to say.

McComber who was the pilot of F-Freddy, poked his head over Robinson's shoulder. 'Off your arses,' he shouted. His voice was bright and cheery. 'Get your

Finger out. Briefing in half an hour.'

'What's the gen?' Stevens asked.

'Essen,' McComber said and his face vanished.

Robinson's face suddenly became hard and lean. We all sat for a long moment, feeling baffled and betrayed. Who had voted against lobbing down in Sweden? My heart pounded with fear.

'My God,' Maisen said, shaking his head. 'Essen.'

Chapter 5

The sea shimmered. Oh, Christ, Oh, Christ, I thought, wiping the sweat out from under my flying helmet.

'Cromer,' I heard the bomb-aimer call. 'Dead ahead.'

I stared at the plot line of stars across the sky. Ah, at last, the Cromer light, the coast of Norfolk. Home. England.

'Steer two-six-zero,' Dickson called to the pilot.

I pushed my helmet back and stared out at the night.

Far below I saw the sea shimmering, a white collar of foam upon the Norfolk coast. I wiped the sweat from the back of my hand. My hand was shaking.

Was it only half an hour ago when I thought I was going to die? Christ! Essen had never been worse. A sea of fire, the dark bowl of the sky hung with chandelier flares, red and green and yellow, slashed with a thousand searchlights, row on row of searchlights, right into the target, and all the way out, never wavering, and when the machine was conned I was sure they were going for a Burton, way out of the lights. Even now I was still panting. I put my head down on my hands. There must be two thousand or more flak guns at Essen. This was my ninth mission to Essen, in two tours of ops, and the opposition was worse than ever. Through all the spears of searchlights, the night fighters had come swarming like dark fish, soaring in and out of the lights, thirsting for blood.

Jaynes in the mid-upper gun turret and I in the tail turret cried out sharply in the darkness as the aircraft rose and fell, calling out the position of night fighters, yet the sound of our guns seemed remote from the turrets, while I tried to keep my mind on giving the pilot the right evasive action. But only God would know when we'd come out of the searchlight belt.

But now all this was behind. We had twisted free of the lights. My guts were dead and empty. I was washed out.

Then I began to feel my breathing become softer and softer. I put my head down upon my hands, felt myself fighting sleep, then suddenly as if in dream a voice roused me, but I did not believe the sound of the voice. I was certain it was all a dream, and soon we would be landing in England. We were past the coast of Norfolk.

'Dive port! Dive port!'

'Watch it, Mack. Fighter six o'clock low.'

'I see him! Green light, keep turning!'

Voices I had heard so often over the intercom. I felt the immense pressure upon my body, forcing me down and down into my seat, pressing my chest and body down and down. Then I saw the night fighter again, a huge dark beast.

'Junkers! Here he comes! Turn starboard!' I shouted.

And that was almost all. The last sound of my voice. Beneath my seat I heard the explosion, the shuddering of the machine, the monstrous boom as of many kettle drums. Then the lurching, the sickening lurch of the machine that told you only one thing, cannon fire had scored, and you were falling, falling through space.

And I knew in that fraction of a second death was there again. Night fighters had followed us back over the coast, and as soon as we flew straight and level, the German machine had attacked, one from the beam, signaling the other at six o'clock low, to cut in on the deflection angle once the Halifax started to turn into the beam attack.

'Keep turning!' I screamed.

I felt the turn, the steepness, but we were going down and I could not move. My chute hung upon the wall. I reached for it, but I could not rise. An immense weight pressed me down.

I gasped and flung myself at the turret wall. I clawed the chute from the wall and clasped it to my chest. My fingers were frantic to find the chute snaps imbedded in my chest harness, but the chute pack slipped away.

The Halifax shuddered violently. My legs were jerked up. A blow struck my shoulder. I saw the glass turret wall shatter across my lap. Then I did a crazy thing; yet even in that second I thought of a tail gunner from Austrailia, doing something even crazier. That day at Abingdon when a Whitley had crashed on take-off, and Pig-Meat, the gunner, running across the field, away from the burning machine had suddenly stopped and ran back into the fuselage, past all his kit bags stacked beside the damn broken door, to seize his new flying helmet in the tail turret and rushed out through the flames across the fields holding aloft his newly issued helmet, beaming triumphantly.

So now in a clattering metallic noise as I saw the glass perspex shards skittering across my knee, I had a sudden crazy feeling that I must not discard my helmet. I unplugged it. I looked at the cord in my hand, but in that instant I came back to reality. I twisted my body, seized my chute, snapped the chest pack to the harness and struck open the metal door behind me and swung the turret around. Cold air blasted at me front and back.

But my mind was still paralyzed. Then as I heard a crackling noise, like a heavy ice moving in a monstrous river, fear enveloped my body. Prickly fire of fear ran over my head and shoulders. My guts and legs became water. We were falling in flames. A face materialized in front of me, reddish, skin and hair reddish, with a bulbous nose. The nose appeared to be screaming. It was Billy Jaynes, the gunner from the mid-upper turret. His mouth gaped, bellowing in the blasting icy air.

'Bail out!' he yelled. 'We're on fire!'

Jaynes shouted into my face. 'Bail out!' I stared at him dazed as a sleep-walker. I felt hopelessly lost. I couldn't move. I stared down at the open darkness behind me.

We're done for, I thought. Jaynes hit me in the shoulder. He shouted 'Jump! Jump!'

I felt a bump. As I tumbled out backward, I saw briefly the expression of dazed bewilderment on Jaynes' face.

Then I was falling, falling, Christ, falling until the fear in my guts turned to an ecstasy.

Did I pull the ring? I looked up and saw a shower of sparks, like a comet falling in a long arc down through the darkness. Is that it? Are they all dead?

There was no moon, and I could not see the ground. I was inside a huge round ball of darkness with the lighter side above. Inside the dark globe, I swayed gently, and then far away I heard an explosion, and out of the sound my mind wakened, thinking at once: It blew up, and what did they say at school about landing? I turned my head looking for the crash of the Halifax, thinking, keep your legs together, bend knees, roll on shoulder. I saw a gout of flame below, off to the west, glowing up into the darkness.

Suddenly a tree loomed. I jack-knifed my legs, but before I could clench my body into a ball, the ground slammed into my legs. I smelled the damp odor of soft, plowed earth as the parachute dragged me along a deep furrow, and

49

then in the stillness the parachute canopy collapsed. I lay on my face, panting, my heart hammering.

I did not remember rising, nor wiping mud from my hands. I knocked the release mechanism free with my fist, and shed the parachute harness. I stood there feeling as if the war were over and I would never have to fly again. I wondered where I was. I could not recall how long it had been since I had jumped. I looked at my watch. The crystal was smashed. I must have struck the edge of the turret, bailing out. Then I began to smell my own sweat. I stank. Slowly, a feeling of elation began to grow inside me. A sense of profound happiness came over me. I still did not feel pain in my legs or back from the shock of landing. Then I thought of the others, the pilot wrestling the dying monster. Was Robinson dead? He'd held the machine steady with flames all around him. That must have been why Jaynes was trying to bail out through the tail turret. He'd been cut off by fire at the door and bomb bays.

In the darkness there was no sound and then into the silence came the far-faint drone of an engine, and as it came closer, the droning sound mounted into the roar of four engines, and then above the trees, perhaps at a thousand feet, four lights apparently suspended in the darkness, descended, passing. I watched the lights, checking the motion of the machine against a star, keeping the North Star in the corner of my eye. Going toward an air base. But where were the others?

I longed for a cigarette, and felt in my flying boots where I usually kept them, but they were gone. I kicked away the folds of the chute and began to walk North, along the furrows. God, God, I thought, happy and amazed, I'm alive. Am I the only one from the crew? Will I have to fly with a new crew? The thought suddenly terrified me. It was always the new crews who got you killed. It took at least fifteen missions to teach you how to survive. Maybe they would screen me, send me to an Operational Training Unit, down in Buckinghamshire, to train sprog crews. Perhaps the war would end by the time the tour of training was completed. What a fool I had been volunteering for a third tour. What was I trying to prove? That Mack Norton was more invincible than any other flier in the RAF? A big hero? No, I knew my fate; I'd wind up as a spare gunner flying with any crew that needed a gunner and that was the surest way to get killed. Sooner or later you'd get sent to Happy Valley, or some bloody Ruhr target and cop out with a sprog crew on their first mission.

The muddy field ceased. My boots struck grass, and I went on across the meadow. Through a break in a crest of trees, a house loomed, a thick square of dark against the lighter sky.

I paused. No sound. I found the walk and went to the door and rang the bell. At once light shot out from an upstairs window. Then the light was gone and a voice called down through the darkness. It was a woman's voice.

'Who's there?'

'I got shot down.'

'Who are you?'

'Mack Norton. I'm an air gunner.'

'I'll be down. Are you all right?'

'Yes. I bailed out.'

I waited and it seemed that many minutes passed and still she did not come down, and the house remained dark. She doesn't believe me, I thought. I began to shiver with fatigue and cold, and the longing for a cigarette grew inside me. She's afraid, I thought.

Suddenly the door opened. The woman stood against the light. I blinked. The light blinded me.

'Come in. Come in.'

I followed her into a sitting room, filled with tuck-pointed velvet chairs. On each of the fireplaces bookcases and books gleamed against the dying embers.

'What happened?'

'Intruders followed us over the coast.'

'Did the others get out?'

'I don't know.'

'There was an explosion up north.'

'Probably our kite going in.'

Though I had been in England three years, the conversation of English people still seemed unnatural in certain circumstances. All their dialogue seemed based on a series of phrases for certain codes of action as if life were a play script for each act; whether it was the weather or the war, they seemed to have set lines. To receive any personal opinion from them was as easy as catching a greased pig. Play the scene in their manner, just as if nothing has happened.

'May I use your phone?'

She did not answer. I looked at her. Her hair was chestnut colored. She wore a soft blue dressing gown. In the firelight, her eyes looked greenish. 'Yes,' she said abstractedly.

Then, 'My husband's away in the desert.'

'Tanks?'

'Yes.'

'Rum,' I said, playing the Englishman.

'Worse than flying.'

'At least we get a warm bed at night.'

'Care for a drink?'

'I could use one.'

I walked to the fire and leaned over. My hands felt boney and cold, yet my body felt light, almost weightless. I was aware of my breathing, soft and steady, of my hands turning slowly into each other, feeling the warmth of the firelight seep into the veins of my wrists.

I felt dream-like, standing there in front of the fire, a woman in the other room, all the fear far away. Where were the others? I had seen so many burning on engines, crashed after take-off, running screaming on fire across the fields. Was that what they were doing? I closed my eyes, dipped my face to the glow of the embers.

I heard the woman putting a decanter and glasses down on the table.

'Water?' she asked. I shook my head, without opening my eyes.

'A cup of tea?'

'No, straight whiskey.' I opened my eyes.

God, I thought, watching her bend over the table, amazed by her presence, as if she had come from another world. Her lips so red and soft and full. Her shoulders and breasts smooth and round beneath the dressing gown, and as she leaned down the golden soft hair on the nape of her neck caught the fire light.

'I better call in,' I said, but I did not move.

I stared at her face, the curve of her cheek, the soft cloud of her hair, and I thought of the wild nights I had wasted on so many leaves, drinking, whoring, longing always for somebody until I had met Joan. But is it only the hour? The time? The circumstances that gave her this lovely look? How easy it would be to dream of her. Suddenly I longed to hold her, to touch her hair as I would hold Joan.

'The phone is in the hall,' she said.

I rose.

She handed me a glass.

'Thank you,' I said.

The whiskey tasted cool and fiery, seeping down through all my veins, my very skeleton in my flesh seemed to sigh and shudder with pleasure and relief.

'Pour yourself another.' She touched my arm. 'What's the base number? I'll ring it for you.'

I gave her the number and poured another drink. My stomach and chest felt heavy and tired. I sat back in a deep chair. A vast lassitude crept over my body. I sipped and closed my eyes.

I felt myself falling asleep, dreaming of nuns in dark habits coming down the street in the summer; I was nine, and the boy next door saying they were all dead women, walking dead women, all of them in black, walking slowly, under the green trees, two women in black, coming along the sidewalk toward my house, and I was alone, and the dead women were coming to get me, to take me away; I could hear the summer wind in the trees, and see them walking toward the house.

A hand, a voice, roused me. I felt my body twitch and jerk. I woke thinking it was the night before the attack on Lorient when they had scrubbed the mission because of weather only to wake the crews again at midnight for one o'clock take-off, and I started up violently, thinking, oh, no, oh, Christ no, we have to go.

'Your squadron's on the phone,' the woman said softly.

I looked up at her. I rubbed my face. I stood up above the fireplace and saw my face in the mirror. But it was not my face. The eye sockets were cavernous. The cheeks were streaked with mud and grease. The hair was matted with sweat. I went swiftly to the phone.

'Hello,' said a voice.

It was Southworth, the squadron adjutant, a flight-lieutenant air gunner who had lost part of his left arm over Lubeck two years before.

'We got hit coming in,' I said. 'Intruders.'

'Are you all right?'

'How's the crew?' I said.

'Where did you bail out?'

'Half a mo', Bob,' I said and put the phone down and went into the sitting room.

'Where am I?' I asked.

'Sharpe's cottage. Three miles south of Rockton-Higby.'

I told Southworth, and standing there I was suddenly aware the woman was close beside me in the dark and her arm was touching my arm. I touched her fingers.

'Where's the crew?'

'All over the countryside,' said Southworth. 'But they're alive.'

'What about the squadron?'

'Grawert's gone for Burton.'

'McComber?'

'Fighters pranged him over the Wash. The gunner just called in from King's Lynn.'

McComber, I thought. More than seventy missions, including Crete in Wimpeys.

'I'll send a lorry for you,' said Southworth.

'Okay,' I said. 'See you at breakfast.'

I put down the receiver. I did not know I still held the woman's hand. I stared at her.

'What is it?' she asked.

'They've had it,' my voice said.

I looked at her, then down at my hands. I felt the warmth of her flesh, the shape of her face in the darkness. I had known many women, but I had never been in love until Joan. She seemed unreal now. I needed the warmth of this woman now. Her face was soft and silent. I longed suddenly to feel the softness of her body, to know I was real and alive.

But I did not move, for back in my mind I felt Joan again in the touch of this woman's fingers.

Now as the sweet soft odor of her struck into my body I was filled with that great forgotten joy of being alive. I wanted to press my lips upon her throat and breasts to feel her soft limbs killing all the dead feelings inside me.

But we're all dead, I thought. All dead, burned, smashed, lying out on the moors, scorched like roasted meat, lying on engines, burning in gasoline, headless, flesh seared, split like turkey brown roasted thighs. I would never see this woman again. Perhaps even now her husband's body lay in a smashed tank somewhere in the desert. I longed in the darkness for her hands to move. For her to take the blame of my thoughts of Joan. I will never see her again, and she waits, waits, waits. She pressed her lips against my throat. I felt her fingers tenderly touching the nape of my neck, and in the soft odor of her hair and the sweet taste of her cheek, the beat of her heart came to me. I embraced her longing for our bodies to melt into each other. Now, now, I thought, tomorrow, tomorrow night. More frightened now of flying than ever before.

My hand touched her breasts. One of her hands came slowly away from my neck and loosened her robe. The soft warm, round globe of flesh glowed in my hand and I felt my whole body sigh and heave. My lips touched her nipples, and she stood above me, stroking my head as my tongue tenderly anointed her breasts.

'Oh, darling, darling,' she said softly.

I felt bodiless, her nipples sweetening in my lips.

Then for the first time I had a dark, swift deep sensation of the silence in which we stood, as if the silence were a substance, surrounding, enveloping us like water, rising slowly in the room, higher and higher around our bodies. I had never known such silence in three years, only excitement and tension, engines, gun-fire, voices. The silence was frightening.

'Come here,' she said softly. She paused and loosening her robe, cast it upon the floor. I saw her body white in the darkness.

'There isn't time,' I said. 'I'll come back.'

'Let them wait.'

'They'll knock on the door.'

'I'll tell them my brother drove you to the field.'

I kissed her. 'I will drive you later,' she said.

I undressed in the darkness. Her body was cool and white; Oh, God! God! I heard my flesh screaming the words as I came into her, feeling immense relief, her loins slowly taking the tension away. I thought I heard her cry softly. Then feeling her anguish was gone, too, the anguished longing for her husband, I touched the long cooling smoothness of her arm, as if she were no longer there, only the smooth long arm, reminding me of my life, and then again my desire kindled, until she turned slowly, bathing my lips, making me think of waters beneath the falls, my mouth upturned, under Minnehaha Falls in that long ago dead summer, standing, face up-lifted, cooling sunburned eyelids beneath the falls, beneath the back spray of the falls, as I looked out through the sunlit falling torrent of water; Oh, God, Ah, I thought, now tasting her soft sweet lips, as if the sweat and sunburn of my face were cooling beneath her lips and in the memory of cold spray falling back upon my burning skull.

'What will they do with you?' she asked.

'We'll get a new aircraft.'

'Fly again?'

'I have to finish the tour.'

'How many missions have you done?'

'Two tours. Sixty.'

'Third tour?' she asked.

From far away came the sound of an engine, a truck. We lay in the darkness listening.

'We better dress,' I said.

'Tomorrow,' she said. 'Will I see you?'

I touched her lips, her face, with my fingers. 'I don't even know your name,' I said.

Her smile curved against my cheek.

'And I don't know yours.'

'Mack Norton,' I said.

'Mary Wayne,' she said. 'Tomorrow?'

'Tomorrow,' I lied.

Chapter 6

It was dawn now, and though the strain and fear of the night was gone, I did not feel any better. In a kind of blind stupor of fatigue I could not feel anything. Only numbed, beyond any feeling or emotion. My eyes were bloodshot and did not seem to focus correctly. I sat on the edge of the iron cot in my Nissen hut, and looked with a kind of blank hopelessness at the flying boot on my right foot. Dazed and weary I had pulled off the boot on my left foot, and then too tired to move, I just sat there, leaning forward a little, staring at the boot on my right foot, having the feeling it was not even my foot. Not even my body, I thought, but now in a little while I'll bend down and pull the other boot off. But not yet. And I stared numbly at the wall, my mind blank. Then thinking began again; lean down and pull it off now. Still I did not want to move. Did not want to do anything. Never to do anything again. Never to have to eat, sleep, drink or make love again. Just sit here and stare dumbly at the booted foot.

But after a long moment I moved, swallowed, and heard invisible feet coming along the hall beyond the wall; then the door opened; Dickson, our navigator, who lived in the next room, looked in. 'Hey, the discip sergeant wants to see you.'

'Everybody back okay?' I asked.

'Made it,' he said. He looked dead beat.

'What's the discipline sergeant want?'

My eyes blinked, focused.

'Me?' I said cold, motionless. Then suddenly in quiet astonishment, 'For Crissake, I haven't been to bed yet.'

'Yeah, I know. Don't tell me about it. I haven't either. Look, all I know—the discip wants you.'

'Okay.'

'We're the only crew who got back.'

I laughed idiotically. 'Yeah?'

'Well, we're here.'

I laughed. 'Yeah. Because we're here.'

Dickson went away. I listened to his footsteps die along the hall, then stooping, I reached and pulled the flying boot on to my left leg and stood up.

I combed my hair and put my cap on the side of my head, and looked at my face in the mirror. Pale. I needed a shave and about ten hours sleep. I hoped there wouldn't be a call on tonight.

Outside it was cold and raining. I went along the road to the Flights, my battle dress collar drawn up high about my neck, my shoulders hunched against the wind. Why the hell would the discipline sergeant want me at this ungodly hour? I had never heard of anyone being called down to Flights after a raid. People went to bed then. It did not seem reasonable. But then so many things didn't have to be reasonable.

I turned into the Flights building and saw Olcott, the discipline sergeant, in the hall.

'Want me?'

'You're on a charge,' Olcott said.

'A charge? What the hell for? I haven't done anything.'

'Maybe that's just it. You haven't done anything.' He patted me jocosely on the chest. 'Maybe that's just it,' he grinned.

I turned on him angrily. 'You're pretty goddam funny.'

Olcott stopped smiling. 'Funny enough to take you into the C.O's office. Your cap.' I handed him my cap.

Then we were marching into the C.O's office, Olcott leading the way.

At the far end of the room the C.O sat thickly behind his desk. He did not look up as Olcott and I entered.

When Olcott gave my name the C.O finally raised his head.

'You may go, sergeant.' He looked down at his desk again.

After Olcott was gone the C.O still did not look up. He mused on the desk top, tapping his pencil against his lower lip.

Finally, after a long deliberate pause, he looked up and cleared his throat.

'Norton,' he said. 'I called you here this morning because I think you need a lesson. Etchually,' he leaned forward against the desk, pointing his pencil at me, 'as a matter of fact, this entire squadron needs a lesson. Because you're aircrew, you think you're little tin gods, don't you?'

'No.' My voice was a monotone. I felt myself slipping back into a numb dark abyss.

The C.O tapped the pencil against his lower lip, and slowly said, 'Norton, how long have you been in the services?'

'Three years.'

'Mm. Three years,' said the C.O. He gave a little humming laugh. 'Three years. What did you do before the war?'

The bastard, I thought.'

'Nothing. I was on welfare,' I lied. 'Couldn't get a job.'

'Not much discipline, was there?' The C.O laughed, feeling he had made one of his little jokes. 'You like it?' he went on. 'Would you like to remain in the Services after the war?'

I didn't answer.

'Well?' he said archly.

'I'm tired,' I said.

'You're tired?' The C.O leaned forward a little further on his desk. 'Oh, you're tired?' he repeated. Then he looked down at the sheet of paper on his desk and picked it up and began to read to himself. When he looked up at me, he said, 'It might interest you to know, Norton, that I'm tired of you. Do you see this?' He tapped the paper with his pen, then leaned forward, his eyes glittered and he thrust a finger at me.

'Perfect record!' he said. 'My squadron had a perfect dress regulations record. Did you or did you not wear your battle dress pants in town?'

'Well, uh, I—'

The C.O waved his index finger wildly, thrusting it toward me, his voice imperious. 'Did you or did you not? Answer me, yes or no.'

'I've only got the one pair of pants... They were at the cleaners...had to wear battle dress pants in town to get 'em...only pair I had...' My voice failed. My legs felt like water. Shit. My eyes blurred, my ears whistled.

The lousy crud of the Service Police. Chicken shit dress regulations. How nice and polite and understanding they were when they stopped me on the street in York. 'We'll just take your name,' they'd said. No, no, they'd insisted, don't give it a thought. Just a matter of form. Sure, sure, we understand. Only pair of pants you've got. The lousy, lying, two-faced rotten cruds, sending my name in on a charge. In despair and impotent hopeless outrage I felt like crying, but I felt too tired to cry. Too weary to speak, I stared down at my feet.

The C.O leaned on his elbows on the desk and surveyed me. His mouth opened slowly. In a measured clipped tone he said, 'Norton, I'm going to give you ten days. Ten days confined to camp. I've been fifteen years in the Air Force.' He leaned back in his chair. 'I started out as an aircraftman second class. I've been all through the mill, and I don't care if you flew last night, I'm going to have discipline around here. Do you understand?'

I did not say anything.

'Do you understand?'

I did not speak. I could not understand how people could be like this. I thought of all of us terrified in the Halifax, the aircraft staggering back across the English coast in the dark, on fire, with the undercarriage shot away and the radio gone and no aileron control.

After a long moment I said 'Yes,' quietly, and looked past the C.O with an air at once queerly detached and serene, an expression profound and tranquil, while I listened to my voice going somewhere beyond me. 'Yes, I understand,' nodding my head dream-like. 'Yes... Is that all?' The C.O looked at me.

'That's all. Report to the Office of the day every evening at 1900 hours. You may go.'

I stood, not moving, in a kind of trance, my eyes empty and dazed.

'You may go!'

I saluted like a robot and went out,

moving with the airless, oblivious quality of a sleep-walker. My eyes seemed to be open on nothing, and I blundered dumbly along the hall, bumping against the wall, and then out into the cold air with the thin icy rain waking me from wherever my mind seemed to have gone. I felt myself walking on in a vacuum in which time and distance seemed to have ceased.

When I reached my room I lay down on my cot with my eyes closed, feeling as though I wanted to cry a little, but I could not even find strength enough to curse the C.O.

Chapter 7

I lay on my bed with my clothes on. I lay there smoking, looking up at the ceiling. I knew it was hopeless to close my eyes. I would not be able to sleep. I was dead beat but I could not sleep. I lay there a long time, thinking about our crew, wondering who had voted against aborting to Sweden. We would need a mission at least as far east as Kiel to make it credible. But who had voted against it? Would Robinson know? Could he tell by the printing on each ballot? Probably not.

Christ, why was I afraid to quit? Afraid to die and afraid to quit? But tired of trying to live up to the picture of myself, the intrepid young airman. Now I was so damned ashamed. All I wanted was out. Some clean way out, but I didn't want to feel like a coward. Well, hero, suck on your medals now. How do you quit without feeling like a bloody coward? No, to hell with England. Let them save themselves. What did one more flier mean? No, that wouldn't wash. Being a coward hurt, and quitting meant you were a coward and I was a damn coward if I quit.

For an instant I could see myself going to the C.O and asking to be taken off flying. He would have a fit. Then there would be a court martial. And I would be sent to the Glass House. From what I'd heard about the Glass House, dying was easier. You got clubbed by the guards, and did everything on the double, including going to the toilet.

'Sir, I can't polish my belly button anymore, I want to quit.'

That would set him off. I'd get two years in the Glass House.'

'Sir, I want to be grounded. I'm afraid to die and I don't give a crap about England anymore.'

But I felt so damn old, really old. I couldn't remember the person I had been three years ago. I lay there half dazed, thinking like that, and suddenly I must have fallen asleep. I began to dream, yet knowing I was dreaming, but liking that I knew it was a dream; hearing music across summer air above a lake, the sweet sound of jazz falling in soft waves down through the elms where the edge of the lake met the drooping boughs of the trees. A girl's face in silhouette against the darkness and the water and light from the water flickering in her hair, and the music coming softly. Somewhere an orchestra was playing.

Suddenly the sound of the sea filled the dream, and the wind crying cold over the Yorkshire moors. No, it was the gray cold of the sea wind off Friston, and below the sea pounded against the white cliffs. And in the noise of the sea I saw clouds passing over the moon, and then black Messerschmitts diving, the whining roar of their engines rising to a crescendo that seemed to pass out of the realm of sound. Long threads of fire coming at me, going through me, but there was no pain. I woke up sweating and shaking. I opened the black-out curtains. The sun was shining. Never had the grass looked so brilliantly green, the trees so beautiful. I felt strangely rested. I started to whistle. There wouldn't be any missions for at least two weeks. It would take that long to form up a new squadron. I whistled, making my bed. Then I went down the hall to Robinson's room. He was sitting up in bed reading *The News of the World* with his head against the wall.

'What's the gen?' I asked.

'Pretty duff.'

My heart sank.

'What do you mean?'

'We'll be operating again in a couple of days.'

'Impossible. They can't take that many sprog crews and train them for ops in a couple days,' I said.

'No sprogs. Group is sending over what is left of Seventy-Six Squadron, and Operational Training Command has a couple of experienced crews who've finished screening periods. So they're joining us.'

After a tour of thirty missions crews were screened for a couple months, which meant they were taken off combat status and sent to operational training school to instruct green aircrew.

I said, 'Who voted against Sweden?'

'I don't know.'

'Can't you tell by the handwriting?'

'No. Remember I asked everybody to print.'

'How many voted No?'

Robinson raised one hand, smiled, made a V for Victory sign with two fingers.

'Okay,' I said and went straight out the door.

'Mack!' he yelled, but there was nothing he could do, and nothing more I wanted to know. I went down the hall. The door to Folkes's room was open. He was sitting on the edge of his bed, polishing the buttons on his tunic.

'Bob,' I said. 'Do me a favor.'

'Anything but money.'

'How did you vote on the trip to Sweden?'

He didn't look up. He polished a tunic button harder.

He said, 'I'm for it. I voted yes. We've had it.'

'Thanks.'

Dickson lived in the next Nissen hut. I saw smoke coming out of the chimney from his stove. I looked over at the roof of the outdoor toilet next door. The wood roof was gone again. Somebody had stripped it off for firewood.

Jaynes was in Dickson's room. They were both kneeling on the floor rolling the dice. Pay day in two weeks. Ever since I'd introduced crap shooting to the squadron Dickson and Jaynes were losers. They didn't know the odds and I wasn't

72

about to tell them. They also didn't know how to control dice if somebody rolled them on a blanket instead of against the wall. They were practicing rolling them on a blanket.

They turned their heads and looked over their shoulders at me. Dickson was grinning.

'Dumdum here owes five hundred quid so far,' Dickson said.

'On credit,' said Jaynes. 'You'll never live to collect it.'

'Listen,' I said. 'I want to ask you something seriously.'

'Shoot,' said Jaynes and Dickson rolled the dice. 'Come on. Fever! What do you get in the swamps, baby? Fever!' He rolled the dice again and up came seven. 'Keeerap!' he bellowed and slammed the dice down on the blanket. Jaynes picked up the dice, cackled them in one hand, blew on his hands.

'Big seven for daddy!'

I leaned down and put my right hand on Dickson's back and my left on Jayne's back and pushed. Both fell forward on their chests. I gave Jaynes a gentle nudge in the butt with my shoe.

'Listen,' I said. 'How did you guys vote about lobbing down in Sweden?'

Jaynes rolled over on his back, raised his right hand. 'Yes.'

73

Dickson nodded his head up and down.

'Something's screwy,' I said and turned toward the door.

'What's the trouble?' Jaynes said.

'Tell you later.' I went out the door fast and slammed it shut. I didn't want them to know I was going to Larry Stevens' room. He was at the other end of the Nissen hut. I went out the door nearest Dickson's room and slammed the outer door so they could hear me leaving. Then I went swiftly around the Nissen hut on the far side to the door at the opposite end.

I opened Stevens' door without knocking. He was lying on his stomach reading the *London Times*. He turned his head. He looked sore.

'Bloody hell,' he said. 'Don't you Yanks have any manners?'

'You know the colonials.' I shut the door. 'Listen, Larry. There's something I've got to know.'

He sighed, turned on his side, propped his head on one hand. He looked bored.

'Well, get on with it.'

'How did you vote on the Swedish deal?'

'None of your business.'

'Please, Larry. I've got to know.'

'Why?'

'Just tell me yes or no.'

74

'Why?'

'I think something's fishy.'

'Such as?'

'Well, if everybody voted yes, why didn't Robinson say so?'

'How do you know they did?'

'I won't know until you tell me how you voted.'

'Yes.'

'Yes, what?'

'I voted yes.'

'For Crissake,' I said. 'Somebody's lying. I voted yes. It was Robinson's idea, so why wouldn't he vote yes?'

'Did you ask him?'

'No reason to. It was his idea.'

'Obviously, somebody's lying,' Stevens said in a bored voice. 'So what?' He rolled back on his stomach. 'Mind you close the door, please.' He flattened the *London Times* and started to read again.

Outside it was almost dusk. This was the time we would be getting in the trucks to ride out to our aircraft if we were operating. It felt wonderful not to go. The night was mine. No worry. No fear. But something was really fishy. Somewhere a stink, but I couldn't put my finger on it. Somewhere a stink. Somebody was lying. Maybe two people were lying. But why wouldn't they vote yes? Well, face it, I thought, somebody isn't afraid, that's all there is to it. Somebody hasn't lost confidence. Somebody believes in what they're doing. Believes enough to die, but it was easy to believe that way if you still had that wonderful feeling of being invulnerable. Ah, to have that again as I had felt in the beginning of the war. To believe you would never be killed or wounded. Somebody else might, but not you, and then to know the terrible truth. Then to go on flying you had to be dumb or courageous. I was no longer courageous. I wanted to live. I didn't want to die for anybody. But you're too ashamed to admit you're a coward, I thought.

Then it struck me. It was strange the way it happened, but I couldn't put any of it together then. But it was strange the way it happened. Have you ever just been walking along and for no reason at all the words from an old song will start running through your head?

It was kind of like that, this strange thought that seemed to come out of nowhere, but later I knew what had caused it. In the dark sky I found myself watching a Halifax making an approach to land, blinking its wing lights, red and green, just two stars, red and green, suspended in the darkness, then moving down through the darkness. How like stars they were. *Heinkel, Heinkel, little star, how I wonder what you are,* started running through my mind, and for a reason I'll never know I suddenly started thinking how at the end of each briefing we sometimes would have to wait five or ten minutes.

'We'll have the German colors of the day for you in a few minutes,' the intelligence office would say. We would sit quietly waiting, wondering what the Luftwaffe Very Signal colors would be tonight. Red-red? Green-red-green?

Then if we were conned in the searchlights we would fire the German Very signal colors. And the Germans would think it was one of their fighters and pull away the searchlights.

But what had happened over Essen? My skin crawled and prickled along the back of my neck. We had been conned in searchlight beams. We had fired the correct colors, but the searchlights kept us pinpointed and the flak burst all around us.

Christ, I thought, doubting my thoughts for a second. Could it be possible the Germans had somebody who had infiltrated bomber command just as the RAF apparently had somebody in the Luftwaffe who wirelessed via Morse code the German colors of the day to us?

77

And the Germans knew that we knew their colors of the day and then changed them after being notified that we had received them? Was it possible?

Slowly, very slowly, I began to wonder. Why were the night fighters always waiting for us? Why didn't the colors of the day work any more? Why were our losses so high?

Did the Germans have an agent in the RAF who wirelessed them time and position of our target?

Why not? If we could have an agent over there sending us their signal colors, why couldn't they have an agent among us?

Why did they always seem to know the path of the bomber stream? *Why were our losses so high?*

Darkness shrouded the earth. The stars hung cold and remote. There was no sound in the sky. I began to shiver. God, we didn't have a chance if they knew our targets! Was it possible? What chance was there to survive if the Germans knew our moves? But if I quit there was the Glass House, worse than the American chain gang.

If I went on flying, I would die for sure. Goddamn it, I said aloud over and over again. I'm trapped. Completely trapped. I began to sweat.

Chapter 8

Now, two nights later, beyond the moving tip of the port wing as the Halifax Bomber turned slowly, rearing big on its tires, on to the flare path and into wind, I sat as the gunner in the mid-upper turret, looking out between my guns. I saw the green signal light flash by the control tower. A quickening of the heart, a terrible feeling of loneliness in the cold Yorkshire dusk, as quickly gone as felt, swept away into the sound of throttled engines. And below the turret, on the grass near the flare path, a clotting of dark figures—crews not on 'ops', the C.O's car; already a few hands half raised in a gesture of farewell, lips shaping 'Cheerio!' 'Good trip!' 'See you at breakfast!' Engines roared, fuselage shuddered, green light flashed 'Go' in the twilight. Behind the rear-turret, grass trembled, flattened...

The old worry was there, would I return tonight? Ah, hell, only to Italy? All the reassuring descriptive phrases entered my head. 'Piece of cake.' 'Only light flak.' 'You know how the Eyties were at Genoa.' 'No night fighters over Turin...very feeble if there are fighters.' All the remembered encouragement of the intelligence officer at briefing, filled my mind... Then I remembered the last two trips on Essen... Kite all shot to hell...Jesus Christ!

I felt the cocking toggle catch, heard the clash of the breech block sliding home, felt the strange queer feeling of guns cocked and ready to fire; cold exhilaration! Of course I'd make it tonight. Foolish worrying. No point. Should have mailed letter to Joan this afternoon. Soon as I get back...

I looked out on the dying sun to the West; orange light laked an immeasurable sky, profound, tranquil, empty, the world dying. World empty. Lonely, remote as a gull, the machine passed, moved steadily across the evening. Reaching, fumbling with gloved hands, I found the raisin bag in a little iron tray to my left, squeezing a few into my mouth, under my oxygen mask. I spat them out almost at once. Damn! Seeds! What had happened to all the seedless raisins that once were issued? I felt annoyed. I stretched, cramped.

'Hello, Dickson! How about a course to the coast?'

'Okay, George. Just a second.'

Dickson up ahead, bent over his navigation table; an old family guy, I thought, ought to be home with his wife.

I put the cocking toggle back in its clip.

'Okay, George. Course one eight six magnetic.'

'Righto! I say, could you give me E.T.A to the coast?'

'Be with you in a minute.'

'Righto, boy.'

Good old Robinson, I thought; fine skipper.

In the rosy sky ahead I watched another bomber hover seemingly motionless, following, a mile away. That night at Essen! Good old Robinson. Best damn pilot for the worst damn places. Caught in the searchlight (Oh, God! This is it!) Where were they all now? Cook, Clark, Jake? Faces in old Messes, faces in other bunk houses; names on a casualty list. Rostock, Hamburg, Dusseldorf, Ruhr! They were all out there somewhere. Not even the recall of their faces meant anything anymore beyond the mere fact of their only and simply being recalled as dead. Gone.

Climbing steadily now, feeling the earth go away farther and farther, and far below, through a break in the clouds, a glimpse of a river, silver, shining, twisting. If you were going to go you were going to go, I thought. Only fools believed rosaries and rabbits' feet would help. A toss of a coin. You were in or out of the game. But it was not as easy as that. What if you lived with your arms burned off?

Dickson's voice squeaked over the intercom.

'Hello, George. We're crossing the coast, or should be, if we're not. New course is one two seven magnetic.'

Then Robinson's light, crisp, cheerful voice. 'Oh! I say you chaps! Here it comes! Huns glorious greeting!'

Far ahead to starboard somewhere, I knew not where, as leaning forward in the turret I saw the searchlights and flak. Light flak, I thought at once, seeing a few long bending strings of red lights, swaying and climbing above the clouds, while shafts of light probed, sabred, fingered and pointed into the darkness. A few flashes of fire, smears of white light shone briefly ahead through the clouds and vanished like white blossoms snatched suddenly away. 'Jesus! Jesus!' I was saying to myself, breathing hard, thinking, 'Heavy flak, very little, must be somewhere near the mouth of the Somme!' Cramped, waiting, I crouched forward, moving the turret from side to side, standing now, looking down, far down to the clouds below on both sides, knowing I was panicking slightly, holding to myself mechanically, out of practice and experience, wishing that for a moment some flak would burst near. Everything would be all right then. It was being away from it that bothered me. A taste of a few close bursts and I knew I would feel better.

Folkes's voice from the front turret. 'Flak ahead, George. Turn sharp starboard.'

Jaynes's voice: 'That's miles away!'

I was studying the sky above the starboard rudder when I heard Folkes's voice: 'Hello, George. Some searchlights ahead.'

I quickly looked out between my guns.

An hour later, eyes swollen and ass numb, I held in one hand my frozen oxygen tube, feeling kernels of ice under the pressure of my hand, cursing the tubing, hoping it would clear, as I listened over the intercom to the usual night's debate concerning our position. Robinson was asking Dickson where we were, trying almost in vain to keep his tone courteous. Dickson's irritated voice explained halfheartedly he wasn't sure of our position, but would have it in a minute.

After a moment Dickson asked Larry Stevens, the wireless operator, to get an accurate bearing. Stevens replied that something was wrong with his wireless. I looked out at the full moon, and far below at the moon-lit field of level white cloud. I released my oxygen tube and discovered happily I could breathe without gagging in my mask; the ice had melted. I started thinking sleepily of Joan, her thoughts, her speech, her beliefs. What a fantastic woman she was. Her lips, her soft cheeks, her black lovely long hair, her perfect straight legs. What a good sound her voice was.

I yawned, looked out at the dark side of the sky. Robinson informed the crew we were heading into a fog. Dickson told Robinson a course to fly. Worried, I decided Dickson was a little too young to be a navigator, especially, I felt, after some of the hellish spots he steered us to, the searchlight- flak-lighted nights we'd been caught in over Dunkirk and Boulogne. I felt there was no excuse for Dickson having positioned us there; it frightened me, even now, to remember those nights. I hoped nothing like that happened tonight. I thought of the night George, our original bomb-aimer, had been killed, and what a piece of luck we'd had not being killed the same night; just one piece of flak through George's skull. And George's funeral, the cold, long march to the cemetery with the bagpipes squeaking a lament all the way, and the animal-like sobs of the relatives, and the monotonous mourning speech of the Minister, and George's coffin with

'Age 19' on the brass plate. I felt tired and cold.

Later, with the mid-upper turret facing forward, the guns pointing ahead along the fuselage, and looking out past the astral dome, the wings dark, and engines filling both sides of my vision, I saw the Alps straight ahead, a monstrous, silent jagged crest against a faded starlit sky, and far below, as I stood up in the turret to look down, the valleys in front of the Alps were great lakes of darkness. Here and there I saw a single light twinkle and was reminded of passing over the scattered lines of lights a few minutes before that marked the streets of Berne.

I looked down at the great streaks of snow on the brown mountains thrusting up ahead and on both sides, thinking the Alps were not so stirring and of far less importance than the possible presence of a night-fighter. The Italian night-fighters were weak. But there was the full moon and the clear sky. Even the most infirm pilot in the most ancient fighter could take a crack at a bomber on a night like this, with all the elements so favourable.

'Jesus Christ!' suddenly crackled over the intercom; and in a tone of admiration and astonishment Robinson said, 'My God! Dickson! You're dead on track. Look!'

Turning the turret aft, I looked out along the fuselage, past the nose and saw ahead, far off beyond and above a scallop cut out of the wavy top line of the Alps, the first glowing, pink reflection on the sky of Turin burning in the valley, and the snaking, turning, twisting, climbing threads of light red flak barely appearing above the line of the Alps.

'I don't know how I did it,' Dickson was saying. 'I didn't know where the hell we were when we came south of Paris. It's just luck, that's all.'

Everyone insisted it wasn't luck, that Dickson was a wizard navigator. The tenseness of waiting partly gone, and now having almost half the trip completed, brought everyone in the crew over the intercom with his particular compliment for Dickson. Everyone was happy and partly relieved.

I swiveled my turret aft and looked ahead beyond the nose at Mont Blanc as indomitable and unmovable and misty and snowy as anything I had ever seen, dead ahead, while the aircraft, with its natural illusion of not appearing to move forward, but to face motionless, the peak moved up slightly, and I wondered would we make it? Then as we slowly climbed, the peak seemed to diminish downward, to pass under the machine though the peak was still twenty miles away.

'We'll make it by five hundred feet,' Robinson said.

'Christ,' said Folkes. 'Looks like we're going to run right into it.'

'This old kite feels like it's going to come right out and groan if I pull it up anymore,' Robinson said.

'Give it a boot in the fanny and let's get over the fucking hill,' Jaynes called from the tail turret.

Folkes yelled 'We're over!' and then I saw Turin and the fires, the city walled dark on all sides by mountain slopes, and a machine ahead dropping flares, descending in a slow burning glow. One, two, three. I counted the flares, and wondered why, and who the hell would be dropping flares this distance from the town. Must be in trouble, I thought, hearing Robinson's comment on the light flak. 'Oh, I say, here comes those Christmas-tree doo-dads.'

Simultaneously Folkes shouted 'Weave, Robby! Hard to starboard. Heavy stuff coming up, pretty close behind!' I looked out and below and saw the yellow blobs of flashes, and decided it was close, and watched the round balls of smoke dissolve and get further behind as the machine moved steadily toward the target.

'Lovely, isn't it?' Folkes called from the nose. I saw down through the darkness, squinting, straining my eyes, the long white mounds of incendiaries marking the target. Pressing my forehead against the perspex, as if it would enable me to see better, I made out, through breaks in the smoke covering the city, the curving, small dark lines of streets and caramel-size squares in minute regularity that were the tops of houses. Then I saw the docks—ten grey square fingers, enveloped by smoke, and the moonlit glint of water underneath. Yes, I thought, it was lovely all right, and I sat down. It was more lovely than Bremen or Hamburg, or Duisburg or Cologne or Essen. Yes, it was lovely because the Italians couldn't hit you, and I never felt more certain of anything in my life. Yes, it was lovely, and it was the Fourth of July and a Hollywood premiere, and they couldn't kill you over the target and you'd get back all right, and maybe you wouldn't even see any fighters on the way home. Maybe, but you doubted it. They were sure to be up now, waiting at the French coast.

I sat stiffly and watched the flak burst below and harmlessly to the rear.

'Bombs gone,' I heard Folkes's voice. 'Let's get the hell out of here. Those guys stink but they've still got guns.'

Robinson laughed. 'Let's fly through one of their searchlights for the hell of it. Bet

88

you two to one they turn it off when we do.'

Balls, I thought, what a mad bunch of goons. Let's get home.

An hour later, munching a raisin as comfortably as my oxygen mask would permit, I crouched down on the end of my spine trying to find a portion of my ass that wasn't numb. I settled my weight on the bottom of my right thigh and fought to stay awake. It's all over now, I thought, we're good as home; I slipped another raisin under my oxygen mask and munched slowly and watched the fog obscure the wing-tips. An immeasurable, depthless sea of milky vapour, I thought, while I fished with my tongue against the roof of my mouth for the raisin that was stuck there.

Only one hour, I thought gratefully, feeling happy and confident. And suddenly all fatigue dropped away, and as if to prove to myself I was ready for any emergency, I swivelled the turret around, making search of a sky filled only with fog.

Forty-five more minutes to the French coast, I thought, and probably every little Focke-Wulfe in France is now tooling around looking for us. I checked the light in the reflector sight and heard Dickson's voice.

'This wind's a bitch, Robby.'

'Well, where are we? Do you, by any mysterious luck, have a vague idea where we are?' Robinson asked sarcastically.

'Fly one three zero magnetic. Radio compass has packed up. I think we're south of Paris.'

'That's just ducky,' answered Robinson more sarcastically.

'Have a course for you in a minute,' Dickson said in a hurt voice. 'These winds have got me all screwed up. The met's all wrong.'

Folkes's voice cut through Dickson's words.

'For Crissake! You're not kidding! We're not *near* Paris, we're *over* it!'

And looking out past the rudders, I saw the first eighteen black puffs of heavy flak, thinking, Damn close, frightened.

Jaynes's voice contained that quality of confidence given only to crap shooters accustomed to rolling consecutive naturals.

'Turn starboard, Robby. It's pretty fucking close.' I felt and saw the wing go down and the level clouds below and there above and behind five hundred yards away, I watched eighteen more black sausage shaped bursts of heavy flak that hung as tightly together as black night-fighters in formation. I thought, with a sense of relief, Well, that's one battery fired a round. Now to get the hell out of here. Any battery who could get our altitude and range so closely at sixteen thousand feet with one volley were dangerous to the point of getting a direct hit. Then I was swinging the turret around to starboard, the wing tip up, the sky and stars now above my left shoulder. I saw the flashing patches of light that were flak bursts on the clouds. Suddenly I saw the sky and stars directly behind and above the rudders and knew we were diving.

'Weave, Robby! For fuck sake, weave!' Jaynes's voice was level and collected, yet desperate.

I swung the turret from side to side, darting my gaze, thinking, wondering. When, when, when, are they going to hit us? In fear and sweat I crouched and watched, feeling completely helpless, the dark puffs of flak bursting now at regular intervals on both sides of the aircraft. Then I heard explosions like the dull thud of a brass drum strike one resounding boom directly under the turret.

'Jesus, Robby!' Jaynes was calling. 'That was close! Everything okay?'

No answer.

'Hey, lads! Can you hear me? Is everything okay?'

'Well, we're not dead, are we?' someone

said over the intercom.

I felt the sweat around my stomach and chest. I wondered how much altitude we had lost and started a careful search of the sky knowing we were still in the night-fighter zone.

'Anybody know a nice comfortable place to cross the coast?' Robby asked.

Everyone was momentarily happy again. 'You mean no flak, no searchlights, no fighters?' Folkes asked in a light innocent voice.

'Are you kidding?' Jaynes said sourly.

I looked over the side, felt suddenly that far down in the darkness I saw a pattern of lesser darkness, like a map of lace against the bottom of the dark space.

I called, 'It does look like something below us. The sea or something.' I pressed my face against the perspex glass and squinted desperately. Was I fooling myself?

Yes, I decided, looking down again to make sure, seeing rippling white waves, yes, sure it's the sea, I told myself.

'Damn sure we're over the Channel,' I said.

'Okay, boy,' Robinson's voice suddenly cheery. 'Good-oh! Thanks much.'

I lounged against the butts of my guns, drowsing, fighting sleep. I slapped my cheeks, shook my head. Jaynes's voice startled me awake like a hot needle passing through my guts. 'Mack!' I looked out on a sky filled with searchlights, swinging, searching, probing, dozens of white spears against the black sky. I sat staring, swinging the turret back and forth.

'Weave, starboard!' I yelled, crouched, watching ten searchlights bending and fingering across the sky toward us, seeking, coming on steadfast. Beyond and on all sides I saw other searchlights, moving, swinging, darting, looking for us. Suddenly, the clouds opened above, and moon and stars shone, and the searchlights were on us. Blinded, I twisted to one side and ducked my head and looked around the side of the armour plate placed above the guns.

'Weave! Weave!' I was calling coolly.

Fighters'll come up through their own flak, I thought. I felt dead, yet knowing I would fight and do what I had been taught to do. I looked around the plate of armour, watching between the searchlights for fighters while I saw the stars wheel and spin and the sky whirl. Where are we? I was terrified again. What are we doing? Stars appeared below. Searchlights seemed to have two ends. Which end was attached to the earth? We were inside a hollow ball, the entire inside of which was lined with darkness streaked and criss-crossed by searchlights, speckled by stars, the ball continually rotating in all directions. I closed, opened my eyes against the lights, blinded.

Then suddenly the searchlight was out of eyes but there were innumerable lights groping toward the plane from the port side, and heard Folkes' voice, even and controlled, 'Keep weaving, Robby! They've got our altitude,' while flak bursts in white balls of smoke hung momentarily suspended then dissolved in the searchlights.

Then the port wing dropped and I knew the machine was diving to port. Would we get away, keeping my eyes on the groping searchlights. Balls! Balls! Balls! I thought, and heard my voice, 'Keep turning, Robby! The stuff's right behind us!' The machine bounced, lurched.

'Christ!' The searchlights were in my eyes again. Maybe this is it! No, no, no, this isn't it. The beam swerved. They're not going to get us. They won't. They won't. They won't. They mustn't. 'They will,' another voice repeated inside my head. 'They will.'

I gripped the gun control column, thumb of my right hand lightly resting on the firing button, waiting, waiting, panting and sweating, then holding my breath.

There was no sound over the intercom and the searchlights caught and glared on the turret and again, for the third time, I saw our tail and rudders lift, and a section of the sky widen and continue to widen under the tail. Watching the flak I could not even think to know we were diving. Nothing in my mind told me we were diving. My eyes saw the change in positions of sky and plane, but I only sat and stared out between my guns and waited, watching for a night-fighter. Let the heavens roll around. Watch for that bloody shark in the night.

'Keep weaving, Robby.' My voice was hoarse and tired. Then I felt the shuddering jar and heard the dull drum-like 'Boomf' underneath of flak exploding right under us.

'They got us,' I called in the casual tone, too tired to sound anything else but reconciled to the belief that now only a few more moments waited and a direct hit would kill all of us.

In the glare of light, the shape of the fuselage thrust back from the turret, its lines as definite as though painted white. More searchlights rushed across the darkness, seeking an alliance with those already on the plane. I leaned my head against the plate of armor and waited. How was it going to come? Blow up? Engine on fire? Tail shot off? I pressed my head hard against the armor plate and started making plans for bailing out.

'Robby, for Crissake! Do something!' Jaynes's desperation call was feeble. Searchlights held us. Flak came on, unceasing. 'Keep weaving, Robby. Keep weaving,' somebody called.

'Sorry, chaps,' Robinson said suddenly, as if he were pleading for forgiveness. 'I did the best I could,' and I saw the rudders and tail come level, then bisect the dark horizon.

My head pressed hard against the armor plate. I waited. Only a minute more. Robinson was giving up. Sure sign. All over. Sonofabitching luck! Goddam! Robinson giving up. Anybody'd give up, Robinson gives up. Nobody do anything if Robinson can't. I raised my head and looked out into the searchlight. Get a fighter, anyway. Bastard! Light left my eyes. Sky went topsy-turvy. Stars wheeled, spun, and after a moment I saw not far behind, searchlights flattening, reaching, flattening. We were free! They couldn't reach us. I wanted to scream, shout with happiness. Free! We made it. Probing, sabring in vain, the searchlights arced across the darkness, and I sat jubilant.

'Robby!' I called. 'That was beautiful. Wizard!' Compliments filled the intercom. 'Christ, what flying!'

'Good show, Robby.'

Ahead, beyond the English Channel, thrusting up in the fog, two stationary searchlights crossed, bisecting each other. England! I thought, knowing a sense of relief similar, I was sure, to anything Columbus might have felt at the sight of America. Oh God! Oh God! Oh God! I'm happy! I felt the words repeated over and over in my head, and heard Folkes calling 'That must have been Calais.'

'What a bright boy,' Jaynes interrupted dryly. 'What the hell did you think it was?'

Where were we? What part of England? Larry Stevens, the wireless operator said he was unable to decode the last ground message which was telling us where we were and where to land. I cursed him.

What a fool I've been, I thought. How easy it would have been not to have volunteered. Dopey kid. Yet I knew I could not quit; that when they called me out tomorrow, and the long dark road of days ahead, I would be going. Dusseldorf, Emden, Brest, Bremen, Hamburg. A sudden white arc of a searchlight swept up into the fog for an instant, then vanished. Down, down we rushed into the smoky fog. I stared out into milky soupy fog, waiting.

'Robby! There's a light blinking L.

Robby to port!' Folkes's voice sang out.

Then suddenly the light vanished. Fog, depthless, soundless, immeasurable. Wings enveloped again. A wingless fuselage rushing down into nothing. Ring sight redly luminous. Seven aircrew seated rigid, braced, waiting, watching.

'Anybody see anything?' Robinson asked. No answer. Then 'Hello, Upton, Hello Upton. This is J Johnnie calling Upton. Can you give me cloud base, please?' No answer. 'Hello Upton. Can you give me cloud base please... Hello...'

I saw Robinson's hands on the control wheel sweated inside his gloves. We waited in our positions.

'For Crissake, Larry,' Robinson bawled to the wireless operator. 'Get group and get us Q.D.M to base. Find out where we are.'

'Half the Royal Air Force is on the air trying to do that same thing,' said Stevens.

'Ready, chaps,' Robby called. 'I'm going down through. We're at three thou. Watch for lights.'

I swung the turret around and looked out over the motionless propellor of the port inner engine. Directly ahead, at right angles to the aircraft, a searchlight thrust a horizontal path of light through the fog, pointing the way to the aerodrome. Below the ground was dark, completely lightless. The wing dipped, came level again. I swallowed, my throat filled with a dry copperish taste.

Suddenly the searchlight swung around, and I saw our astral dome and fuselage glitter, and heard Robinson cursing.

'The dim-witted bastard! Putting it in my eyes.' Suddenly below the fog dissolved. Lights! Thank God. The ground!

Ahead the black lane of the runway between the spaced yellow flares, and off to the right, a light blinking red. No, no, I thought wildly, standing bolt-upright, suddenly afraid.

'Go round again!' I wanted to shout. 'You'll never make it.' The flare path was still below and to the left. 'We're going to overshoot. We're going to prang!' I shouted. The sound of engines throttled back filled the intercom. On the intercom I heard Robinson panting furiously, 'Aaaah —Aaaah,' holding his breath under the strain.

'Okay, chaps. Brace yourselves. Might be a bit ropey landing,' Robinson said.

Steady, Robby steady, I thought. Steady. Easy. Christ, don't try side-slipping this kite on three engines! Robby! Robby!... The machine dropped suddenly.

My God, we're going to prang for sure!

My heart hammered with fear.

Then suddenly I saw the beacon on the ground blinking green. We're okay, I thought. The wheels touched, the machine bounced, became airborne again.

Almost at once Robinson shouted: 'Back! Back!' He clenched the control wheel. 'Pull the throttles back!'

'Home, we're home,' I murmured, crazily happy. Robinson was calling the control tower. 'Hello, hello, this is J Johnny. We have just landed. Could you tell me where to park it? I will repeat. This is J Johnny... Will you...'

'How'd you like that one?' Jaynes laughed over the intercom. I watched another aircraft coming in to land, caught in the directing searchlight.

Robinson braked and opened the throttles on the starboard engines and slowly turned the aircraft off the end of the flare path. We climbed out.

'Who's buying beer in the Mess?' Jaynes yelled, exhilarated as we walked across the field to the Intelligence Room.

'Hey, what drome is this?' Stevens yelled. He was grinning goofily, looking around in the darkness.

Later, as on many nights before, the truck moved away from the Interrogation Office. Seated in the back on the floor, I looked out into the cold Surrey dawn and thought how wonderful the warm food would taste in the Mess. My mouth filled with saliva. Oh, God, it was good to be home again.

Chapter 9

I woke in the dark, shaking, hearing music. A hand, a voice roused me. I was lying on my back. The surface was hard. When I rolled over my neck and shoulders ached.

'Mack,' a voice said teasing. 'Wakey, wakey! Tea and cakey!' But it was not the mocking voice of the duty sergeant that roused us every morning with those words over the tannoy system back at the squadron.

Then I realized I was not at the squadron. We had landed last night on a Spitfire field on the coast of the English channel, a field with grassy runways. I was lying on a billiard table in the squadron Mess. Maisen and I had slept on it because there weren't any beds available in the squadron Nissen huts. In the dark somebody was playing the tune 'Dancing in The Dark' on a phonograph somewhere in the room. The song before I fell asleep seemed sad and mournful. It made me feel very old, out of the dead time of my summer high school days.

'Let's get some breakfast,' Eddy Maisen said.

I rolled over. 'I'll be along.' I listened to his footsteps. Then suddenly in a shock I realized I had never asked him how he had voted concerning desertion to Sweden. I sat up quickly.

'Maisen,' I called. I jumped off the table. He was out in the hall. There were sleeping figures back on the carpeted floor. He turned, halted. There was a dark smear of oil on his cheek.

'Tell me,' I said in a low voice. 'How did you vote about Sweden?'

His lips cracked in a smile.

'Vote?' Then he grinned, balled one hand into a fist, and held it in front of my nose. His thumb stuck up. 'How else, chum? You?'

I gave him a thumbs up.

'I'd like to know who the sod was who vetoed it,' he said. Then he slapped me on the shoulder. 'See you at breakfast.'

'I'm going to kip in a little more.'

I stood in the hall. He went away. So I was alive again, alone, standing in a strange hall, on a strange squadron. Where were we? What field?

I went to the door and looked out across the brilliant green grassy field. There were the Spitfires, a long line glistening in the sunlight on their stork-like legs. They seemed to lie in a hazy pearl-like glow. The brilliant sunlight glazed the field. I looked at my arms, the black hairs rising from my flesh. I was alive. I was back again.

I opened the door and stepped outside. On the grass, beneath the trees were patches of sunlight that flickered and faded and grew bright again. I could see our Halifax across the field, huge and black, rearing high above the Spitfires, a ghastly big, black bird above the shining silver sparrows. My heart said, 'You're here, you're here...alive.' I narrowed my eyes against the bright sunlight. I felt my nerves tighten. I might be shot for deserting. Did they ever shoot airmen deserters? I did not know. No, they were sent to the Glass House. I might as well be dead. No, anything was better than being dead. Than being Never. I felt my face brighten as if with a fever. I would not fly another mission. I would never get in a plane again. It was all over. I would never fly again because they could not make me fly again. I was through.

For an instant the field seemed to darken as the sun passed into a cloud, and then it was bright again and I was walking over the grass, turning up a dirt road, leading into a forest. I went on between the trees. Big beech trees on each side of the road. From time to time I heard music and for an instant, I thought it was the phonograph back in the Mess, and then I realized it was bagpipe music—it was up ahead of me.

Before I saw the column, the bagpipes wailed again. Then the rutted lane curved and I saw the pipers. Above the company of Highland Light Infantry, the thin high notes of pipes streamed back upon the still air like the crying of dying birds. Then suddenly there was no sound in the blue sky, only echoes of the pipes crying, mournful and sad.

I walked along behind the pipers. Sunlight came through the trees in long yellow pencils of light. Then I was walking too fast. I slowed. They were walking the slow tread of the dead march. Ahead of the column a flag-draped catafalque moved, horse drawn. Suddenly the sun burned away clouds and the sky glared down, vivid as glass.

Abruptly the bagpipes ceased. In the silence there was only the sound of marching boots, the tread sullen and muffled, the slow march of the dead.

The pipers turned as the track curved. Suddenly I felt shame and regret for having told myself I would never fly again. I belong there...in the coffin...I must not fly again. I must not fly again.

Still there was only a single sound in the air, the soft shuffling tread of marching boots. Then the crying shriek of pipes came again. For a moment the catafalque paused, flag-draped, bearing a single wreath of flowers.

Then the column moved. At the turn in the dirt road I saw three women in black, with veils over their faces, standing with heads bowed as the column passed. Mourners. Perhaps mother, wife and sister. They were keening, their anguished cries rising sharp and terrible above the sound of the pipes, then swept away into the high sunny air.

The column went on. Sunlight lay thickly over the grassy slopes. The sky was a curved dome of glass. The sound of the women mourning went on, their sobbing mounting to a furious animal wail that seemed to pass completely out of the realm of human grief until it became one with the crescendo scream of bagpipes.

I followed the column steadily across the field. The sun was rising higher. The golden glare of sunlight poured down. The wind in the field beyond the marching column was quieting as if silence were a substance like water slowly coming toward us over the field.

Roofs of a little town beyond the field

were visible between the tops of trees.

Then I saw the church, the spire sticking up above the hayfields, above the red-tiled roofs of small square stone houses. An old church, an old town; a hamlet, six or seven hundred years old.

The bagpipes ceased, and after a long interval of silence, from beyond the trees behind us, filling the air, came the sound of Rolls-Royce Merlin engines starting up with explosive snarls. The roar of the engines rushed into the peaceful sunny stillness like a burst of artillery fire; the thought of tomorrow hooded the mind with a sense of despair, a memory of old disaster.

Then the sound of the engines faded as the Spitfires became airborne, just receding, steady, far faint vibrations. Again the bagpipes wailed.

I followed the column between rows of small, gray stone cottages. In the doorways the men and women leaned, their faces grave, musing, with a curious watchful expression that was almost akin to suspicion. The bagpipes faded, died. The dead man's march again, the soft muffled tread of marching boots. Fifty paces with the pipes playing, and fifty paces of silence with the cadence of boots pacing the distance to the grave.

The column turned into the front of

the churchyard, stopped in the grave yard behind the church. The pallbearers, lifting the coffin from the catafalque, stumbled. The church spire upthrust against the sunny air seemed to tilt suddenly above the grave. I put my hand against the wall.

Suddenly there was no sound, no wind. I looked at the chaplain standing at the head of the open grave. I wanted to look down into the grave. I looked at the little black prayer book in the chaplain's hands.

I walked slowly toward the grave. Nobody moved. Nobody seemed to notice I was there. I stopped and looked down. The grave yawned down into the cool gloom of the moist earth. A face I had never seen stared up at me, a blank dead face I had never seen before. Then it was gone suddenly. I felt myself sway at the edge of the grave. I felt dizzy. Then the acute surge came over me, as if my blood were suddenly too hot. I stared down into the black earth in the bottom of the grave. A hand touched my arm drawing me back.

I heard the chaplain's voice rising higher and higher, soaring over the bowed heads around the grave. The voice went on in the sunlight, rising and falling. I could not hear the words, only the singsong voice, fading at last into the sunny morning air.

Suddenly I heard a clash of metal and wood. I watched the pallbearers lower the coffin. Somewhere a bugle blew, slow, mounting notes, echoing in the distant hot stillness, inevitable with death and tomorrow.

Then the column of Highland Light Infantry was forming up again, bagpipes bobbing along the dusty road. I looked at the people in the open doors of the cottages. Their faces were empty as the blank face that had stared up at me out of the grave.

But above them, seemingly beyond the town, the bagpipe music rose, soaring into the golden light of the sky, a bright, lifting dancing tune. The burial was over. The grave closed. For an instant I felt a sudden ease, an illusion of old strength, old confidence. I'm okay, I thought, I'm okay.

I walked slowly toward the air field. The column was marching quickly, playing a lilting song. The column vanished on the dusty road through the woods. I wasn't okay. The plate was cracked. You might glue it together again, but it would never be the same plate.

When I reached the woods the column was gone. I could hear the music. It seemed far away. I went on among the cool beeches, the soft, checkered sunlight until I heard a voice.

'Mack.' I turned. The road was empty

and my name came again; and I knew the voice. I was dreaming.

'Joan,' my mouth said. 'Joan.'

'Mack,' the voice came from the trees.

Then I saw Joan standing in the middle of the road. I walked toward her to be sure she was real. I stood in front of her. I sensed a sudden kindness in her face, pity in her eyes. My nerves tightened and I seemed to come awake suddenly and I stood back from her. I did not want her to touch me. I wished she would go away. She was speaking in a voice I had not heard before, words I did not know, and I had caused it.

'Go away,' I said. 'Goddamn it! Go away.'

'Mack,' she said in a frightened voice that seemed to taunt me. I did not want her to look at me. I had forgotten this was her aerodrome. I had forgotten I had not known where I was when I had wakened on the pool table. She was spying on me now. She knew I was going to quit. I didn't even have to tell her. She could see it in my face. She knew. She would tell my friends and her friends. They would tell everybody I was a coward. I had quit. Light seemed to slowly darken all around me. Oh, Christ, everybody would know it. To hell with them! I would run away. I wouldn't have to take their accusing looks.

I wouldn't have to look at her watching me with her damn kindness and her damn pitying eyes. No, she wasn't going to make me feel worse with her kindness and her pity.

'Get out of my way!' I pushed her arm, but she caught my wrist and held me. Strange, for an instant, I wanted her kindness and her pity. Her lips glowed, stopped me for an instant in which I saw her strangely the way I remembered seeing her the first time in my life.

In that fraction of a second I knew her as winsome and shy and beautiful. I remembered her white shining knees, her silky, satin breasts.

Her fresh, rosy cheeks. I felt tortured by the vision. I was lost. I must hide my feelings. I was lost. All the things my love was made of were lost. Darker shadows moved out of the trees over the road. Waves of leaves rippled over the ground. I could not bear her kindness and her pity. I was lost. I shoved her away.

'Find somebody else!' I heard my voice shouting into her face. 'Forget me! Forget me!' I ran past her!

'Where the bloody hell have you been?' Robinson asked when I ran into the Mess. 'We've been looking all over for you. Come on, let's go,' Robinson said. I saw him wink at Dickson.

The field was bare. The sky was silent. We went on toward our huge bomber. It looked like a black prehistoric reptile with wings, rearing high into the wind on gigantic vulture-like legs.

Chapter 10

God, did we celebrate that night when we returned to our own squadron Mess. It was as if we had wakened from a dream to find ourselves already drunk on waking. The Mess was roaring with beer, beer, beer, our bodies still wet with fear that could have been washed out of the turrets with hoses, our guts still cold that might have been sloshing now in bloody water on the floors of our turrets.

I stumbled and somebody helped me lie down in my bed in the dark Nissen hut. I passed out and dreamed. My body was being washed out of the gun turret with a hose.

I was frightened because I knew I was dreaming. I was seized by the dream, and I could not escape from it. The dream made me feel real.

Ah, the dead are always there, I thought,

like the snow leopards; the fucking 109 rolled into my tracer. Goddamn it! My right guns were jammed. A fucking 110 was firing, coming in from starboard. Got him in my ring sight now. His wings fill the ring sight. Point blank. But he won't stop. Threads of fire laced around my face. He won't die. He's going to kill me. You shit! Die! You fucking 110.

Then I fell out of the bomber, and I was tumbling, falling away from the spinning earth, in my wet fur flying suit. Free from flak and fighters. Ah, at last not to die, to be hosed out of the turret, a pile of blood and guts washed out onto the ground. But then I was back in the turret again. The fighters were there. Fucking goddamn fighters. Kill the German bastards! Kill them! fuck you, you Hun bastards! The air quivered. Stick your medals up your ass, you Hun bastard! Light and fire shimmered into me through the plexiglass of my turret.

Then suddenly in sleep I saw the German's body, all black and swollen, floating in the North Sea, his sides slit like fish gills, the sea drinking his blood.

I felt shaky in the morning. I thought it was just a hang-over. Silence all around me. Then in the silence I felt bubbles rising in my head. I ducked my head under the blanket. And then the questions started coming at me, floating in the bubbles inside my head.

And if you run away???

And if you never fly again?

You're dead?...

When did you die?...

I lay quietly in bed with my head under covers. I opened my eyes, pressing the dark blanket against my forehead. Did it really matter? Would anybody die because I wouldn't? What if somebody died in my turret because I wasn't there? I must erase the thoughts. To hell with all of them. Somebody must die. Not me.

But would they all die?

Would they burn, cook, fry, be blown to pieces, lose their arms and legs?

My thighs pressed together under the blanket. I must not think about answers. My head was too light. I couldn't follow my thoughts.

My God, I thought, I'm going out of my mind.

My brain shrank smaller and smaller like a pea in the dark under the blanket. How could I ever learn to live without fear and shame? How could I ever learn to forget the past? I must get up. I mustn't lie here. Must get up.

I jumped out of bed to take a pee. Outside a big rabbit came out of the bushes and put his finger to his nose and yelled, 'Hey! Booby!'

I ran back into my room. I squinted at my face in the mirror. It looked too bright and shining. I tried to assess it. My eyes were big. I could see shame rising in them. Why was I such a miserable liar? I waited anxiously for my face to change in the mirror. It wouldn't change. I spat at the mirror and wiped off the spit. Then I saw my eyes again in the mirror. They were dimming as if weeping. I ran away from the mirror.

I dressed fast and ran out the door and there on the grass was Flying Officer MacDonald's Pit-Bull, with a black ring around his right eye, sitting on his haunches, holding a tin cup with a slot in the top. He raised one eyebrow. His right eye glinted.

'Penny for the Guy!' he shouted. 'Penny for the Guy! Help a worthy cause!' I spat at him.

He shot away on all fours and disappeared around the rear of the Nissen hut. My heart pounded. It couldn't be true. I couldn't have seen and heard a rabbit and a dog. I must see the medical officer. But that pink little tongue, those long back paws.

'Hoy!' shouted a voice from the doorway of 'B' flight barracks. It was Sergeant Jaynes. 'Some ale left, old cock.'

I stared at him. Somebody who had flown the mission had gone for Burton. The beer they had purchased before the mission to celebrate their return Jaynes had swiped out of their rooms.

'I gotta see the M.O,' I said.

'What's the trouble?'

'I got the whammies.'

'Come on! Six bottles left!'

Maybe a beer, I thought, it was supposed to be soothing. Maybe a couple of beers would help. The whammies would go away. I'd sleep.

I opened the door of Sergeant Jaynes's room. He was sitting on the bed with a bottle of pale ale in each hand.

'Ah,' I said, sipping the cold ale. 'Whose beer is it?'

I drank one bottle straight down.

'One for the road,' said Jaynes.

'Got to go,' I said, feeling it coming on again.

'Drink up,' he shouted.

I looked at him and then it happened. Sergeant Jaynes turned into a red-cheeked man wearing a flat-top old fashioned derby which he doffed and twirled on the end of his cane. When I saw it was Winston Churchill the beer choked in my nose. My guts started to heave. I felt cold all over.

I jumped up. Winston Churchill took out a cigar and sniffed it just before lighting. His eyes were bloodshot and red-rimmed.

He gave me the V sign with two fingers. I ran out the door. I must get to the medical officer. I felt sick. My guts felt hot and my skin felt cold. I felt my skin jerking.

Then a man in a Gestapo uniform stopped me. His eyes were black and shining fiercely, black as his uniform. It was Rudolph Hess. Like a man in a dream, I saw myself watching him.

'So Winnie won't see me?' he hissed. 'Think you can win this war?'

'Listen, Mr Hess, I'm only a—' It was all a dream. It had to be. I must be in bed dreaming, thinking I was here.

'If I ever get you in Germany,' said Hess, 'I'll—' He drew out a black jack and length of rubber hose. I grabbed the rubber hose.

'Help!' I heard my voice screaming at two pilots passing. 'Hess is going to get Churchill to make a deal and betray England. Help me kill him!'

I swung the rubber hose at Hess. He fell on his knees. I kicked him in the stomach. I shouted at the pilots to hold him but they ran, suddenly turning into

116

ostriches. Rudolph Hess suddenly became a small ape, with blood running out of his mouth.

I rushed away, terribly depressed, and ran into Dr Berins' office, past the line of waiting airmen and told the nurse I must see the doctor at once.

She took me straight in.

'What's the trouble, lad?' he said, patting my shoulder. 'Sit down. Sit down. Take it easy now.'

'I just saw Churchill and then a friend turned into Rudolph Hess and there's a dog out there soliciting funds for Guy Fawkes Day.'

'Where did you see this?' he asked quietly.

'At the Cowes regatta,' I heard my voice say. 'Winnie was standing on top of a yacht twirling his derby on a cane at the crowd.'

'Is that all?'

'I beat up Hess and left him down the street. He'd turned into an ape.'

Then I felt Dr Berins' fingers on my eyelids.

'Open your eyes,' he said.

I opened my eyes and looked at Dr Berins.

'Oh, my God,' I said. 'Look at yourself. You've got pointed ears.'

'Yes,' he said softly.

'There are horns growing out of your skull.'

He caught my wrist and pressed his thumb against my pulse. I jerked my arm away.

'Nice try,' he said. 'Who told you about tonight's operation?'

'Piece of cake,' my mouth said.

'Actually, yes. Paris. But what will you pretend to see when you hear you're going to Essen again?'

His voice sounded peremptory, cold and harsh.

Just then the nurse came in. She was covered with yellow fur and big black spots. She was swinging her tail and walking straight at me with her tiger teeth dripping saliva.

I shot out of the office and ran all the way back to my room and slammed the door and locked it and lay down on the bed. I felt my skin jerking again. I felt cold all over and then suddenly my stomach heaved and I vomited over the side of the bed.

The next thing I remember somebody was pounding on the door.

Robinson's voice. He sounded angry.

'Open up, you dimwit!' he shouted.

I opened the door a crack. Robinson pushed it open and I staggered back from the blow. His face was white with anger.

118

'What the bloody hell are you filling the medical officer with?'

'It's true.'

'Bloody hell! Don't you realize if you keep up this bull they'll finally believe you and mark you unfit to fly? And they'll give us a sprog gunner. We'll have to go to a rough target with a sprog gunner. He'll get us killed!'

'You'll get killed anyway.'

'Shut up,' he said. 'Take these.' He handed me two pink pills. 'Get some sleep. We're on tonight.'

'What's the target?'

'Paris.'

'Piece of cake,' I heard myself say automatically. I took one pill and slept. When I wakened I remembered it was pay parade day and I'd missed it. I started to feel sick again. I sat, staring at the wall with a kind of quiet horror. It seemed to me I would not be able to stand up. But I must stand up. I must get my pay. Then I heard my boots hit the floor and I was standing. I moved.

I caught the squadron accounts officer just as he was leaving his office. He gave me my pay envelope. He stared at me.

'How're you feeling?' he asked. I felt him watching my eyes.

'Fine, fine,' I said quickly and once out the door I started to run toward the Mess.

I knew what I had to do. There would be the pay day crap game. I had to break it. Get enough money to desert. Hide out in London. I was panting when I ran into the Mess. There was a crowd around the billiard table. Cries of the dice shooters. Eddy Maisen had the dice. He was yelling, 'Fade two quid!'

'Gotcha,' I shouted and pushed somebody aside and leaned against the edge of the table.

A voice beside me said, 'Did you hear the gen? Ops are scrubbed tonight.'

I was looking at Maisen. He was cackling the dice in one hand, blowing on his knuckles.

I felt my head turn. I looked at the face beside me. The face was strange, unreal, a dream face. 'Ops are scrubbed tonight,' the face said. No, I thought, we'll go. They don't scrub ops anymore. They just say that. You go when the weather clears.

I looked back at Maisen. 'Shoot!' I said. 'You're faded!'

Chapter 11

Maisen bet another quid on the come. His point was eight. Somebody said he was hot. Nobody would fade the come bet. He shot a four for the come bet. I had him faded. He crapped out in two rolls. I picked up three quid. Then a Canuck named MacDonald had the dice and got a hot roll going for two points. Nobody seemed to know the odds. What the hell. It was a new game to the British. MacDonald doubled his bet on his roll and I faded half his bet. Three quid. The odds were against him making his point three times in a row, unless he was red hot. He rolled box-cars first and I picked up a pound, ten shillings, and he shot another three quid, trying to get his money back.

'Coming for a six,' he said, rolling the dice between both hands. 'Come on, six, baby.'

He rolled an eight, then a ten, and then a seven and crapped out.

'Shoot five,' said the next roller. It was Dowman, a big Englishman, a big winner at cards. Maybe he'd figured the dice odds by now. He was a crafty poker player, always a winner.

I didn't like the way he was blowing on the dice, holding the dice in one fist, the fist pressed tight against his lips. I'd seen hustler's switch dice like that back in the states. Blow on the dice, slip the loaded dice into your hand suck up the honest dice. That was the trick.

'Don't do that,' I said.

Dowman took his hand away from his lips.

'What the bloody hell!' he said. His voice was innocent but mean.

'Don't blow on the dice,' I said.

He pressed his lips against his fist again and blew on his hand as if his knuckles were cold.

I picked up my pound notes.

'He's all yours,' I said.

Dowman wiped his lips off with his left hand, and cackled the dice in his right hand. I watched his left hand. It hung down by his side, the fist balled. He went on cackling the dice in his right hand.

'Come along, lads!' he shouted. 'Get on the gravy train!'

Two pound notes fluttered onto the table.

'Who wants the other three?' he shouted. No takers.

'Come on, Norton! Get on the gravy train!'

'Shoot,' I said. 'You're off for two quid.'

He dragged two pounds. 'A pound open!' he shouted, shaking the dice up beside his ear. I watched his left hand. It hadn't moved. It still hung straight down along side his leg, the fist balled.

He dragged the pound note. I watched his hand release the dice. They were small dice, small enough to hold in his mouth. The dice tumbled swiftly across the table, caromed off the side cushion.

'Seven!' Dowman shouted. 'Shoot the six!' he yelled. 'Get on the old gravy train!'

He could only get betters to fade three pounds, so he dragged three one pound notes and cackled the dice. 'Seven, seven! Come eleven!' he cried as he flung the dice across the table. His point was eight and he made it after two rolls and dragged three pounds. He stood there waiting to be faded, blowing now on both his hands, cupped over his lips. When he drew his hands away saying, 'A quid open,' I saw his left hand dangling against his thigh, palm open. After he was faded he rolled an eight but he couldn't make the eight and he crapped out.

123

Not a bad hustler, I thought, he cleans up but loses three quid back to make it look honest.

I went around the table and tapped him on the shoulder. He turned his head. I drew my left hand across my lips and beckoned him with the forefinger of my right hand.

'What do you want?' His black eyes were cold and hard.

I didn't say anything. I drew the palm of my left hand across my lips again and jerked my head. He walked away from the table and I moved out of hearing range of the table.

'That's a nice trick,' I said. 'Where did you learn it?'

'Up your jacksey, Yank!'

He turned and I grabbed him by the shoulder and spun him around. 'Get your ass out of that game,' I said in a low voice. 'Or the next time you get the dice I'm going to open your left fist and show everybody where you've palmed the straight dice.'

His pupils pin-pointed and the tip of his tongue moistened the edge of his lower lips. I looked at his eyes. He knew I knew his game: loaded dice in the mouth, slipped into the hand he was blowing on, and the straight dice palmed into his left hand and kept there until he switched dice back by holding both hands up to his lips before his last roll.

'Make up your mind,' I said. 'They'll kick you into a hospital for six months if they find out you've been cheating.'

'Friend,' he smiled, putting a hand on my shoulder. 'It's all your game tonight. You hustle them this pay day, and they're mine next time. Okay, Yank!'

I didn't move his hand.

'I may hustle them,' I said. 'But I don't cheat them. I just know the odds.' I pushed his hand away and returned to the table. He departed.

'Dowman!' shouted a short dark Flight Sergeant navigator. 'Where are you going? Come on! I want to win back my money!' But Dowman vanished through the open hall door.

There were about two dozen airmen around the billiard table, standing two deep, some playing their bets over the shoulders of others. I figured there were about four hundred pounds in the crowd. If I played the odds right I could take out at least half. If need be I probably could take out all of the money. But why leave with that rotten a taste in my mouth. I felt guilt and shame now for what I was going to do, leave them all to die while I got out. At least I could leave them their beer and furlough money. At least that. Please, God, I prayed, don't make me feel like such a shit, take away some of the rotten feeling. But it wasn't much use. The thing to do was to concentrate on my hands, on the crap game.

There was money in the center of the table again and two small red white-eyed dice were rolling.

I held my money in my left hand, ten one pound notes and two folded five pounders.

A little rat-faced curly-haired cockney with small white hands was shooting two pounds. I tossed down two pounds to cover him and a fat Australian gave me a dirty look.

'Hey, joker,' he hissed. 'He's mine!'

I dragged one pound. He tossed his pound note on the table. 'Bloody Yanks.' He gave me another dirty look. 'Figure that joker's ready to crap off so you're jumping on the train.' His face was red and furious, so he must be a real loser so far.

'Shut your mouth and fade,' I said in a low voice.

He started to say something and then the shooter rolled out the dice and came out with a six, a five. He started working on it and made it with a couple threes.

'Four quid open,' said the cockney.

I tasted bile in my mouth, tart, brackish, bitter as gall. I looked at the Aussie. He

126

still looked sore. His eyes were bright.

'Cover him,' I said.

'Drag a couple quid,' said another English voice.

'You're faded,' I said, and tossed four quid on the table.

The cockney puffed his cheeks and blew on the dice. 'Come on for daddy. Big seven.' He snapped his wrists, released the dice. They bounced off the billiard cushioned sides, stopped five.

'What do you get in the swamps, baby?' a Lancashire accent murmured. They'd all learned the crap table lingo. 'Fever. Big fever, baby.'

The cockney picked up the dice and rubbed them on the bald head of the flier standing beside him.

'Shoot,' somebody said. 'Roll 'em.'

The shooter blew on them, then cut them loose.

'Seven,' I said, crowing a little. I picked up the eight one-pound notes.

The dice were three places away from me. I won three pounds before I got the dice. My lungs felt tight. I felt tight and anxious all over.

'Shoot the wad,' I said. I tossed twenty pounds in the center.

'How much?' somebody said.

'Twenty pounds,' I said.

The Aussie said, 'Five pounds covered.'

'Fifteen open. Get on the train.'

'Got five,' somebody said.

Then bills showered on the table. They were out to clean me. 'Shoot, Yank. You're covered.'

I watched each better pull in the bills he had covered. I picked up the dice, shook them a couple times and rolled them backhanded. One came to a stop five up; the other rolled, bounced off the cushion and stopped with the two up.

'Seven from heaven,' I said. 'I'll shoot any part of it.'

'Drag,' the cockney said. 'What the hell do you think this is, Monte Carlo?'

'Shoot any part of it.'

'Bounce them off the cushion,' somebody said.

Then everybody at the table was taking a piece. They wanted their money back. I didn't think I could make it but I was going to go for it. I had the feeling the dice were hot. But a sick, scared feeling filled my guts. I was going against odds. I knew better, but I was going against my own thinking. I ought to drag half or more. Third time around. Odds were I would crap out. I could stay here and keep taking the money in a pound or two at a time and get my hundred pounds. But I could feel the terrible urgency to leave here as quickly as possible. I never wanted to feel scared and powerless and unprotected again as long as I lived. I didn't want to wake up every morning thinking I was going to die that night. I had looked death in the face too long and knew he was there waiting for me. I had to take their money as fast as I could because nobody was going to save me but myself. Suddenly all I felt for all of them in the room was a cold disdain. They were fools to stay here and die. I bounced the dice off the cushioned sides of the billiards table.

'Eight's his point,' somebody said.

I put the dice in both hands and blew on my hands.

'Big eight,' I said. 'Eighter from Decatur. Come on, baby.' I rolled, tasting bile in my mouth. Nine. I picked up the dice. I threw down another five pounds. 'Five quid on nine.'

I rolled three times, came close to crapping out and then the nine came up. I picked up ten pounds. The odds were running out on my making eight. I felt my legs trembling. A vein throbbed in my temple like a bug picking at the inside of my head. It was an effort to release the dice. I felt the strained smile on my face.

'Anybody want to blow on these babies for good luck?' I held the dice out in the palm of my hand.

'Shoot,' somebody said. 'You're holding up the game.'

'I'll give you some luck,' a voice said as a hand came down hard on my right shoulder. I looked back, just turning my head. It was Dowman. He leaned quickly over my shoulder and blew on the dice.

'Make that eight,' he said, 'and I'll cover everything you want to shoot.'

I rubbed my face with my left hand. That bastard Dowman could really get on my nerves. I was a chump to let him rattle me. I shook the dice, feeling my heart getting smaller. My face felt as if it were drawing in, skin tight over the bone. If I lost I was finished. The game wouldn't go on long enough for me to win it all back a little at a time and that was the smart way, double your bets, win, drag, double, win, drag. I felt something hammering on my brain. Drag. Drag. Drag. I took a deep breath and cast the dice.

Dowman screamed. 'Big eight! Big eight!'

A collective sigh came from the ring of faces around the table. Dowman said, 'I got sixty quid says you're a loser, Norton.'

I saw the wad of bank notes in his hand. He tossed them onto the center of the table. I picked up the dice, felt them. They were the same. I thought maybe he

130

might have had somebody switch them at the end of the table. I knew nobody had touched them after they turned up eight.

I picked up all my bets, counted the money. Sixty quid. I tossed it in the center of the table. 'Shoot it,' I said. 'Roll for high dice.' I tossed one dice to Dowman. I watched his hand. He shook the dice and flicked it across the table. It bounced off the cushion and came up five. I held out my hand for the dice and picked them up when somebody at the far end of the table rolled it back. Same dice. I shook the dice once in my left hand and rolled a four.

'Your dice,' I said and handed Dowman both dice.

'Don't blow on them,' I said. There was no sound in the room. Cigarette smoke swirled over the table. I looked at all those pound notes. One hundred and twenty quid. Passage to freedom. Dowman shook the dice. His mouth twisted down in one corner, sneering. I had that terrible sick gone feeling again in the pit of my stomach. He rolled the dice quickly. One bounced off the cushion came to a stop six up; the other rolled diagonally away from the end of the table and into the crevice under the rim of the cushion and cocked with the five facing up.

'Tough titty,' said Dowman.

'Cocked dice,' I said.

'Bull shit!' he said in a choked voice. He reached for the money. I leaned across the corner of the table and grabbed him by the tunic in one motion. He rolled his head to one side and my fist went past his ear and somebody grabbed my arms and held me.

'Shoot it out,' a voice said. I pulled my arm away.

'Your dice, Dowman,' I said. 'Shoot.' The dice were still on the table. I picked them up and rolled them down the table to Dowman. 'Shoot!' I yelled.

He picked up the dice and lifted his hand to his mouth, puffing his lips.

He looked at me over his gnarled big fists, his eyes blistered with hate. 'Shoot,' I said. 'You're holding up the game.'

He shook the dice three times and flipped them the length of the table. They came rolling down in front of me and bounced back off the cushion and came to a stop together box cars up, two sixes face up, looking right at me.

I reached for the money.

'That's the game,' I said. I looked at Dowman. 'Unless you still want to shoot.' He walked away.

I didn't count the money. I stuffed the bills in my pockets and walked out of the room. It wasn't dark outside, but as soon as it was dark I was going to make my move. London by morning.

Chapter 12

It was a beautiful evening. I felt child-like, so free, sitting at my window, looking out at the dusk coming far away. So free at last. All in the darkness I would go.

I looked up at the high white creamy clouds, the upper edges still sparkling in sunlight, turning rosy gray, edged with tender whiteness. The whole sky made me think of the sea and all the clouds became islands, surrounded by blue light, each cloud motionless now against the darkening horizon. I watched as the light faded, and I thought of the hundreds of islands off the Danish coast the evening we ran over the Baltic to attack Stettin, the sky scarlet and radiant before dusk. Then high above us over the dark earth the first evening star shone. We were going perhaps to our death but the beautiful summer evening made it all seem like a dream, death so remote and unreal.

I started to pack my kit bag, shirts, socks, shoes, shaving equipment, and then I went to get my civvies. Brown sports jacket and gray flannel trousers. They should have been hanging on the hook by the door. They were gone. I felt sick and lost. I couldn't get to London unless I wore civilian clothes because I didn't have a furlough pass. If the special air force police stopped me my goose would be cooked without a pass. Bloody hell, who'd copped my clothes? I could kill him! There was only one thing to do. Steal a pad of passes from the executive officer's office. Were the administration offices locked after dark? I'd have to chance breaking in, but only after it was dark enough outside.

When it was, I went down the hall carrying my flashlight and opened the door and stepped out into the night. I could smell the fields, the odor of buckwheat. The Yorkshire fields lay silent. I went along the road to the squadron headquarter offices, a thick dark square block of buildings. No lights. All the building windows were blacked out.

As I lifted the latch gently on the door of the building, I thought I heard something move in the hall. The hall was dark. I eased the door open a few inches more and listened. No sound, and no light from beneath any of the office doors along the hall. The first door on the right would be the Wing Commander's Office, then the Squadron Leaders' offices, and the third door would be the door to the Executive Officer's office.

I snapped on the flashlight and tiptoed along the hall, pausing every few feet to listen. Officers were rarely here at this hour, either before and sometimes briefly after a mission. But what if one came in now? My heart clenched. Damn it! Nobody was going to stop me. I felt a strange kind of pure and impersonal outrage at the thought of somebody trying to stop me. The fools. But even in that brief rage I felt it was only to cover the twinge of guilt inside me that kept pushing up.

I put my head against the surface of the Executive Officer's door. What had been the sound in the hall? Just imagination. The door was open an inch. I pushed it fully open with the toe of my shoe. I put the light immediately upon the desk at the far end of the room and walked straight toward it. God, what if he locked his desk drawer? I had to get a pad of furlough passes, at least a few to safeguard against the RAF special police checking passes in the railway station.

One pull and the desk drawer opened and I scanned the inside. There was a pad of furlough passes in the lower right hand corner. I tore off half a dozen passes. As I reached to close the drawer I heard the sound again, just a faint scraping noise like a needle scratching on stone momentarily. I started to bring the beam of the flashlight around to the corner behind me. I felt suddenly trapped. Somebody was in the room.

I felt weak, scared, a terrible sick gone feeling. Blood rushed to my head, blinding me. I turned my head, looking for the sound. I never had time to see him: just a black huddled shape, seen in the wobbly glare of the flashlight beam. A blinding explosion went off just back of my eyes as if my head were blown off. I felt as if my ears and eyes had popped off. All the shaft of light in my hand ran down to a pinpoint of darkness. Then I didn't know a thing.

When I came to I was laying flat on my back beside the desk. When I opened my eyes I looked up into blackness. I got up on my knees, leaned there against the side of the desk, feeling faint. I touched my jaw and cheek. Then I remembered the dark figure in the room. I was more scared than before. Who had seen me? Who was in the room? Why had he been there? I knew I hadn't been unconscious too long. Whoever had been in here wasn't going to call the police. He would have to blow the whistle on himself as a prowler.

I stood up and bile rolled up in my stomach. I knelt down on my hands and knees and I thought I was going to throw up and stopped myself. I felt along the floor for the flashlight. It was under the desk. I flicked on the beam. The furlough passes were scattered on the floor. I picked up each one carefully and searched the room for more. My skin felt tight and hot, but I closed the office door.

Outdoors I started retching but stopped myself. The stars filled the sky. The cool air fanned my eyes. Who had slugged me? But that wasn't important. Getting to York to catch the Edinburgh-London train. That was important.

The sick, scared feeling left my stomach. I walked slowly back to my hut, because I remembered: operations had been scrubbed. The squadron would be in the City of York, knocking back pints of mild and bitter in Betty's Bar. I hauled out my kit bag, tied it on my bike, and started peddling for the City of York, ten miles away.

Chapter 13

I cycled along Stoney Road, sweating and tired, the York street full of airmen, swaggering, shouting, singing in the dark. I hopped off the bike and pushed it over the cobblestones, avoiding pub doors, passed the DeGray Rooms Dance Hall and looked down the street at the Station Hotel, looming big and dark. I left the bike outside the station and looked at my watch. Ten minutes to train time. I went into the toilet and standing there taking a piss I suddenly remembered the furlough passes weren't stamped. I took out my pen, dated the pass, scribbled a fairly good forgery of Squadron Leader G.C Saxton's signature and strolled out onto the platform beneath the glass roof and looked up and down the tracks. No special police on the platform. They were probably back in town. With flying operations scrubbed the city would be full of aircrew. I bought a ticket, returned to the platform, waited.

It had always been exciting waiting for the train on furlough. But I was scared now. I felt like a thief. I stared at the faces around me. They did not look at anybody. A sense of dread swept over me. I felt the need to move, but nobody moved on the platform. They stood under the dead Yorkshire sky, listening. I longed even to hear a footstep. Nobody moved. I felt they were listening. They had nothing to do but listen for the sound of the train. Would Beryl be in London? She might be up in the Midlands for in Bristol trying out a new play for the London West End Theater. How long ago I had met her. So long before I loved Joan. Jesus, I felt so damn old now. But how good she and her lover Terry had been to me on leave, always taking me from pub to pub, buying me beers, putting me up over the weekend in Cheyney Mews, those short alleys the British called mews, with a garage at the end, an apartment above the garage, so bloody chic, but what a blessed respite from the Yorkshire Nissen Hut. And up the street by the Battersea Bridge, all those good pubs, Chelsea Arms and the Murderer's Arms and the Blue Cockatoo. Beryl had to take me in if I got to London. I knew why she must.

I didn't see the RAF special policeman. He came from behind me. Nor did I hear him. I didn't know he was there until I heard his voice. I was standing along at the far end of the railway platform. The light was dim, almost dark.

'Sergeant,' he said, 'may I see your pass?'

I started to jerk around. I stiffened and turned slowly. My pass was in the upper left hand pocket of my tunic. I unbuttoned the pocket slowly. I handed him the pass. He snapped on his flashlight and studied the pass. Without lifting his head, he said: 'Where's your gas mask?'

'Blimey,' I said, and snapped my fingers. 'I completely forgot it.'

There was a rule, all soldiers, airmen and sailors on leave must carry gas masks. Usually we used the canvas bag to hold our toilet kit. Jesus, I could get stopped in London.

He started writing a complaint ticket from my furlough pass. The ticket would go to the squadron, giving time and place of the complaint.

Suddenly he stopped writing. The beam of his flashlight just as suddenly struck me full in the eyes. Blinded. His voice was cold, peremptory: 'Where did you get this pass? The date should be stamped.'

Keep cool, I thought.

'Squadron warrant officer made it out,' I said. 'The executive officer was away. Call if you want to check it.'

'At this hour?' he said.

I closed my eyes against the blinding

glare of the light as he said, 'I'll have to hold you till morning.'

I looked over my shoulder. There was no one near us. This end of the platform was deserted. We were standing right on the edge of the platform, just above the track.

'Come along, sergeant,' he said, and he reached to take my arm.

'Half a mo,' I said. 'Let me get my kit bag.' I bent down and slung the kit bag over my shoulder. I was still crouched when I swung the kit bag. A high wide arc, with the draw strings looped around my wrist. The force of the bag caught him right across the side of the head and he flew off the platform.

I glanced up and down the platform. No sound, only blurred shapes far away at the opposite end in the dim light.

I looked over the edge of the platform. Sonofabitch of a cop! Anybody who would be a service policeman was a creep in my book. A bunch of creeps. Those bastards sitting in our Mess late at night eating steak and eggs they had pulled off the blackmarket, sitting there with the aircrews coming in hollow-eyed, half dead from a raid. Sitting on their perfectly polished asses while we got a lousy piece of Spam. Nazi Finks in their paratrooper boots they would never earn in battle.

141

The policeman lay on the track face down, one rail creasing his stomach. The London train would cut him in half. For a fraction of a second I wanted him to die, for all the special policemen to die, to be gutted under the train. Then I thought maybe the poor bastard might have a wife and kid, trying to live on his two pounds a week salary. Christ, I thought, and me running away, taking my guilt out on this poor bastard.

I dropped down from the platform. I found his flashlight, stowed it in my tunic pocket. I lifted his body off the track and shoved it up onto the stone platform.

I grabbed him under the arms and dragged him to the end of the platform. I jumped down and reached back and dragged him off the platform. His feet plopped onto the ground. I dragged him along beside the rails, his feet dragging in the cinder path. I pulled him over into the bushes and snapped the flashlight on his face. A worm of blood crawled down his jaw from the corner of his mouth. He was breathing. He must have struck his head on the rail or ties. I took off his belt and tied his wrists behind him, then removed his boots and socks. Gag in place. I lifted his eyelids. In the glare of the flashlight I stuffed his socks in his mouth, used his bootlaces to tie the gag in place. I lifted his eyelids. In the glare of the flashlight beam his eyeballs rolled whitely. I felt his pulse. It was steady, so was his breathing. I heard the far-faint sound of the train humming along the rails.

I turned and ran back to my kit bag, scouring the floor for my furlough pass. Jesus, he must have it in his pocket. The humming sound of the approaching train reverberated faintly and then stronger and stronger along the track. I ran down the platform into the bushes. The policeman had not moved. I searched his clothes. The furlough pass was not there. Get to the train, was all I would think. Get on that train.

Chapter 14

The train compartment door slid open. The man closed the door behind him, turning his back. He was quite short, perhaps five feet five inches. Even through his soft bottle-green tweed suit his body looked spare. As he turned, the light caught the glint of a gold watch chain across his vest. He wore a derby, not raked. It sat impeccably straight upon his long, narrow skull. Beneath his arm

143

an umbrella. In his other hand he held a newspaper. The clothes were Saville Row. He looked to be fiftyish.

'Good evening, sergeant,' he said genially. His voice was English, but not British; the rising inflection was in it, but there was something else, too, foreign in the inflection. I had been so long among British voices I knew his accent and inflection had been acquired.

His lips moved slowly apart in a studied, calculated warm smile. I had never been spoken to before on a British train by a stranger. This man obviously wasn't English. He was too open and friendly. The English were afraid of strangers. Bad manners, you know, to speak with strangers in the same compartment, though you might be starving to death together.

He sat down across from me. The light was dim in the compartment. He crossed his ankles, lifted his newspaper.

Ah, the English, I thought, with all their stuffy social relationships. Everybody look straight ahead on the train, no questions, please; don't complain, carry on, good show. I was tired of carrying on, Good Show. To hell with it.

His head came up slowly over the top of his newspaper. I smiled at him. Ah, I had committed the unpardonable British social gaffe. Fuck 'em all, the long and

144

the short and tall. Carefree joy seized me.
I was out of it. I felt light-headed as if
I had downed a couple shots of whiskey
after being on oxygen for five hours. I felt
reborn.

'Hey, Mac,' I said. 'What do you do
for a living?' I thought I would pull his
leg by impersonating the completely rude
American.

Over the glint of his rimless half-glasses
his eyes gleamed with amusement and
mockery. Then the heavy lids of his eyes
closed to reptilian slits. His voice was soft
and slow.

'I'm in diamonds,' he said. 'What do
you fly?'

'Halifaxes.'

'Good aircraft?'

'As good as any.'

'Not as fast as the Lancaster, are they?'

'Not quite.'

'Isn't the Lancaster supposed to make a
new mark to carry a remarkable load?'

'No Lancs around us,' I said. 'They're
up in Lincolnshire.'

'Oh, yes.'

'What do you do in diamonds?'

His small pearly-sized teeth glinted in a
quick smile.

'Actually, very little. The war, you
know.'

'Do you dig them?'

145

He laughed, very jolly. 'No, no. Just cutting stones.'

'Are you rich?' I asked. I really didn't give a damn now what I asked. He was getting his leg pulled. I wanted to goose him a little.

He chuckled. 'Well, you might say so.' He flattened his newspaper of his lap. 'You're an Ameddican, aren't you?'

I pointed at my shoulder flasher.

'Where are you from?' he asked.

I looked at his reptilian eyes.

'Tell me,' I said. 'Where are *you* from?'

'London.'

I laughed at him. 'You're not British. How long did it take you to develop that accent?'

He smiled. The mockery was still there in his greenish eyes.

'Rude Ameddican,' I mimicked his accent. 'I bet I can guess where you're from. Bet you a quid. Say something.'

'Five quid.'

'Five to one,' I said.

'Guess,' he said.

'Say "Can you con can you ki can you constansti. Can you ople? Can you pople? Can you Constantinople. Spell it with two letters." '

He shook his head. 'I'll give you three guesses where I was born.'

His inflection wasn't quite right for

146

an Englishman. Nor was he European. I had heard many French and Polish fliers speaking English. No, he wasn't French or Polish. Nor colonial. Nor Aussie or Canadian. He had the British rising inflection, but it was manufactured along with his broad 'a'. His inflection didn't stay up there. It dropped off at the end of a sentence.

'Five quid to a quid?' I asked and he nodded his head.

'Carolina?'

'A bit off, old boy.'

'You are American?'

He nodded his head, extracted a long cigarette holder from an inside coat pocket and a gold cigarette case. He held out the cigarette case. I shook my head.

'Massachusetts,' I said.

'You won five quid, old boy.'

He produced a gold lighter from his vest, and slanting the cigarette holder upward from the corner of his mouth, he lit the cigarette. I watched him inhale deeply, blow a plume of smoke across his face.

'Care to triple your money?' he asked. His eyes watched my face.

'What's the bet?'

'What city?'

'Come off it,' I said. 'I'll take the five quid.'

He reached inside his jacket and drew

out his wallet. It was stuffed with five pound notes. The eyelids lifted. Again his eyes gleamed mockingly as he handed me the five pound note.

'How did you ever get into diamonds?' I asked.

'Went out to the Gold Coast after college,' he said. He appeared to settle back for a moment but I could still feel his eyes on me. Suddenly in a soft voice he said, 'Are you on Mark Three Halifaxes?'

'Sometimes,' I said. 'Depends on what kite's ready to go.'

'Are you using the new G Box?'

At first I wasn't sure I had heard him. I felt hair prickle along the back of my neck.

'What?' I said.

'The new G Box.'

How the hell did he know about it? He was in diamonds, not aircraft manufacturing. The newspaper had not mentioned the new G Box. We had only just started to use it on the squadron. It was a radar electronic device giving out a radio beat which enabled the navigator to get a navigational fix instead of using the old way of getting a navigational plotting fix from a loop bearing taken by the wireless operator.

I laughed. 'Never heard of it.' Well, I might as well pull his leg a bit. But how would he know about it unless he was with air ministry. It was still a public secret. Strange he should know.

'You know,' I said, 'I don't fly anymore. I'm with the Royal Air Force morale squad.'

His beady eyes blinked, seemed to go out of focus a moment, and his lips opened as if he was going to speak. But just as slowly and quite carefully, he closed his lips around the upthrust cigarette holder. His gaze became disinterested, quite blank.

'Not many people have heard of it,' I lied. 'Actually, I've done two tours of ops. I got screened into the morale squadron. Pretty tricky operation. Hard on the old body.'

'How's that?'

'Well, you know how civilians wonder about what they read in the newspapers. "Five Hundred of Our Aircraft Attacked Dortmund Last Night." Lots of people wonder if it's true. Especially when Jerry is plastering them back day and night.'

'Oh, yes.' His eyes were watching me closely now.

I said, 'Well, at night a couple of fly boys, we go around from pub to pub, letting the people ask us how's it going over against Jerry, are you giving him hell, mate? We work factory towns mostly, building up morale among the workers. We give them the old thumbs up bit and tell 'em, we're knocking hell out of Jerry and it won't be long until Jerry packs in.'

'Do you really?'

'It's not easy,' I said. 'We lost two lads last month. Cirrhosis of the liver.'

'I say! Actually?'

'Ectchually,' I said, mimicking his British country gentry accent, but the mimicking went right over his head. Later I realized that he had deliberately ducked it.

At the time I thought I was pretty funny. Pulled the wool over this bugger's eyes. But I was the stupid one in the train compartment. Not this dude with the orotund British accent.

'Where are you staying in London?' he asked.

I shrugged. 'Don't know. One of the service clubs probably.'

That was the least of my worries. Beryl would put me up at her flat. The problem was not to have my pass checked at Kings Cross railway station. Either stay on the train and get off later after the train had been in the station an hour or jump off in the yards before the train entered the station.

It was still dark outside. The train was running fast and smooth. I lay back on the seat and closed my eyes and tried to keep from thinking. But all I kept thinking about was how to get some civilian clothes. Well, Beryl would know about that. You couldn't buy clothes without clothing coupons and only civilians had clothing coupons. There must be a black market. Beryl would know about that, too. Then I thought about Joan. That was over. But was it? I loved her. But I couldn't see her. She wouldn't stand for a deserter. No help there. I thought about her some more and wanted to sleep. I was tired but I couldn't sleep. The more I thought about Joan DeMarney the worse I felt. I would never see her again. She wouldn't talk to me now. Her home had been bombed. One brother dead at Dunkirk. She was very bitter about the Germans. She hated them. I had quit. No, if I loved her I would fight. Jesus, I wanted to live. I wanted her, too. You can't have it both ways. Quit and you lose her. She was like Desmond Porter when it came to hating Germans. I thought about Desmond, dead six months now, pressing home an attack on Dortmund, with one engine conked, running in through the searchlights on three engines. His gunner had come back through Spain and told how Desmond kept screaming obscenities at the Germans right down through the searchlights with the Halifax streaming flames out of two engines after the flak caught them in the searchlights.

I opened my eyes. The compartment was empty. I was alone. It was strange. I couldn't remember hearing the compartment door open or close. I must have fallen asleep. But I didn't remember sleeping. I looked at my watch. We would be getting into London. I lifted the blackout curtain. Rooftops swam past. We were in London, running through north London. I was chilled and hungry. The train seemed to slow but I wasn't sure. Then after a while I felt it was definitely slowing. I looked beneath the window shade. Rooftops passed beneath the window. I turned out the compartment light and put the shade up. My stomach turned over with hunger.

But even then I couldn't stop thinking about Joan. I would never see her again. I couldn't see her again. She wouldn't see me. Then I could hear the rails clicking. The man without a country. Only in a uniform I did not want to wear anymore. The man without a girl. Just a man alone trying to stay alive. I sat there listening to the rails clicking beneath the carriage. I was out of it. But if they caught me I would be in prison. Maybe better in prison. No, they would not catch me. How would you get home after the war? There must be ways. How would you eat after your money runs out? There must be forgers in London who could make me identification papers.

But guilt went away and fear came in to replace it. It was light out now, gray light, the color of water, beyond honor, beyond help. I had left my friends. I hoped they would not die. It was my war, but I was afraid. They must die alone. Maybe some of them were too afraid to quit. Where would they go? I wished the damn train would slow enough so I could jump before it rolled into the station. The police would be looking for me in the station. I must not go into the station. I wondered what the air force would tell my parents. Missing in action. Desertion. Probably nothing. Maybe I would never get home again. Maybe we would lose the war. The way it was going in the Western Desert it looked as if we were going to take a long time to win it.

I wondered if the United States would ever get into the war. Their airplanes wouldn't be any help now. They didn't have any aircraft that could fight over fifteen thousand feet. They better stay out until they had the Rolls Royce engine for their machines. I would never see Joan again. The train was going very slowly now. I eased the door open. The wheels made a clacking sound. It was safe to jump. There was a big embankment beside the track; I could see houses below. I

153

opened the compartment door, tossed my bag and jumped. The ground was soft and I rolled over twice and saw my bag rolling down the embankment.

Chapter 15

I rolled down the hill. I found my kit bag in the bushes behind a little brick house. The bag was up against the garden wall. I slapped the dirt off my knees and took off my tunic and shook the dust and dirt from it. I picked up my kit bag and went through the garden gate. It was still early morning. There was a gate on the other side of the garden and I opened it and stepped out onto an empty street lined with trees. I saw a double decker bus coming down the street. I stood at the bus stop and got on. I took a seat downstairs in the back. There were two soldiers with Royal Artillery insignia on their battle dress jackets sitting up front.

'How far?' The conductress asked me.

'Green Park,' I said.

'You'll have to catch the tube.'

'Where?'

'I'll tell you when to hop off. Five pence, please.'

I felt like a masquerader. I had the feeling somebody could see I was no longer in the service even though I was wearing a uniform. 'Come on,' I told myself. 'You're getting spooky.' The elation of being free had gone away and there was nothing now to take its place, perhaps only a little fear about being caught. I watched the brick houses go past. The two soldiers were drunk and laughing. I felt very far away from them. Last night seemed a long time ago. I was asleep without knowing I slept when a hand touched me and even before I wakened I felt my body jerk, and then I sat bolt upright. It was only the 'clippie,' as they called women conductors on the buses.

'Next stop,' she said. 'The tube station's just around the corner.'

'Thank you.'

'Have a good leave.'

'Thank you,' I said and wondered how she knew I was on leave.

Well, of course, you didn't see air crews in London unless they were on leave. I was getting spooky. I had to get out of this uniform. I could get off the tube at Green Park and pick up a taxi in Curzon Street or right on Piccadilly, but I didn't want to hang around Piccadilly. There were too many air force police walking in pairs along there.

I got off the tube at Green Park underground station and walked over to the Ritz Hotel but there weren't any taxis.

I started walking up to the Hyde Park Corner bus stop. In a few minutes a Chelsea bus came and I jumped on. It was safe up here. No air force police this far away from Piccadilly. The bus swayed, picking up speed in Knightsbridge. It felt wonderful to be back in London, like the first day of a long furlough.

I heard the wheels of the bus spinning over the pavement saying, 'London... London... London... London...' What the hell did I have to worry about? I was free. If they caught me, they couldn't send me back to die. How lucky could I be to be right here.

I got off the bus at the corner of Oakley Street and Cheyney Walk. I went into the Chelsea Arms for a beer. I had spent many hours in here on leave. The bartender was a short old man who wore a square-topped derby when he was off duty. I leaned on the bar.

'Mild and bitter, please,' I said.

'Spot of leave?' he said, topping the glass, pulling the spiggot again.

'Convalescent,' I said.

He slid the beer across the bar. 'On me,' he said. 'Where'd you get shot up?'

'Kiel.'

'No, you.'

'Arm. Leg.'

'Weren't you shot up before?'

'No. You must be thinking of somebody else.'

He had a good memory, damn it.

'No, you copped it over Kiel once.'

I grinned and looked at him over the rim of my pint glass.

'Everybody cops it over Kiel. Seen Beryl and Terry?' I asked.

He raised his eyebrows.

'That's it,' he said and smiled. 'Friends of yours, aren't they?'

'Have you seen them?'

'I think Beryl's in Bristol. Trying out a Noel Coward show.'

'What about Terry?'

'He goes to a gymnasium every day. He stopped drinking. He's getting ready for a new show.'

He squinted at me strangely and rested his elbows on the counter.

'How much leave do you have?'

'Two weeks,' I lied.

'Two weeks?' He looked at me strangely, watchful.

'We got shot up over Dortmund. Skipper's a little flak happy. He's gone down to St Ives for a rest.'

'How many tours of ops have you done?'

'This is my third.'

He whistled softly. 'Pushing it a bit, aren't you?'

I didn't want to think about it.

'Another pint, please,' I said.

'Have it on me,' he said.

'No, that's all right.' I put a ten shilling note on the bar.

He pushed the ten shilling away. He leaned over and drew another pint and set it on the bar.

'What're you going to do?' he asked.

'Live it up,' I said. 'Suck up a few pints. Take it easy. Sleep in the mornings.'

'You won't sleep much at night. Jerry's coming over again.'

'To hell with Jerry.'

'How's the war going?' he asked.

I laughed. 'You read the papers.'

'I mean, are you dropping a lot of bombs?'

'They're catching it,' I said. 'But I don't see the bomb plots.'

'What?'

'Well, they have these WAAF types,' I said. 'They look at all our bomb photographs. Make a big mosaic. They wear watch repairer eye pieces. Magnify the photos. They make a complete layout of the bomb area. Can tell if we pranged it or not.'

'Those pathfinders must be something.'

'Wizard,' I said. 'We missed the docks at Hamburg couple weeks ago. Pathfinders lit up a resort town on a island. Intelligence claims we killed all the mistresses of high Nazi officials in Hamburg.'

He didn't say anything. He drew himself a pint and raised his glass and touched mine. 'Here's to more dead Jerry whores.' We clinked glasses and drank.

'I have to go,' I said.

'Take care of yourself. Have a good leave,' he said.

I went outside and stood on the corner. It was a beautiful morning. I walked across the Chelsea Embankment and looked at the Albert Bridge. The sun was shining on the Thames, and big white clouds were coming up in the high clear sky. Never to go away from this. Just to stand here warm like this, the breeze blowing off the water. Never to go back. Or maybe the woods near Abingdon beneath the hot sun in the shade of old beech trees on the grassy forest floor. Just lie there and look up through the shade of the trees at the sunlight, listening to the breeze high up in the branches. But it was impossible.

There were a lot of other good places in England. But how long would my money last. What the hell would I do if the war stopped? Well, it wasn't going to stop. Maybe the United States would come in. I went back across the Chelsea Embankment and along Cheyney Walk to Cheyney Mews.

Terry and Beryl had a pretty little house in the mews. It belonged to a member of Parliament who was out in the Western Desert with the Guards on tanks. His wife was a sculptor. I had never seen them. I didn't know where she was, but right off the small entrance hall was her studio filled with busts and figures covered with white shrouds.

I knocked on the door. It looked like a doll house from the outside. Inside there was a pretty iron stairway that curved upstairs to two bedrooms and a bath.

I knocked again and the door opened. Beryl shook both my hands.

'What're you doing in London?'

'Got some leave.'

'Come in. Come in. We heard you were dead.'

'Where'd you ever hear that?'

'Follansbye. That blonde Spitfire pilot.'

'That's funny,' I said. 'He went for a Burton last month.'

'How are you, Mack?'

'Couldn't be better.'

'How long do you have?'

'Couple weeks. Could you—'

'Of course, you can stay with us.'

'How's Terry?'

160

'The bastard is out in the provinces.' She smiled. 'Good play. They'll probably bring it into the West End next month.'

She took my kit bag and set it against the wall.

'Have you had breakfast?' she asked.

'Couple pints.'

'Come on,' she said and I followed her into the kitchen. Suddenly I had the feeling I had left something somewhere. Then I remembered.

'I'll be back in a second,' I said. 'I left my cap in Chelsea Arms.'

My cap was still on the bar. The bartender held up my cap and smiled as I came toward the bar. At the far end of the bar a grey-haired man of about fifty in a brown tweed jacket and grey flannel pants stood with one foot on the bar rail. His cane rested against the front of the bar. He turned his head and looked at me casually and then looked away.

'Thanks,' I said and took my hat and went outside. I started across the street. Suddenly what sounded like a twenty millimeter cannon shell exploded behind me. *Bop. Bop.* For a second I thought I was dreaming. Then I heard another shell. A big *bop*. I started to run across Oakley Street. Then I saw a closed car coming down Oakley Street. At first I didn't realize what it was up to. When I started running

161

and the car crossed the pavement onto the wrong side of the street I thought maybe the driver was drunk. Then I realized the loud *bop, bop* I had heard had been the sound of the car backfiring, and the car was coming straight at me.

I dived hard for the sidewalk curb. Out of the corner of my eye I saw the car swerve toward me on the sidewalk and I got to my knees and scrabbled furiously along on the sidewalk like a bear on four paws and dived behind the corner wall just as the car came right across the corner of the sidewalk, the tires shrieking in a skid as the car slid sideways into the street.

I watched it shoot swerving along Chelsea Embankment headed for Chelsea Bridge Road. It roared, skidding around the corner of Flood Street, vanished.

The whole thing made me feel weak. I got up and ran down the street and shoved the door open. I felt as if somebody had hit me in the back of the head. My legs felt weak. I knew that sound of gunfire had scared me badly, only it wasn't gunfire. I put my hand on my forehead and I was sweating. I wiped my forehead and leaned against the stairway railing. 'Christ!' I said. 'What the hell goes on?' Were they drunk or were they trying to kill me? Or both? It was more dangerous than over Essen if London had any more drunk drivers like that. Why would anybody want to kill me? I tried to remember the faces of the driver and the man beside him but couldn't recall if there had been two faces in the front seat or one. I thought there were two but I wasn't sure.

'What's the trouble?' Beryl said. 'Are you sick?'

'Seventy missions and I damn near get killed in London!' I told her what happened.

'Why would they drive on the sidewalk?' she asked. 'They must have been drunk.' I wiped the sweat off my forehead again. I shrugged. 'Maybe they don't like Americans.'

'Ghastly.'

'Scared the bloody hell out of me. All I need, go for a Burton on leave.'

'Have some breakfast,' she said. The kitchen was small, under the stairs on the first floor. I sat down at the table. Beryl sat across from me and smoked and drank tea. There were two huge fried goose eggs on my plate. They had to be goose eggs. They were so big.

'Where did you ever find these?'

She raised one eyebrow and winked.

'Black market, dahhling.' She dinched her cigarette in the ash tray. She was a striking-looking brunette, about thirty-five, a character actress. I remembered a swarthy, tall man who brought silk stockings around to her dressing room one night in the Savoy Theater.

'That Maltese?'

She smiled.

'Eat your eggs,' she said.

I was terrifically hungry. I was eating now. The big eggs were golden yellow on top and the whites were pure and smooth. The tea was hot and delicious with condensed milk and sugar in it. I drank two cups and ate three pieces of toast with butter.

'You must have one fine black market in the theater,' I said. 'I haven't seen butter and sugar in two years.'

'Did you have enough?'

'Plenty. The eggs were wonderful. Do you ever get any bacon?'

'We'll see. You're sure you're not hungry still?'

'I'm full.'

I leaned back in the chair and loosened my belt and unbuttoned my tunic.

'What's the matter, Mack? You don't look well.'

'Just tired.'

'Rough missions?'

'Oh, you know.'

'Well, you don't look well.'

'I'm fine.'

'Mack, what is it?'

'What's what?'

'You're always so cheery on leave.'

'I just missed getting killed. It's a little unnerving.'

'I don't mean that. Are you in trouble?'

'Just pooped out.'

'No. There's something else.'

I looked at her and then I looked away. At first I didn't know what was happening to me. I didn't understand it then. I felt my eyes begin to blink and they kept blinking faster and faster and then my throat started to fill with salty liquid and all of a sudden there wasn't anything I could do about it. I was crying, then terrible gasping sobs. I couldn't stop myself. I didn't know until a long time after why it had happened. I was crying for the dead, for my shame at having left them, for my shame in deserting the living. There was no other way I could get it out. I sat there rocking back and forth sobbing in the kitchen chair. I felt Beryl kneeling beside me, putting her arms around my shoulders, patting my back. I felt like a child and I could not stop crying. I had never felt so weak and humiliated.

'I can't...I can't...stop...' I heard my voice breaking, trying to excuse myself. 'I'm sorry, Beryl. I'm sorry, Beryl. Oh,

JesusJesusJesus Oh, GodGodGod! I can't stop...I can't stop...'

I felt her patting my hand. I couldn't look at her. It felt good to have her patting my hand. Slowly, oh God, so slowly, I stopped crying. My chest went on heaving and heaving up and down, making no sound.

'I'm in a jam,' I said, coughing. 'I've got to get some civilian clothes.' I tried to stop coughing. It would not stop.

'Don't worry,' she said.

'I haven't any clothes coupons,' I said.

'Piece of cake, laddy.' She stood up and poured me a cup of tea and went to the cupboard and brought out a bottle of whiskey. She poured a big shot into the tea. The telephone rang and she went out of the room into the studio. I heard her speaking, but I could not hear what she said.

'Oh, Christ,' I said to myself, and I started to cry again, 'I'm here, and they're all dead.' Goddamn it! I could not stop the damn choking crying. I couldn't stop. I sat there letting it wrack me, just letting it go. There was nothing I could do, but just let it go. It went on and on and I thought my chest was going to break. Then it started to stop, little by little, until there were only little sobs left inside me, coming small, slowly.

Chapter 16

I woke up. It was dark in the room. The blackout curtains were drawn. For a second I didn't know where I was. I sat up, trying to remember when I had fallen asleep. I got up and went to the door and out into the hall. I felt groggy, but rested. In some strange way I even felt a little different. Already I was changing but then I was not aware of it. I've escaped, I thought, and for the first time in that moment there was no guilt in me. I didn't think about that change until later when I seemed to have become a different person.

'Beryl,' I called down the staircase. I leaned against the bannister. She came into the hall. Back of her was the man I had met on the train. He was not wearing the green tweed suit. He wore a black shark-skin Saville Row suit.

'How are you, Mack?' said Beryl. 'Won't you come down?'

'I could use a drink.'

'Aren't you lucky. Charles just brought some Scotch.'

I walked down the stairs.

'Charles—' she started to say.

'We've met before,' I said.

'I say. On the train.'

I shook his hand.

'Charles Seymour,' said Beryl. 'Mack Norton.' She put her arm through his arm. 'Come along, Mack. We'll fix you a drink.'

I followed them into the kitchen. There was a bottle of Glenlivet on the kitchen table. She filled my glass with scotch.

'I'm going to need some water, Beryl.'

'Help yourself,' she pointed at the sink.

I sipped some of the Scotch off the top. About a quarter of an inch. I turned on the tap and filled the glass with water.

'Here,' Beryl said, lifting the bottle of Glenlivet. 'Isn't that beautiful.' She lifted her glass. 'Long live the Scots.' She put her arm around Charles Seymore's shoulder. 'Charles, you're beautiful.'

'You must do a show for me, darling,' he said and kissed her cheek.

'I thought you were in diamonds,' I said.

'He's in everything,' said Beryl. 'Aren't you Charles? Of course, I'll do a show for you.'

'You'll be very funny in it,' he said.

I looked at my glass. It was half empty. But nothing had happened to me. The Scotch didn't take me any place. I was watching Seymore. He was a strange looking guy. His eyelids were so wide and thin. I wondered if the sunlight came through the eyelids easily.

'Come on, Mack,' she said. 'Fix us a drink. Let's go in the studio, Charles.' She handed me her glass and his glass, and they strolled out of the room. She had her arm around his shoulders but she wasn't fawning over him. They were very comfortable together.

While I fixed the drinks I heard them talking. I poured the whiskey slowly, leaning against the kitchen table. I felt tired and lonely. I started thinking about Joan. It made me feel more lonely. Beryl came into the kitchen and put her hand on my shoulder. I felt low.

'You deserted, didn't you?' she said.

I didn't say anything.

'Don't worry, Mack. Everything will be all right.'

'Sure.'

'We'll get you identification papers. Clothes.'

'How about a trip to America?'

'Don't be funny.'

'What the hell does Seymour really do?'

'A little bit of everything. Theater. Business.'

'Must be a good business.'

'Two shows running right now.'

'He told me he was in diamonds.'

'He is. Would you like to make some money?'

'Diamond smuggling?'

'Stop trying to be funny, Mack.'

'Funny money?'

'Look, I want to help you.'

'Where's Terry?'

'God knows. Some place in the provinces with a new play. Listen to me.'

'O.K. Money.'

'I'll talk to Charles.'

She went out of the room. I heard them talking in low voices. She came back smoking a cigarette. She had a box in her hand about the size of a shoe box.

'It's a present from Mr Seymour,' she said. She had a five pound note in her hand.

'I've got money,' I said. She handed me the five pound note.

'Get a taxi. Go to the Savoy Theater. Stage door. Ask for Mary Alice Towner. Give her the package. Don't give it to the stage doorman.'

'What's in it?'

'It's just a present from Seymour.'

'Why doesn't he deliver it?'

'Stop asking questions. I'll talk to you

later.' We went downstairs into the studio. I had the five pound note in my pocket.

'You give my best to Miss Towner,' said Charles Seymour.

I wondered why he didn't send his chauffeur with the package.

'I say, Mack, would you stop and get some beer.'

'So long,' I said. I went out the front door. There wasn't a taxi along Cheyney Walk. I walked almost all the way to Cadogan Place before I found a taxi, and then I got out in Trafalgar Square and walked up the street to the Savoy Theater.

The stage door was open. An old geezer was sitting on a broken chair just inside the door.

'Miss Towner?' I said.

He looked at the package. He stuck out his hand.

'I'll see she gets it.'

I smiled. 'This is personal. I want to see her.'

He scowled and jerked a thumb over his shoulder. 'Room five.'

It was cool in the hall. I knocked on the door and just when I was beginning to wonder if there was anybody in the dressing room a woman opened the door. She was tall, with a broad face. Her eyes were puffy and she smelled of gin.

171

'What do you want?' Her voice sounded scratchy and gruff.

'Box from Mr Seymour.'

She smiled and her eyes lit up.

'Oh yes. Thank you. Will you have a drink?'

'No thanks,' I said.

'Take care,' she said and shut the door.

Outside I walked along looking for a taxi and somebody called my name from behind. I turned around. It was Jim Evans. He was a Canadian pilot, and I hadn't seen him for nearly two years, not since Operational Training Unit at Abingdon. He came up smiling and we shook hands.

'I thought you were dead,' he said. 'Somebody said you were.'

'You hear that about everybody.'

'Remember Robinson?'

My heart kicked over. How long since he had seen my pilot. Robinson had been with us at Abingdon.

'Sure,' I said. I watched his eyes. But they were bright and cheery and innocent.

'What a way to go,' said Evans. 'Home on furlough and a car ran over him in a blackout.'

'Where'd you hear that?'

'Saw his wife yesterday. She's in London.'

'Jessica?'

'Where you staying?' he asked.

172

'Green Park Hotel,' I lied.

'Give me a ring,' he said. 'I'm at the Cumberland. I've got a date in half a mo.' He punched me in the arm and grinned. 'Take it easy, Mack.'

'See you around.'

I walked on toward Trafalgar Square. Robinson dead. I ought to feel something but I couldn't feel anything, not even lucky that I was alive and he was dead. Hit by a car in a black out. Robinson must have completed nearly two tours of operations, shot at, crash landed, baled out once, landed in the Channel once. Then goes for a Burton in a blackout with both feet on the ground. It was all fate. No pattern to it. Just fate. Run into a stray flak burst not even aimed at you, gunned by a night fighter. When your number was up, it was up. The thing to do was keep out of the numbers game as much as possible. I counted the pigeons for a while in Trafalgar Square and caught a taxi back to Chelsea. I felt better.

Chapter 17

When I returned Charles Seymour was gone and Beryl was lying in bed reading a play script. I stood in the bedroom doorway.

'How did it go?' she asked.

'What's Mary Alice's problem?'

'Gin.' She put her book down. 'Did you see her?'

I nodded. She patted the bed. 'Come here and sit down, Mack.'

I went and sat on the edge of the bed.

'We're going to have to make some plans for you,' she said. She wasn't a bad looking woman for thirty-five, but she looked old to me. She put her hand on my knee. 'Seymour has a lot of friends. I think he can help you.'

'How?'

'Like that present to Mary Alice today. Silk stockings.'

'Is he in the black market, too?'

'Now. Now. Don't get nosey, darling. He likes to make people happy.'

'Those eggs made me happy.'

'Yes, darling. Those were good eggs. From Mr Seymour.'

'And you make him happy?'

'I play in his shows.'

'Everybody's happy.'

'You need a job and money. Mr Seymour said that one of his assistants was blown up by a bomb two nights ago. You might fit in.'

'Delivery boy?'

'Very perceptive, darling.' She leaned forward and kissed me cooly on the forehead. It was more than a motherly kiss.

'We're going to a party tonight.' She smiled and her dark eyes sparkled. 'Claridge's. Champagne. Lobster.'

'There's a war on.'

'I told you Mr Seymour knows his way around.'

'Around everybody.'

'It's his niece. She's getting married. A Dutch boy.'

Suddenly I felt tired.

'I'm going to take a nap.'

'Go on. I'll wake you?'

I went into the other bedroom and undressed. The sun was shining. I drew the blackout curtains and got into bed. I was really pooped out. I thought I could sleep right away. I closed my eyes and everything started going around in my head. Running away. Joan. How long would the war last? We were stalemated. It might take another hundred year war. Well, that would take care of that. No, I thought, get some sleep, play it day by day, mission by mission. There was no other way. It wasn't long until I was asleep. For the first time in a long time I didn't dream. I slept as if I were drugged.

When I woke up it was time to go to the reception. I asked Beryl what clothes I should wear and where could I get civvies at such short notice.

'Wear your uniform,' she said. 'Nobody's going to ask you for your leave pass at Claridge's.'

'I must be jumpy.'

'You really are, you know.'

I got dressed and we took a taxi to Claridge's. The doorman had more medals than a general.

'He must have been a general,' I said. We walked into the lobby.

'Who?'

'The doorman.'

'He's an old Coldstream regimental sergeant major.'

'He looks like a general.'

At the ballroom door Beryl showed our invitation card. The doorman gave me a snotty look. I could see why when we were inside. The ballroom was jammed with dancing couples. There wasn't even a Lieutenant in the room. Nothing below a Captain or a Flight Lieutenant and lots of red tabbed staff officers.

'I might as well be naked,' I said.

'What's your trouble?'

'Majors, Majors everywhere. Not a Flight Sergeant in sight.'

'Let's get some champagne and lobster.'

The waiters were busy serving champagne. Behind the barmen the long white table was loaded with empty bottles of Mumms. Beryl took two glasses off the waiter's tray and handed me one.

'Cheery-oh,' she said. The champagne was beautifully cold. The American jazz music thudded over the buzz of voices all around us.

'Cheers,' I said and touched her glass with mine. We drank almost a bottle before we started on the lobster. We sat down, eating the lobster and drinking more champagne. Beryl put her plate on the edge of the table.

'Let's dance,' she said. I got up and we danced. She pressed herself against me. The champagne and her slim hard body made me feel horny. She drew back her head and looked at me and smiled.

'I say, Mack. How long has it been?'

'Quite a while.'

'They didn't scare that out of you.'

'Not quite.'

'I'll have to do something about that.'

'I've got a girl.'

'Where?'

'She's in the WAAFs.'

'Serious?'

I nodded.

'You won't be seeing her for a while, will you?'

I didn't answer.

'What'll she say when she finds out you deserted?'

'Do we have to talk about that?'

'She's a patriot?'

'Her brother was shot down over Biggin Hill. He was on Spits.'

'You can't go near her. She'll turn you in.'

'Probably.'

'Don't be shy with me, Mack. Terry's going to be away at least a month.'

'Let's dance.'

'I like this,' she laughed. 'Just standing here.' I pulled her closer and we danced. I was horny as hell, and hadn't thought about sex for days. I wondered what was happening to me or what had happened.

'Let's go home,' she said.

'Let's get some more champagne.'

'Are you in love with her?'

'That's right.' I stopped dancing and took her arm and steered her through the crowd.

We drank three more glasses of champagne and watched the crowd. There were bags of Admirals and Group Captains and a couple of Brigadiers. The war seemed very remote despite all the uniforms.

'I thought booze was rationed,' I said.

'All you need is money.'

'Christ, they're starving to death on the squadron.'

'Come off it, please. Let's go home.'

She leaned against me and I drank more champagne.'

'I have to spend a penny,' she said. She put her glass down on a table and went out.

It was getting more crowded and noisy. Suddenly I wondered why I hadn't seen Charles Seymour. And who was his niece? Who was the bride? I had another glass of champagne and a woman's face came toward me over the shoulder of a man and I thought I was dreaming.

'Jessica,' I said.

She was small and dark and pretty. She saw me and smiled and it was a sad smile and she gave a little wave of her hand. She was dancing with a man in a dark suit. They moved on through the crowd.

What the hell was she doing here? Robinson dead only a few days. Did she know I had deserted? I better get out of here. I looked around for Beryl.

I got in with the crowd along the bar. I could barely move. That was good. I was screened in front by a row of men along the bar and two rows of people behind me. I stood there, not moving.

I did not turn my head. I just kept looking straight at the bartender who was busy. The crowd in front of me gave way and I stood against the bar and took a glass of champagne and leaned forward.

'Mack,' a voice said. It was Jessica. Her smile looked bright but her eyes were sad.

'I want to talk to you,' she said.

Oh-oh, she knows.

'What is it?'

'Not here. Let's dance,' she said. She took the glass out of my hand and set it on the bar. She took my hand. I put my arm around her waist and we moved out among the dancers.

'Are you smashed?'

'A little.'

'You look it,' Jessica said.

'I heard about George. I'm sorry.'

The band was playing 'I Can't Get Started With You.' We turned and circled at the end of the ballroom. I stopped dancing and stood against the curtain.

'That isn't it,' she said.

'Really, I'm sorry. I heard about the accident.'

180

'Who told you?'

'Evans.'

'Who's Evans?'

'He was at Operational training with us at Abingdon.'

'What did he say?'

'It was an accident. A car hit him in a blackout.'

'It wasn't an accident,' said Jessica. 'I was there.'

'Take it easy.'

'No, it wasn't.'

'Let's get a drink.'

'Listen to me, Mack. Listen.' She caught my right hand. She held it between her hands. 'I saw it. He was murdered.'

'Take it easy, honey.'

'No, it was quite deliberate.'

'Did you tell the police?'

'Coroner said it was an accident. Hit and run.'

'You need a drink,' I said.

She looked straight at me.

'I know all about you, Mack.'

'Well?'

'Maybe you were smart to desert.'

'How do you know it was an accident?'

'Do you know what happened to Peter Dickson yesterday?'

'What *is* this?'

'Dickson is dead. Hunting accident.'

'Come on,' I said. I was used to seeing

people die in the air or hear about old friends shot down in flames that all death seemed only a matter of luck. And if it were murder, all the deaths I had seen seemed to make murder not too serious. Somebody died. Somebody lived. I felt indifferent to death now. I didn't want to be upset by it. I was free of death. I wanted to keep the feeling.

'But it wasn't a hunting accident?'

She nodded. 'Peter's uncle doesn't believe it.'

'What are you doing here?'

'My father works for Mr Seymour. He thought it might do me good to get away.'

'Where are you staying?'

'Green Park Hotel.'

'Across from Flemmings?'

'Mack, get out of London. Something's odd. I don't know what it is.'

'Hello, Mack.' It was Mr Seymour. He had come up behind us. 'May I have this dance, Jessica?' He led her onto the dance floor and called over her shoulder. 'Enjoy yourself, Mack.' They went away into the crowd. I started back to the bar. She's all shook up, I thought. Jesus, maybe we're safer flying combat. I couldn't believe it. Gone for Burton. Double accident. Hell, nothing unusual. It would happen to anybody. I was wrong. I didn't know it then.

182

'I've been looking all over for you,' said Beryl.

'I saw Charles Seymour.'

'He's a darling.'

'I'm sure.'

'Let's go home, Mack.'

'Not a bad idea.'

Chapter 18

It was still light out when we got back to the house in Chelsea. Beryl was tipsy. I did not want to sleep with her. But where the hell else could I go? I had an idea.

'Have you got any whisky?'

'No,' she said and grinned foolishly and put her arms around my neck and kissed me. I returned her kiss but not with much on it.

'What's on your mind, baby? Stop worrying,' she said.

'How about that whiskey?'

'Not a drop in the house.'

She put her arm through mine.

'Come on. We'll go to the Murderer's Ams.'

The Murderer's Arms was a pub down the street on Cheyney Walk. I didn't want to go but there was no way of talking her out of it.

'They'll be out of booze by now,' I said.

'That bartender is a good friend of mine.'

'He probably waters it.'

'Probably,' she said. We went out. There was no talking her out of it. If the whiskey wasn't watered maybe she would get drunk and I could get her home and get her to sleep before she got any new ideas about us going to bed.

'Hello, everybody,' she said as we came into the working man's bar. There were a bunch of old men standing around wearing old flat top derbys. They were all taxi drivers. Beryl knew them all. They were playing darts.

'Give us two whiskeys, Bert,' she said to the bartender.

'Where have you been?' said Bert. He had a drinker's red nose.

'A smashing wedding. Bags of champagne.'

The bartender looked at me and shrugged. I knew what he thought. Beryl didn't need any whiskey. She was smashed now.

'Come along, Bert,' Beryl said. 'We're parched. You remember Mack.'

The bartender nodded at me. Beryl reached across the bar and took two glasses of whiskey. She handed me a glass and clinked her glass against mine.

'Down the hatch, Yank,' she said.

'You're getting stiff as hell,' I said.

'That's what I want. Something stiff as hell.'

The bartender walked down to the far end of the bar and leaned there watching the old men shooting darts.

'You're a bloody Puritan tonight,' she said.

'I'm tired, Beryl.'

'Bloody crepe hanger, that's what you are.' She tossed the whiskey off neat. I took a drink. It burned and tasted lousy after the champagne.

'Come on, let's go home,' I said. I knew her well enough. She had a hollow leg. Once she had drunk two days straight without eating and she had not looked drunk nor staggered.

'Now you're talking. Yank. Drink up.'

I drank off the whiskey and we went out. It was bright as noon outside though it was nine o'clock in the evening. The sun was still shining on the barrage balloons above the Thames.

She staggered a little as she stepped off the corner curb. 'Left. Left,' she said. 'Give us a little top rudder, darling. I think I'm skidding.'

I got her across the street and into the

house in the mews. She needed help to get up stairs. The whiskey had done it.

'Wow!' she laughed and fell back on her bed. 'Come here, Mack.'

She lay on her back with her legs over the edge of the bed. She was smiling and looking straight up at the ceiling. She held up her arm.

'One moment,' I said. 'I've got to make a phone call.'

I went out of the room and started down the stairs.

'You better come back,' she shouted. 'If you know what's good for you.' Then she laughed: 'I know what's good for you.'

The telephone was in the kitchen. I shut the kitchen door and looked up the number of the Green Park Hotel in Half Moon Street and dialed the number and asked for Jessica Robinson. The desk clerk rang the room number over and over again.

'She doesn't—' the desk clerk started to say. Then: 'One moment, please. Mrs Robinson. Are you Mrs Robinson?'

'Hello.'

'Hello, Jessica?'

'Mack.'

'Oh, yes,' she said quickly. She sounded even more disturbed. 'I'll take it in my room. Hold on, Mack.'

I waited, listening to the wire hum.

186

Maybe Beryl was asleep. Anyway she was quiet. That was something.

'Hello, Mack. What's your number? I'll call you back in a moment.'

I gave her the Chelsea number and hung up. I went to the window and looked out at the Embankment. There were army trucks going by. On the other side of the river the sun was still shining on the barrage balloons. They looked like grey elephants. The telephone rang. I picked it up.

'Mack?'

'What's the trouble?'

'You don't have to believe me.'

'I believe you. What is it?'

'Peter Dickson. His uncle doesn't believe it was a hunting accident.'

'So what?'

'You ought to talk to his uncle.'

'What for? He's dead, Jessica.'

'Somebody murdered him.'

'Jessica, you ought to go home to your folks.'

'Please see him. His uncle. He lives at Hambledon. I only spoke to him on the phone.'

She sounded so desperate.

'Hambledon?' I said.

'It's a little village. Really just a pub inn. Near Henley.'

'I remember it.'

'Then if you don't believe me—will you

call me after you see him? His name is Rodger Belton.'

'Get some sleep. I'll call you.'

'I'll be home.'

She gave me a telephone number at Selby in Yorkshire. I remembered the town. There was a beautiful cathedral and about fifty pubs.

'I'll call you,' I said. 'Get some rest.' I hung up.

I didn't think anything about it then. I just put it away. The way I was putting everything away. The squadron, the dead, my whole life on the squadron. I must keep it away. I went back upstairs. I had put Dickson's death away, just as if he had been shot down and I had come back from a mission and found his bed empty with somebody trying on his boots. He was gone. A new body would fill his bed tomorrow.

'What were you doing, calling your true love?' She was sitting up now, on the edge of the bed. She didn't look so cock-eyed, but she didn't look sober either.

'No, my broker.'

'Don't sell the franc short.'

'I'm going to bed,' I told her.

'You bet you are.' She stood up and put her arms around me. Damn it, I was horny. Would it mean anything going to bed with her? Nothing to her, I was sure,

188

and certainly nothing to me. I thought about Joan. I felt like a shit leaning against Beryl.

'Take your clothes off,' Beryl said. She turned around. 'Unsnap me first.' I unsnapped the back of her dress, and she drew it over her head. She was wearing pants and brassiere. She stood with her back to me, and pointed over her shoulder with one hand at her bra. I unsnapped her bra and she turned around. Her breasts were beautiful, and she undid my belt and put her hand inside my trousers. That was about all I could stand.

Beryl was about ten years older than me. But she had the firm, slim body of a twenty year old girl. She was marvelous in bed. I had no idea she could be this good. She did things for me no other woman had ever done. She knew all kinds of tricks. I don't know how long we made love, nor how many times. She was quite tender and gentle one moment and voracious the next. I felt good afterwards, but I didn't feel anything toward her except a certain passing fondness I hadn't felt before.

I lay beside her and she smoked and looked up at the ceiling. It was dark outside and dark in the room. I could see the red tip of her cigarette. She talked without taking the cigarette out of her lips.

The red tip bobbled up and down in the darkness.

'Do you want to sleep?'

'No,' I said. 'Have you had enough?'

The room was pitch dark. She put her hands between my legs. The tired warrior was quite dead.

She said, 'He'll keep till morning. Are you really in love with this girl?'

'I told you before.'

'Are you sure?'

'Of course.'

'You're very young.'

'I don't feel young.'

'How old are you, Mack?'

'Twenty-five.'

'Oh, to be twenty-five now that Mack has come again.' She laughed. 'You'll get over it.'

'I don't want to.'

'Everybody falls in love in war time. They're either bored or lonely.'

'I love her.'

'I'm sorry, Mack.'

'What about you and Terry?'

She laughed.

'We might even get married someday, he's such a cad.'

'What do you mean?'

'He's always screwing women.'

'I thought you were engaged.'

'God no, we just live together.'

She put her hand between my legs. The tired warrior stirred.

'I say, Mack. That is something. Does your true love appreciate you?'

'You bitch.'

'You bet. Come here.'

She rolled over on top me and the warrior rose to battle. Then I fell asleep. After a while, I woke in terrible pain.

'Jesus!' I yelled. 'You sonofabitch! Are you nuts?' I jumped out of bed. She had touched a lighted cigarette to my navel.

I walked across the room. But there was really no place to go. I was trapped. She giggled.

'I thought you were dead, Mack.'

'Very funny.'

'I'm sorry. How did you happen to meet Charles Seymour?'

'On the train. He was in my compartment.'

'He's certainly interested in you.'

'My future employer?'

'He's very big in London.'

'Diamonds. Shows. Blackmarket?'

'Keep your big Yankee mouth shut and you can sit out the war working for him. He might get you home.'

'What did he ask about me?'

'Nationality, your parents?'

'Irish.'

'Hmm,' Beryl said. 'That's funny. Rude,

191

you might say.' She shook her head. I didn't think much about it.

'Employer's survey,' I said.

And I thought no more of it until I started to drop off to sleep. And then I remembered a rather odd question Charles Seymour had asked me on the train. About the G Box, a new, secret navigational aid. It laid an invisible radio grid over the nearest Continent areas. With a Gee receiver you could plot your position at any time to an accuracy which varied from zero near home to within six miles at a range of 400 miles from the transmitter. It had helped burn down Rostock up on the Baltic. But there was nothing in the papers about Gee. So how had Seymour heard about it? Maybe had friends in the service.

Then suddenly my head said. 'That car! Had somebody tried to kill me? I couldn't believe it. If they had tried and failed, why hadn't they tried again? And for what reason? Nobody drove a car up over the sidewalk unless they were after you or very drunk. The more I thought about it the more it seemed it hadn't been a drunken swerving swipe at me. It had been quite deliberate. And Jessica's husband and Peter Dickson. Murdered? Could that be true? Baloney. Impossible. But was it? Had they been murdered?

The more I thought about it the more I thought about seeing Dickson's uncle. I got out of bed. I had escaped being scared. Now my throat felt tight again. My mouth felt dry and copperish tasting as though just before a rough mission to the Ruhr. I was scared.

'Where are you going?' Beryl said.

'I need a drink of water.'

'Bring me one.'

Chapter 19

'This is it,' Beryl said.

'It has to be.'

I looked up at the sign. Stag and Huntsman Inn. We were in Hambledon, a village about five miles from Henley-on-Thames. I remembered the Inn now. Two years ago I had been here while training on Whitley bombers at Abingdon. The walls of the Inn were plastered white with Tudor beams on the outside. Cromwell probably had slept here. In Buckinghamshire every pub owner claimed Cromwell had been a guest.

I opened the Inn door.

Inside the small lobby was silent and empty. The night before I had told her what I thought about Jessica's story. But I had not told her about the strange questions Charles Seymour had asked me on the train.

I rang the bell on the desk and in came a cheerful white haired old man, and gave us a good room, overlooking the wooded valley. His wife was just as cheerful when I came down stairs to ask where Rodger Belton lived.

'Weren't you here before?' she asked.

'Couple of years ago. I trained over at Abingdon.'

'I thought so,' she said. 'Mr Belton lives up on the hill.'

She gave Beryl a look as if to say, You're not his wife. Beryl ignored her sharp glance and we went out.

It was a beautiful afternoon in Buckinghamshire. Like the August days of the Battle of Britain. The high, hot clear sky was vivid as bluish-white bottle glass. Such a soft day, the unbelievable radiance of so soft a summer. Along the horizon, fat clouds like gobs of whipped cream floated lightly above the woods on the hill. There was something sedate about the clouds. We walked along, up the path through the woods to the hill. There was the sweet wonderful summer soft smell of flowers, roses and phlox. I could taste their colors, red, white, blue and yellow, as if their petals lay upon my cheek like the soft lips of Joan.

'Jesus!' Beryl said suddenly. She dropped down on both knees. God, hallucinating about bombers. A lot of British were spooky if they had been through many air raids. The slightest sound and they were liable to jump off a street curb and dive on their faces.

'Get down,' she said.

I didn't hear or see anybody.

'Come along, Beryl,' I put my hand under her elbow and lifted her up. She swung away and dropped down on both knees and then sprawled on her face.

'What the hell,' I said. 'Come along.'

'Get down! Get down!' she cried.

Her body shivered.

'Lay off the juice,' I said, not wanting to mention irritably now that I thought she drank too much.

She hissed. 'You stupid ass! There's a man in the woods with a gun. He pointed it at us.'

'Balls.'

'Balls, hell!'

'Come on. We'll have a drink.'

I grabbed her arm and jerked her up and walked back to the Stag and Huntsman.

'I thought *I* was spooky,' I said.

'There's a man in the woods, Mack.'

'You're dreaming.'

'Haven't you a gun?'

I had forgotten about it. It was in my kit bag and it was still there upstairs in our bedroom. A standard issue .38 Webley. We could carry it on missions if we wanted to, but nobody ever did. It would give the Germans a good excuse to shoot you while you were surrendering after being shot down. It was a big, clumsy pistol.

'I'll be down in a minute,' I said.

I went upstairs. The pistol was there. I put it inside my jacket. I was wearing Terry's tweed jacket and grey flannel slacks. It made a bulge, but not too much.

Downstairs I took her arm and steered her outside.

'Do you have the gun?' she asked. 'I won't go up there if you haven't.'

I patted my breast pocket. She touched it.

'I still think you're dreaming,' I said.

'No. I saw him.'

I looked up the path through the woods. It was a beautiful wood. There were yellow leaves on the ground under the oak trees but it was like a park, not like the woods back in the states with undergrowth waist high around the trees.

The path went up a hill. There were woods on each side of the path. The trees were oak trees and ironwood. There were patches of sunlight on the leaves beneath the trees. I kept looking right and left, with one hand in my breast pocket. I still did not believe Beryl. She had been in too many London bombing raids. She had spent too many nights in underground shelters feeling the earth reverberating from bomb explosions. She was bomb happy, spooky. Why would there be anybody in the woods pointing a gun at us?

The woods stopped and we went across a meadow into another wood. There were primroses among the trees. Suddenly the woods ended and we stood on the edge of a big flat green lawn.

Ahead, above the long beautiful sweep of lawn, a gray granite Queen Anne house rose, a three storey square bulk against the sunny sky. There were french windows open on the first floor.

A white haired man was sitting in profile to us on the lawn. He was hatless dressed in tennis shirt and long white flannels, and smoking a cigarette in black holder. He did not look around at us. He sat in a white wicker chair. There were two other chairs and on the wicker table in front of him there was a silver tray, a glass decanter of whiskey, two silver cups and a pitcher of water.

'I was hoping you would come,' he said.

We walked toward him but the old man did not turn his head. He blew a cloud of smoke, rose and bowed to Beryl and we introduced ourselves. I gave him a phony name, Steve Cannon.

'I knew your nephew,' I said.

'Won't you sit down?'

'How did you know we were coming?' I asked.

'Mrs Thompson at the inn.'

'I wanted to talk to you about Peter.'

'Sit down. Sit down. Water?' He looked at Beryl and then at me. He poured two drinks and handed us the silver cups. They looked like mint julep cups. There was an inscription on the side, but I did not read it. It was good Scotch, quite heavy.

'How did you know Peter?'

'On the same squadron.'

'Oh,' he said casually.

'Robinson's wife told me Peter was murdered.'

'Oh?' said the old man.

'I talked to her at a party.'

'Whose party?'

'Come on,' I said.

'What squadron was he on?'

'Ten.'

He rose, lifted his cup. He put the cup on the table. 'Come up to the house.' He looked at Beryl. 'Would you mind staying here?'

'Yes, I would,' said Beryl. 'But if you'll fix another drink I would prefer to stay.'

'Do have another, Miss,' said the old man, turning away, glancing quickly over his shoulder, smiling a little.

He beckoned me with a wag of one finger to follow him.

I felt uncomfortable following him across the grass. It was because I had not worn civilian clothes for a long time. The knotted tie at my throat and loose fit of the tweed jacket compared to a RAF tunic or battle dress on ops seemed very strange.

We went up the front steps together. The long hall through the middle of the house reminded me of old southern houses in Alabama, plantation houses, but here the walls were stone. We turned into a circular room. The walls were at least fourteen feet high, but it was not a big room. On one corner wall there were wooden plaques into which were set inscribed silver medallions. Out of the center of each medallion hung a fox tail.

'Would you care for a drink?' said the old man.

'Fine,' I said.

He went to the wall and pushed a button.

'Did you know Peter well?'

'I knew him at O.T.U,' I said. Which meant I had crewed up with Peter Dickson at Operational Training Unit.

'Oh, yes,' the old man said quickly, looking suddenly fragile. He said to the butler: 'Brandy.' The butler went out.

'What do you want to know?' the old man asked.

'Jessica said he was murdered.'

'I believe she's correct.'

'What have you done about it?'

'What's to be done? He stumbled on his shot gun.'

'Do you believe that?'

'Would you mind leaving?'

'I'll have some brandy.'

'Please, leave.'

'What do you value most?' I asked.

'My life.'

'Keep loving yourself, old man.'

'And you don't value your life?'

'You're a wise old bastard.'

'You will become wiser.'

'Who do you think will win the war?' I asked.

'You are stupid, young man.'

'Whose side are you on?'

'Britain.'

'You're full of crap, old man.'

'Please leave.'

'Get the guy out of the woods with the gun.'

'Leave.'

'Tell the truth. Why do you think your

nephew was murdered?'

'Some day America will be a wiser country.'

'You're wiser than hell. And Peter is dead.'

'You are bloody stupid,' he said.

I reached inside my breast pocket and jerked out the Webley. It was a most awkward pistol. I pointed it at his head.

'Cut out the shit, old man. What happened to Peter?'

Chapter 20

The butler came in. The old man shook his head before the butler could react.

'No, no,' I said. The butler saw the pistol. 'Put the tray down,' I said.

'Sir,' said the butler, looking at the old man. The butler was a young man, perhaps thirty. I wondered why he wasn't in the British forces. He wore a dark suit that reminded me of people studying undertaking in America. I suppose the government was short of butler's uniforms at that time. Most of the butlers were in the forces. I wondered if this one had flat feet or perhaps a social disease that couldn't be cured.

201

'Put the tray down,' said the old man. 'Come here.'

'Tell him to leave,' I said.

'Henry, go into the hall. Say nothing. Do nothing.'

I watched Henry turn and leave the room. He shut the door.

'Somebody was going to take a shot at me in the woods,' I said.

'Perhaps.'

'There was a man there,' I said. 'Beryl saw him. He had a gun.'

'Poacher,' said the old man.

'You don't believe that, do you?'

'I might.'

'Jessica said you didn't.'

'Why do you care?'

'I think somebody tried to kill me with a car a week ago.'

'What about my nephew?'

'Jessica said you think he was killed.'

'The coroner termed it accidental death. Hunting accident.'

'What do you think?'

'He was murdered.'

'Why don't you do something about it?'

'There's no real evidence.'

'Then why do you think he was murdered?'

'When one stumbles and falls on one's own shotgun and shoots oneself, it is very

202

seldom the gun is found beneath the body and across the chest of the deceased.'

'Where then?'

'The shot would knock him over, and the gun would fall forward. Usually it would be found lying between the legs. I've seen several hunting accidents. Quite similar.'

'Was he shot with his own gun?'

The old man nodded.

'How would a murderer do that?'

'Take the gun away from him and shoot him.'

'Wouldn't there be a struggle?'

'Not if the person knew him.'

'Did you have the shot charge that he was hit with checked against the gun?'

'Same size shot.'

'Same gun?'

'Quite. There's nothing you can do.'

'Where did it happen?'

'On the path below the meadow.'

'How far down?'

'Hundred yards.'

'Thanks for the drink,' I said.

'You haven't finished it.'

'No thanks. I have to go. Sorry about Peter. He was a good lad.'

'Why would anybody want to kill him?'

I shrugged. 'That's what I'd like to know.' I left him sitting there, and joined Beryl on the lawn. I looked back as we entered the woods, but he had not come out of the house.

'What's the mad rush?'

'I want to see something,' I said.

'What?'

'You'll see.'

The path dipped down through the thick trees. I took the Webley out of my jacket and held it in my right hand with the safety off. I heard sheep somewhere. We crossed the meadow. I watched the woods ahead. It was thick at the edge. We entered the woods and started down the path. I counted the yards. When I paced off a hundred yards I stopped and looked down at the dust. No sign of a scuffle. The dirt was hot and hard packed.

'Stand right here,' I told Beryl.

'What are you going to do?'

'Shoot you,' I smiled. 'Now just stand still. Don't move. Face up the hill.'

I walked away at about ten degrees off right angle from her. I turned around and looked at her and then I looked at the ground and studied the leaves. They were yellow and packed in layers by the seasons and rains.

I looked at the imprint my shoe made. There were no depressions in the soft leaves. Then I saw what I was looking for. I reached down and felt the leaves, then knelt down. Yes, the leaves right here in this spot were loose on top. I lifted a leaf. It was not damp and packed down. Nor was the leaf next to it. Nor the leaves around the first two.

'What are you looking for?' Beryl asked.

I crawled around on all fours and lifted up the leaves that weren't packed down in layers. There were a lot of loose leaves. Somebody had sprinkled them on top the packed leaves. Then I found what I was looking for. A footprint. I lifted more leaves and found another print. The leaves were damp underneath, and there was no way somebody could take away the imprint of boots without digging out all the damp leaves packed in layers. So somebody had sprinkled leaves over each boot print.

There was a trail of boot prints right up to a tree about ten yards from where Beryl stood on the path. Then I picked up the trail again behind the tree and lifted leaves for about five yards. I stood up.

'Come here,' I said. Beryl came over.

'You go to the right,' I told her. 'And I'll go to the left. Look for footprints.'

I figured whoever had covered his tracks had done it only so far and then stopped so the boot prints would show up soon right on top of the first layer of leaves. It didn't take long.

'Over here,' Beryl called. I went over

and looked. Sure enough, there was a clear trail. I raised my head and looked through the trees.

'Whoever shot Peter did it from back there. About ten yards from the trail. Using another gun. Then stuck Peter's gun under him.'

'What are you going to do?' Beryl said. She sounded scared. 'See where the trail goes.'

'God, I don't understand.'

'I don't either. Come on.'

I had tracked deer in Minnesota before the war. This was much easier. You could see by the prints the man wore about a size ten shoe. He was walking, not running at all. There was a triangular steel wedge in the heel imprint of the right foot.

We went down into a little valley and up a hill. The trail was straight and the man was walking quickly but he wasn't running. Where could he have been going? The road was back the other way near the Inn. We went on among the big trees and then up another hill. At the top we looked down the other side to a grove of swamp willows; through the willows I could see water glint about one hundred yards below.

We came out of the woods into knee-high grass and I lost the tracks about ten feet into the grass. Wherever the killer had stepped the grass had sprung up.

I was looking down into the grass when a gun went off. It was a shot gun. I heard the shot whistle past. I grabbed Beryl and flung her down and lay down beside her.

'Don't move!' I said.

'Jesus!'

'Twelve gauge.'

'I didn't see anybody.'

'Stay down!'

'What are you going to do?'

I slithered forward, using my knees to push me along. As I lifted my head the gun went off again. I thought I saw somebody moving through the willows. There weren't many automatic shot guns in England. In fact, I had never seen one, but you could load a .12 gauge double fast. Whoever was shooting was using a double.

I would be a damn fool to rush him. That's what he wanted. At first I thought he was a fool to be firing at this range and then I remembered the sound of the shot. He was shooting buckshot. I crawled to my right and then back to my left and lay still. He was going to wait me out. I stuck my hand up and fired a shot. I rolled away. Shots hissed through the high grass. I lay still and thought about the drunken British soldier who had told me how he out waited a sniper during the retreat before Dunkirk. He was pinned down, and if he moved the sniper would get him. He didn't move for five hours. Finally the sniper moved and he nailed the sniper. It was as simple as that. We probably would have to lie here until dark. But that wasn't simple. It meant about six hours.

I lay there about fifteen minutes and lifted my hand and fired down into the willows and rolled away to my left. There was no answering fire. I was sure he was still there. I crawled back to Beryl. Her face was sweaty and white.

'Who could it be?'

'Christ knows,' I said. 'Can you crawl backwards?'

'I could fly right now.'

'Keep your head down and crawl backward into the woods.'

We started wriggling backwards, keeping our heads down. We crawled and stopped and listened. There was no sound. We crawled backwards for a long time.

'When we come out of the grass, just lie still until I tell you.'

'What?'

'I'll tell you.'

We lay there five minutes. The big trees were a few feet behind us.

'I'll get up first,' I said. 'It's a long shot. But if he's there he'll fire.'

I waited another minute, counting the seconds. Then I whirled around and in the same motion, sprang up and dived for the woods. I rose slowly behind a tree and looked out. There was a thin line of water through the willows. There was a river down there. I couldn't see any shape in the willows.

'Come on,' I whispered. 'Crawl and dive.'

Beryl was quick. She was probably quicker than ever before. In a second she was behind the big tree next to me. She didn't look out.

'Let's get back to the Inn,' I said. She clutched the tree with both hands. There was only one thing to do. Walk away from her. I turned and started dog trotting back through the trees. She wailed something and I heard her running and then she was beside me and we were both running.

'Get behind me,' I said as we came out onto the path. We started down the path to the Inn. I held the Webley in both hands. It would need two hands to get off an accurate shot. The barrel jumped to beat hell when I had fired it.

'Hurry up,' I said. Going along the path, I felt someone might suddenly step out from behind a tree and fire on us. The shooter might have circled around behind us by this time. I walked slowly, looking back and forth into the woods on each side of the path. Then I saw the Inn. The chimney stuck up over the tops of low trees. We came out onto the lawn and the sun was shining on the roof. It was a half mile walk to the railroad station.

'We're not going to walk to the station today,' I told her. 'We'll get the morning train.'

The door of the Inn was open and we went inside. I rang the bell and told the old man we would be staying the night and asked if we could eat in our room. He looked at us and nodded. He did not say anything about the gunfire. Maybe he was deaf, but he didn't look nor act deaf.

We went upstairs and I opened the bedroom window and pushed back the shutters. I could see across the lawn down to the sandy road that led to the railroad station. It was possible we could get on the train tonight. But I didn't think the shooter would wait around all night for us. No, he would try something different. He would go away. There were hundreds of ways to get at somebody in the London blackout. But I couldn't understand it. Then I thought about the black market.

'What's Seymour's competition?' I asked.

'There are dozens of producers.'

'No. No. The black market.'

'Darling, that's just a side line. An accommodation for his friends.'

'That's what you think.'

'Do you mean—?'

'Sure. But why the hell would anybody take a crack at me with a shotgun? I haven't even gone to work yet for Seymour.'

'I'm going to tell him.'

'Don't tell him a damn thing.'

'We ought to tell the police.'

'Great idea. Then I go to the Glass House.'

'I'm sorry, Mack. I'm so scared.' She leaned against me. I looked out the window. I did not believe the gunman was still around. He didn't have to be. Maybe he wasn't trying to shoot me. Just scare me. But why? Did he think I knew something I ought not to know? Did he think I was somebody else? How did he know I was here?

'Did you tell anybody we were coming down here?'

Beryl shook her head. Then only Jessica knew, but who knew she had talked to me on the phone if she had used an outside phone? It beat the hell out me.

Still, somebody had shot at me. Could he have hit me if he wanted to, on that first shot? Buck shot would kill at fifty yards with a heavy load. Yes, he was in range. Maybe he was a lousy shot.

I shut the window and lay down on the bed and Beryl lay down beside me. If I went back I would get a year or more in the Glass House. Pissing and crapping

211

on the double, getting kicked in the ass by guards. But it was better than being dead. I fell asleep and dreamed about being back in the States during pheasant hunting season, until Beryl woke me and said supper was ready. She had a tray with slices of buttered bread, real butter and jam, poached eggs on toast and a big pot of tea. I felt punchy from sleeping. But I got up and shot the bolt on the door. We ate and sat on the bed and watched it get dark outside. Then we lay on the bed fully clothed, listening to the darkness.

It was a long night. I didn't think anything would happen but I wasn't sure. I wondered what I was supposed to know about something but didn't know, though somebody thought I knew something I wasn't supposed to know. I tried to remember everything that had happened to me since I had deserted. Then I slept.

I was awake before dawn. I shook Beryl, unbolted the door and we went downstairs. I left money for the bill on the counter. We walked along the sandy road to the station. There were open fields on each side. I felt safe here, but I gripped the Webley in my coat pocket. The train was on time. All the way to London I kept thinking about Charles Seymour,

212

trying to remember something he had said
to me.

It was raining when we came into
London.

Chapter 21

I went up the stairs to Charles Seymour's
office. It was in the Strand, near Bedford
Street. It was almost noon, the day after
the night at Hambledon. He had phoned
Beryl in the morning and said if I was
ready to go to work he would see me. His
name was on the door, but the door was
locked. I knocked and waited. A minute
passed. I looked at my watch and knocked
again. There was no answer. I put my ear
against the frosted plate glass. I thought I
could hear somebody in the room.

'Mr Seymour,' I called.

There was no answer. Somebody's
inside, I thought.

'Mr Seymour,' I yelled and knocked
hard on the glass.

What the hell was going on? He had
called me. I was on time.

'Who is it?' a voice called.

'Mack,' I said.

'One moment, please.'

There was another long pause. A door opened down the hall. A man came out, turned, locked the door. He wore a bowler hat and a dark pin-striped suit. He walked past, looking straight ahead. He was dark, swarthy, Italian or Greek, I thought.

The door made a clicking sound and swung open. I went in. There was a reception desk, chairs, paintings on the walls of rural English scenes. Straight ahead was another frosted glass door. It was closed. I turned the knob and opened it.

Mr Charles Seymour sat behind a big mahogany desk. Behind his head was a painting of a British warship in a big gold frame. On the walls were framed photographs of stage and screen stars and one of the Duke of Kent that was autographed.

Charles Seymour looked small behind the big desk. He smiled faintly, but his eyelids did not move, just a faint curve at the corners of his lips.

'I'm happy you came,' he said.

His eyes were half-hooded by the lids. The little smile left his face.

'How many missions did you have to go to finish another tour?'

'Too bloody many,' I answered.

'Ten?'

'About that.'

'I hear the flak and night fighters are quite severe,' Seymour said. He leaned forward and put his elbows on the desk and stared at me.

I looked at the Duke of Kent. He had visited the squadron once. But he was more inclined to visit the fighter boys. I wondered if the Duke knew that most of bomber commands old lags were dead, the regulars from 1938–39. Most of the experienced crews from pre-war training were gone. Whatever they did, they were done for in the end. Two tours was too many. Only Lady Luck mattered.

Seymour saw me looking at the Duke of Kent's photograph.

'I understand,' he said, 'it was safer on fighters during the Battle of Britain than in bomber command now.'

'I wouldn't know.'

'My friends at Ministry tell me.'

'Let's get on with it,' I said.

'Yes,' Seymour said. 'You're anxious, I'm sure. Cigarette?'

'No thanks.'

'You still look tired.'

'I am.'

Seymour lit a cigarette, waggling the flame out.

'Haven't you ever smoked?'

'Nope.'

'How do you hope to get out of the

country when the war is finished?'

'I haven't any idea,' I said. 'But I'll think about it.'

'You'll never get out of this country,' Seymour said.

'I've got out of a lot of places.'

'You even sound a little English.'

I shrugged and sat there looking at him.

'I can help you if you want me to,' Seymour said.

'How?'

'I help a few friends.'

'I don't want to get nailed in the black market,' I said. 'Then I'm really up the pipe.' I could feel my teeth grinding.

'It's up to you,' Seymour said.

'When do I start?'

'Tomorrow night.'

'What do I do?'

'Just what you did the other day.'

'What kind of stuff will I be carrying?'

'That isn't your business.'

'I don't like it.'

'Take it or leave it,' Seymour said. He leaned back, glanced up at the ceiling. He looked very bored. He blew a cloud of smoke. He could get in a lot of trouble if I got caught. The cops could squeeze me. Why would a theatrical producer be involved in the black market? Must be some big dough in it.

But there was a lot of money in the West
End theater. London was full of plays. The
theater never had it so good. There were
plays going all over the West End. Still
what choice did I have?

'What's the pay?' I asked.

'Twenty pounds a week.'

I whistled softly. Christ, that was more
than a squadron leader made. Sure as hell,
there was a damn good risk involved. But
how could I refuse?

'Twenty-five,' I said.

'You don't make that in a month now.'

'You certainly must be taking care of
your friends.'

'You could be dead now.'

'Could I have twenty pounds?'

'Surely,' Seymour said. He opened his
wallet and counted out four five pound
notes and handed them across the table.

I took the bills and put them in my
pocket.

'Go to the back bar of the Café Royale,'
Seymour said. 'Sit at a table. A man will
contact you. He will ask you if you've ever
tried a Pimms Cup. Say, "Yes, you like
number two." '

'Will I see you again?'

'Perhaps, but not in a business sense.
This gentleman will be your contact.'

'Does Beryl know the operation?'

Seymour smiled.

'She works for me. She is a fine actress. She will not discuss this with you. Nor do you discuss it with her.'

'What if I get nailed?'

'Don't worry about it.'

'Sure thing.'

He smiled and his eyelids lifted.

'The odds are much better here than in bomber command.'

I stood up. 'O.K.' I told him.

'See you around,' I said. I turned and went out. I heard him get up and shut the door. I closed the outside door.

I went down the stairs and out into the Strand in the gray light of the street. It was cool and the buildings looked dingy and old. I walked along Bedford Street to Leicester Square. I went along under the trees in the square toward Regent Street. The air felt heavy, as though it were going to rain. I looked at the people in the street, watching for RAF police, but there was no need now that I was in civvies. Still I felt jumpy.

I went in the door of the back bar of the Café Royale.

There was a crowd at the bar, mostly actors. A lot of them were fairies. Standing between a couple of fairies was a Major of a Guards regiment and a 51st Highlander Captain. They were laughing and touching glasses as they drank. I sat down at one

218

of the tables in the corner. A waiter came over and I ordered a Pimms Cup.

'One or Two?'

'Number two,' I said.

After a while the waiter came back from the bar carrying a silver cup with a slice of cucumber sticking up the side. I paid him and tipped him and he went away. I sipped the drink slowly. I didn't like it. Lemon squash in a drink was too sweet. Even a shandy was better on a hot day than a Pimms. No wonder General Kitchener damn near got whipped by the fuzzy-wuzzies in the Sahara. I wondered if Churchill had developed his taste for brandy by being subjected to Pimms Cups before the last great cavalry charge at Omerdurman.

After a while the door of the bar opened and a man came in. He stood at the bar. He took off his light gray Holmburg and set it on the corner of the bar.

'Sir?' The bartender asked him.

'Whiskey. Soda.'

The voices at the bar were louder. The man stood at the end of the bar and read the newspaper. Now and then he glanced over the top of his newspaper and looked at the officers and the actors.

'Oh, George, you wouldn't,' said the thin actor.

The Major and the Captain giggled.

'He isn't ready yet,' said the Major. They all laughed as if one of them had told a wonderful joke.

The man at the bar folded his newspaper and stuck it under his arm. He wore a double breasted black suit. He was tall and sturdy, with black, kinky hair, but his features were not Negroid. Nor did I think he was Jewish or Italian or Spanish or dark Irish. I had never seen a man before with his strange yellowish-dark-olive skin. He had full lips, a high forehead, and a long, straight wedge-shaped nose. He didn't look African. Perhaps Mediterranean. But from where? Levantine?

He picked up his hat and glass and walked toward me. He did not look at me. He walked straight past me. The tables around us were empty. I heard him sit down at the table behind me. It was a small, round table. I heard him flick the newspaper open and brush it against the top of the table.

I called the waiter and ordered another Pimms. The waiter went away.

'Do you like Pimms?' a voice said. It was muffled.

I didn't turn my head. I didn't speak. I waited for the waiter. He put the drink down on the table.

'I said number two?' I looked at the waiter.

220

'It is, sir.' I paid him and tipped him and picked up the cup. I took a sip. God help Churchill, if he'd gone into that last cavalry charge full of Pimms No. 2!

I heard the man fold the newspaper, lay it down on the table. I listened to him pick up his glass and put it down.

'Tuppence ha'panny stamp, my chocolate ration coupon, and—' began the 51st Highlander Captain at the bar, but before he could finish, all four men were guffawing.

'Come outside,' said the voice behind me, screened by their laughter.

I waited for the voice behind me to move. I drank, waited.

'Go on,' said the voice.

'After you,' I said.

The man got up and went out. I waited, sipped my drink, glanced at my watch. One minute. Two minutes.

It was pitch dark in the street. I couldn't focus my eyes.

'Over here,' said the voice. A hand touched my shoulder.

'Come along.'

I looked up in the darkness. Nobody there.

'Take a taxi to Chesterfield House in Curzon Street,' the voice said. 'Flat two-oh-three.'

I heard footsteps going away. I walked

down to the Regent Palace Hotel and waited for a taxi. It was quite a wait. Five whores hustled me, and three men carrying trays and selling razor blades, chewing gum and rubbers, importuned me in the blackout darkness before I hailed a taxi.

The taxi turned into Piccadilly. It was dark, a street of ghosts. Well, you're dead lads, and I'm here. All the best. The taxi puttered along and passed the Ritz, looming big and blacker than the sky, and the taxi turned down Half-Moon Street. Right up the street from the Mirabelle Restaurant the taxi stopped and I got out. I took the elevator up and pushed the bell. The man from the Café Royale came to the door. He was holding a brandy snifter.

'Hello,' he said. His voice sounded British, but there was another inflection in it I could not recognize. He did not have the complete rising inflection of the English.

It was a white apartment. The walls were white. The rugs and furniture were all white. All the tables were glass and metal. The big sofa was milk white. He stood at a small glass bar in the corner of the room. It looked like a woman's apartment.

'Brandy?' he said.

'Fine.'

He brought me a snifter of brandy, then sat down on the sofa and I sat across from him in a big overstuffed silky white chair and looked at him across the top of my glass. I inhaled the brandy. It was expensive and powerful. I sipped it and set the glass down. He smiled but his eyes were cold and hard.

Chapter 22

'I'm your contact,' the man said. His voice was arch. 'Paul Phillips. But don't phone me. I will always contact you through Beryl.' His voice became harsh, peremptory.

'What do I do?' I asked innocently.

He looked sore.

'We're coming to that.'

'Isn't the whole business a bit risky?' I said.

His lips tightened against his teeth.

'That's why you're here,' he barked.

I smiled.

'Thanks,' I said.

He lifted his eyebrows.

'Thank your friends.'

'Mr Seymour?' I said.

His lips opened, closed. He spoke through his teeth.

'Never heard of him.'

Then his voice came again, harsh, peremptory. 'Let's get down to business. It is risky. The government so far has prosecuted forty thousand cases. Ninety percent conviction.'

I lifted my eyebrows.

'That's why I'm here?' I said in a snotty voice.

He smiled. His voice was cheerful.

'Right-oh.' He lit a cigarette. He did not offer me one. He blew a cloud of smoke and flicked ashes into a big glass ash tray. 'Yes, very risky. We're putting you on the theater run. Cosmetics. Rather an easy do. Your contact will be the doorman at each stage door. There won't be any name on the packages. You will keep the name of the receiver in your head. And simply tell the stage doorman who's to receive the package.'

'Okay.'

'How do I get paid?'

'Every week. From me.'

He stubbed out the half-smoked cigarette and sipped his brandy. He reached in his trouser pocket and drew out a slip of paper.

He glanced at the slip of paper a moment and then handed it to me. There was an address on it. 62 Caledonian Road. Buford Machines, Ltd.

'Know where it is?' he asked.

'Near Kings Cross station?'

'Right-oh. Knock three times at the back door. Be there tomorrow morning at ten.' He stood up. I put my glass down.

'Finish your drink,' he said. He stood there. I looked at the yellow abstract painting on the white wall and sipped my drink. He left the room. I heard a door shut down the hall. It was fine brandy. I had never tasted any this old. I was just about finished when he returned. He stood a little behind me.

'All set?' he asked.

I got up. 'See you in the morning,' I said and left.

When I got back to Cheyney Mews Beryl was lying on her bed reading the *London Times*. She had a glass of whiskey and water on the chair beside the bed. I started to tell her about Paul Phillips and she held up her hand.

'I don't want to know.' She smiled. 'I have only two rules here. You have to laugh at my jokes and we don't talk business. Not that business. Only theater and sex.' She patted the bed beside her for me to sit down. I stood looking at her and shook my head.

'I can't figure it. Those were murders.'

'Forget it.'

'Bullshit! Somebody knew I was going there.'

'Stop being so silly. It was just somebody hunting.'

'Very funny, Beryl.'

'Sit down. Be a good lad. Mix a drink. Relax.'

I went into the kitchen and mixed a scotch and water. I stayed in there a while and thought about everything. I had the feeling Beryl knew something. She had been scared in the woods. Why wasn't she scared anymore? Why was her voice so cheery and bright? Oh, crap. I tried to be fatalistic as if I were back on the squadron. If you were going to buy it you were going to buy it. Sure, but that hadn't worked on the squadron either. The trouble was that fatalism was a lot of crap, especially if you knew every day you were going to pack it in sooner or later. And if somebody knew I was going to be in that woods, that somebody would know where I was now. So what was to stop him from taking a crack at me again? I was completely boxed in. My guts felt tight and lousy and I took a big drink of whiskey. It helped a little. I took another big drink to help turn off the thinking and that helped more. When I got back to the bedroom Beryl was lying there naked, still reading the *London Times*.

'Hurry up,' she said, without looking up from her newspaper. 'I could eat you alive tonight.'

She damn near did, too, but all the time she was doing it, I kept wondering why she felt so sexy suddenly. Nobody feels sexy when they're frightened and scared. Something or somebody had helped her get over being scared.

Chapter 23

It was morning and we were in the back room of Buford Machines, Ltd.

'Over there,' said the man standing behind Paul Phillips. He was a dumpy little middle-aged man with a Cockney accent. I looked at the machine. It was in the middle of the floor. At first I didn't recognize it for what it was. It had been a long time since I had been on a farm. Then the dumpy man pressed a button and the machine stirred and I remembered.

It was a cream churn.

'What the hell,' I said.

I looked at Paul Phillips. He spoke without moving his head: 'Number three?'

The cockney nodded. They watched the churn. It was going full speed. A tall man came in wheeling a rack loaded with white lidless jars. After a while the cockney opened the top of the churn and looked inside.

'Abso-blooming-lutely,' he said.

'Fill them up,' said Paul Phillips. 'Come on, Mack.'

'Hoy! Bufflehead!' said the cockney to the tall man. 'Get crackin' before you're back in the chokey.'

Phillips opened the door. I followed him down a long hall to another door. Inside was a dingy office.

'Sit down,' he said. He went behind his desk and rummaged through some paper and handed me a sheet. It was a list of London theaters and their street addresses.

'Memorize them,' he said. 'Throw the sheet away. Don't carry it with you.'

'What's in the churn?'

'Don't stick your hooter out,' he said. I knew what he meant. There had been enough cockneys on the squadron. Don't get nosey, Mack.

'Cliff'll have the packets ready soon,' said Phillips. 'Give two packets to each doorman.'

'How do I get around? Walk?'

'Little Morris out back.' He opened the desk drawer and drew out an envelope. 'Here's your wages. Identity and ration cards.'

I opened the envelope and read the cards. I was Dennis Stockton.

'Do I bring the Morris back here?'

'Keep it at Beryl's. Make bloody sure you're not followed. If you think you're followed, don't make delivery.'

Two days later the cockney told me what the cream churn manufactured for the black market.

'Number one, and out comes tan stocking paint for the birds' legs. Number two speed, hair oil. Number three speed, face cream.'

'What do you use for a base?'

'Same pawky stuff for 'em all. Beeswax and paraffin.'

I drove the theater route every other day. The Strand. Aldwych. Vaudeville. Adelphi. Duchess. Prince of Wales. Haymarket. All the doormen recognized me after the first day.

I didn't see Beryl for a week. She left a note she was down in Wimbledon, rehearsing. The author and producer were cutting the scenes during rehearsal.

She looked tired and upset. There were dark circles under her eyes. She was lying on the bed in her pants and brassiere, reading *The News of the World*. I sat on the edge of the bed.

'What's the matter?' I asked. 'You look ropey.'

She put the paper down and scratched the end of her nose.

'We've been at it day and night.'

'How's it going?'

'We'll open in the West End in about a week.'

Then I saw the bruise on her arm. It was a round black and blue mark.

'Hey, who hit you?'

She glanced at her arm.

'Oh, that. I bumped into a prop.'

'Some prop.'

'Get me a glass of beer, darling.'

I got up and as I turned she rolled over on her stomach and I saw the bruise across the back of her thighs. I didn't say anything until I came back from the kitchen with two glasses of beer.

'Is there a mule in the show?' I said.

'Mule?'

'Who kicked you in the ass?'

She looked upset for a moment and then she smiled.

'My bottom? Oh, Mack, you love my bottom.'

I laughed.

'Fell over a bench,' she said.

'You'd kill them in vaudeville.'

We drank beer. She lay back on the pillow and looked at the ceiling and set the beer mug on her breast bone.

Then later: 'Aren't you lucky, darling.

Did you see the paper?'

'No.'

'They lost thirty-four in Nuremburg last night.'

'Get off it.'

'I'm sorry. Do you ever wish you were back?'

'No way,' I said, and it was true. All of the past was fading. Just as my life in America before combat had seemed like a dream, combat now seemed like a long ago dream. Even the guilt was gone. I was back in civvy street. Alive. That was what mattered. To survive. I had done my bit.

'Odd thing in a pub the other night,' Beryl said. She rubbed her ear lobe. 'What's darkee?'

'Back in the states a darkey is a negro. Why?'

'Well, this flier was in the pub. A gang of us were playing darts. He was quite smashed. And we started talking. He kept mumbling all sorts of things. Darkee.'

'No big deal. Darkee is a code name for an air force lifesaving device. No big secret. It's an emergency radio system for helping a disabled plane get home. Transmitted on a frequency of four thousand, two hundred twenty kilocycles. Your wireless operator simply calls Darkee control and when

231

Darkee gets the signal the controller tell you to circle until Darkee tracks you. Then you get a course to fly on, and barometric setting.'

'Oboe?'

'Come on,' I said. 'Musical instrument.'

'He kept mumbling it was the biggest thing in the air. It would destroy Germany.'

'Never heard of it. Who's this flier?'

'Don't know.' She shrugged. 'He was sozzled.'

'He had a big mouth.'

It wasn't until after the war I learned what Oboe was. It was two radar beams first used on an attack on the Krupps works at Essen. It involved Mosquitoe pathfinders flying along radar beams until the beams intersected right over the Krupps works. Then the Mosquitoes dropped on the intersection red flares that marked the target and the bomber waves would be right on target. It eliminated all navigational guess work by the pathfinder crews. But I had never heard of it then, though later I realized why we had been so successful during the first heavy bombing raid on Mr Krupps.

'He had bags of medal ribbons,' she said. 'He was miserable because he wasn't back on operations. They had him doing some sort of desk job.'

'He had better keep his mouth shut,' I said. 'Sounds like he's sitting beside the horses mouth.'

'Inside it,' Beryl said. 'H-Two-S. What's that?'

I felt the skin prickle on the back of my neck.

'I don't know,' I lied. Where the hell had she ever heard about the newest radar bombing device? Only the Lancasters had it. It was a vast improvement on the Gee Box, a navigational instrument that would give a fix two hundred miles into the Continent.

'Did he mention it?' I asked. She nodded.

'What is it?' she asked in an innocent voice.

'I've heard it mentioned,' I said. 'But I don't know what it is.'

'He was really sozzled.'

The back of my neck felt warm. Why did she care about H2S? It was the first radar screen, a great advance in accurate bombing techniques. H2S was a box with a screen that produced a radar map in the cockpit. The screen showed changing terrain directly beneath the aircraft. You could see clearly coastlines, rivers and lakes, even above thick cloud. It was supposed to show towns and other large features. I had heard about it from a

233

Lancaster air gunner. It was very hush-hush, nothing was known about it on our squadron. Why was she so curious?

'Let's go over to Murderer's Arms and shoot some darts,' I said. She got up and got dressed. We went outside and walked along Cheyney Walk.

'What the hell do you care about H-Two-S?'

'My, why so formidable?'

'Why the sudden curiosity?'

'I don't know,' she said.

'I never met a female yet who wondered about aircraft equipment.'

She laughed.

'Maybe I'll join the forces.'

'That'll be the day.'

She hooked her arm through mine and started to skip. There was a beer garden behind the Chelsea Arms Hotel. We stopped for a beer. 'I am not dead,' I thought, looking up at the sky. It was full of stars. Someone in me kept saying, 'I'm not dead.' I felt like a figure in a masque.

'What's the trouble?' Beryl touched my arm. 'Drink up.'

I stared at the moon and stars.

'Drink up, Mack,' she said. Fear and death were in the sky and stars. But I was alive. I looked at my glass, lifted it and drank. Suddenly we are so old before we ever know what has happened.

Chapter 24

I sat in the back room of Buford Machines, Ltd. There were five of us, all wearing white butcher's overalls. Paul Phillips stood in front of us. Behind him, pinned to wall, was a map of London. He had marked certain roads with different colors and there were Xs at certain spots. It was like being in briefing again. Only this time the target wasn't the Ruhr Valley. The targets were London meat markets. Then I saw Paul Phillips come in the door. He wasn't wearing any butcher's overalls. He's not sticking *his* neck out, I thought to myself.

I had to hand it to Paul Phillips. He looked smooth and he was smooth. The Cockney had told me Phillips was Maltese, which explained his strange British accent. He was dressed in a pin-striped Savile Row suit with a silk shirt and silver colored tie with little black checks in it and one of those little short-brim Jermyn Street hats.

'Everything ready, Alf?' Phillips said to the Cockney.

'Bang on,' said Alf, doing a thumbs up.

'All right, hear this now,' said Paul. 'We have a meat allocators truck in the yard. It's not been pinched. Alf will be the meat allocator.'

Phillips turned and pointed at each of the Xs on the map.

'We're going to take these markets today. Bobby, you'll drive. You each take turns going into the shop with Alf. I'll be following the regular meat allocator's truck. You hang back a block behind me. If I'm still parked in front of the market, go around the block. Pass on that market. I'll hold up my hand. Straight up. That's the signal to pass. Alf, got your watch set?'

Alf nodded and they looked at their wrists and checked the watches.

'Alf has the delivery times on all the markets. Each man will take two markets with Alf. After two markets, dump your uniform in the truck and get out and go home. Alf will take care of the load and the truck. Got it? Let's go.'

Out in the cobblestone backyard was the meat allocator truck. It looked very official, with the government sign on the side.

The operation was a piece of cake until the last market. And the last two markets were mine. We arrived at each market a couple of minutes after the official allocation of meat was dropped off. Alf went into the market with one of the helpers.

'Sorry, sir,' Alf said to the butcher. 'Got the wrong meat allocation for you today. Back in a moment with the right amount.'

He picked up the allocation that had been left a few minutes before and loaded it in the truck. Everything went well until we hit the last butcher shop in Shepherd Market.

The butcher was a big fat bald man, about fifty, perhaps sixty years old. He looked like a wrestler.

'Wrong allocation, sir. I'll have to pick up what you have, and be back in half of mo with your allocation.'

The butcher stared at Alf.

'Quite,' he said. He came around the counter, carrying a meat cleaver. Right then I smelled a rat. His eyes seemed to get smaller suddenly.

'Twit!' the butcher said. He raised the meat cleaver. 'Get up against the wall.' He wasn't paying any attention to me. I kicked him in the side of his right knee. He screamed and fell down.

As I ran out the door to the right, I saw the police car turning off Curzon Street. The first thing I did running was to start unbuttoning the butcher's overall. I got the buttons loose and pulled the sleeves down and cut sharply into an alley. Only it really wasn't an alley, just a narrow opening between two apartments buildings. I ran out the other end and stopped and jumped out of the overalls. Across the street was a trash can. I jerked off the lid and stuffed the overalls and walked slowly up through the market toward Curzon Street.

A bobby came around the corner at the end of the street. He stopped and looked at me and I kept walking toward him. Then I saw the door to a two storey set of flats on my left and I crossed the sidewalk and opened the door.

There was a stairway. I climbed the stairway slowly. There were a lot of whores in Shepherd Market. Maybe if I was lucky. I knocked on the first door. No answer. I knocked again. I thought I heard the door opening at the bottom of the stairs.

A woman came to the door. She looked like a French whore I had seen working a Bond Street beat with a poodle on a leash. But I wasn't sure.

'How about a party?' I said.

'Tonight.' She started to close the door. I put my foot in the door and pulled out a roll of pound notes.

'Ten pounds?'

She opened the door just as I heard the street door open downstairs. I went into the room. There was a bedroom door open at the far end of the living room. I went in. Everything inside was blue. There was a round mirror on the ceiling and mirrors along the walls.

She came in and I took out the roll of bills again. She looked at it.

'If anybody asks for me or comes to the door asking for a man,' I started to say. I peeled off twenty pounds. 'Nobody's home.'

She reached for the money. I pulled my hand back.

'Wait,' I said. I handed her ten pounds. 'The rest after you answer the door.' She started to take her clothes off. She was wearing slacks and a blue cashmere sweater.

'Hold it,' I said. 'Come here.' I sat down on the edge of the bed. We didn't wait long. There was a knock on the door. I nodded and pointed at the door. She went out and I shut the bedroom door. I looked at the wall and listened. I got up and put my ear against the bedroom door.

'How do I know you are police?' I heard her say.

'Look, ma'am. I just want to ask. Did you hear or see anybody come up here?'

'You can't come in. I have a friend.'

'Don't bluff.'

'Will you go away, please?'

'Go away.' I heard her shut the door

and wait a couple of minutes in the living room. I opened the bedroom door slowly and she turned her head and put her fingers to her lips. Then she pressed her head against the door, and after a long moment, she opened the door and stuck her head out into the hall.

She shut the door and said: 'He's gone. I don't want any trouble. Why are they after you?'

'Is there a way out?'

'I'll show you. Give me my money.'

I handed her ten pounds. She took it and stuck out her other hand, palm up.

'Another ten pounds for the back door,' she said. I hesitated.

She looked at her hand.

I gave her the ten pounds. She went to the door and opened it, and looked back and forth along the hall.

'Hey,' I said jokingly, 'What about my party? It's paid for.'

'You're getting out of here. Come on.'

I followed along the hall. She stopped at the head of the back stairs. There were twelve steps down to the rear door.

'Take a look outside,' I said.

'Get lost.' She turned and went back along the hall.

I tiptoed down the stairs, and leaned against the door, listening. I couldn't hear anything. I turned the knob and inched the door open slowly. As the door opened fully I saw a big beefy Bobby looking straight at me.

'Come on, chum,' he said. I kicked him hard in the stomach and as he went down I ran over him, stepping on his stomach. I ran three steps and saw I was in a cul de sac, the alley open at one end, up which the cops would come, and a wall at the other end, fifteen feet away.

I started for the wall, and heard the cop blowing his whistle. I didn't look back. I leaped and caught the top of the wall and pulled up hard and got one leg over the top just as the cop smashed his night stick against my other leg. The calf of the leg felt paralyzed, but I pushed up with both hands and got both legs over and jumped.

The shock of landing knocked the numbness out of my leg and I was running almost the instant I hit the pavement, down a long alley.

Behind me the police whistle screeched. Then I was running full speed, lifting both knees high, and I came out onto Curzon Street.

For an instant I froze and looked up and down the street. I tried to stop panting, and held my breath. I waited for the police to show. I sucked in my breath again and walked slowly along to Charles Street.

I went along Charles Street to Berkley Square. One of my fingers twitched, and I put my hand in my trouser pocket. There was a taxi in front of the Landsdowne Club and I got in and told the driver to take me to the Antelope Pub off Eaton Square. I felt emptied but this was better than the fear of death. I drank three pints fast in the Antelope and walked home along King's Road. Beryl was out. I mixed myself a big double Scotch and drank it slowly and lay on the bed until I fell asleep.

Chapter 25

A voice roused me, a hand. I was lying on my stomach, fully clothed, with one arm hanging over the side of the bed. It was dark in the bedroom.

'Get up,' Beryl said. 'Paul wants to see you downstairs.' I rolled over. I wondered how long I had been asleep.

'What time is it?'

'Past twelve. Hurry up.' Her voice was tense. Then she said quickly, 'Please hurry.'

Phillips was waiting in the sculptor's studio. He was leaning against a white shrouded sculpture. He wore a tweed

242

jacket and khaki pants.

'Get a jacket,' he said. 'I've got a job for you. Hurry.' He looked at his watch. I was still half asleep.

'Come on, get cracking.'

I went upstairs and got a jacket and told Beryl I didn't know when I would be back.

'All right. All right,' she said quickly. 'Have a good time.'

'What the hell are you talking about?'

'Don't keep him waiting.'

'What's the matter with you?'

She stood up and put both hands on my shoulders.

'Please go, Mack. Please.'

'What the hell,' I said. 'What's everybody so antsy about?'

'Don't keep him waiting.'

'So long.'

Alf was in the truck behind the wheel. 'Oy, mate,' he grinned. 'I knew you'd make it.'

'How'd you get away?'

'Shanks mare,' he grinned.

'Come on. Come on,' Phillips said. 'We haven't got all night.'

The truck ground into gear. We turned onto Oakley Street. The street was pitch black. The sky was moonless.

'What's the deal?' I said to Phillips.

'Grouse. Ducks. Whatever we can get. I

have the guns and shells in back. I gather you can shoot.'

'Oh, quite,' said Alfie imitating an upper class accent.

So this was how the big hotels and restaurants still were able to get wild game for special guests. Poachers.

Invoice your luggage, Norton, I thought to myself. Say so long to all. The car rocked. We were on the North Road. I slept, dreaming of streets of gold, thrones of jasper, falling flowers, toppling mountains, stars going out.

When I woke it was still dark, but I could see faint light on the horizon. I rolled down the window, hearing the wind, barking dogs, suddenly a bird song. We are in the moors, I thought. For an instant I thought of Joan, of how we walk in loneliness all our lives, remembering the summer cries of children in the evening. For an instant my eyes blurred. I shook my head, looking into the silence coming across the grass and flowers, through the trees, forcing forgetfulness again into me.

'Wake up,' Phillips said. 'We're almost there.'

Half an hour later it was almost dawn. The blackened wind was gone. We got out of the truck, got our instructions from Phillips, loaded the shot guns, slung our shell bags across our shoulders.

244

The earth of the rolling Yorkshire moors seemed to hold the color of grouse feathers. The sunlight falling through the clouds at random intervals covered the ground with a sheen of speckled brownish gray light like the breast feathers of living birds. As the sunlight slanted between clouds, the morning light failed, but the vast empty land retained an afterglow like that of a shot grouse as the plumage fades.

I looked out over the moors. We're some place north of Whitby, I thought.

A big, tall old man came out of the woods. Beside him was a Springer spaniel. There were no houses, no sound across the immeasurable distances of the moors rolling purple and eternal.

We walked silently. About a quarter of a mile away, a few scraggly trees rose along a cliff above a small lake, almost a pond. I thought of cattle water holes back in the Dakotas.

The tall man stopped and knelt and glassed the lake. His gnarled hands swung the field glasses back and forth, checking the open side of the lake.

'The two gullies,' said the tall man, without removing the field glasses from his face. 'See the top side? The wind is right for us from the bottom. But the birds will see us. We'll have to come over them. Down through the gullies.'

The nameless man was perhaps seventy. He wore faded brown corduroy slacks, a sand colored tweed jacket with leather elbow patches. His face was long, his eyes bloodshot. He was lean, not an ounce of fat, but he looked as if somebody had wakened him too early.

This must be his country. But who is he? Milord's game keeper, working with the London poachers? Milord out in the desert perhaps with Monty? The game keeper making a few quid off the unshot game.

We walked slowly, using the slope of the land to hide us from the ducks.

'Golden Eyes,' the old man said.

'How many?' I said. Golden Eyes are arctic ducks, the last ducks down through the American midwest, after the Blue Bills are gone with the sheet ice thick and solid.

'Hundred.'

'Oy! Oy!' Alf suddenly cried and pointed. Then the deer were there. They didn't come into sight; they were just there, ghostly reddish streaks, already running, having seen us in that split second before we saw them. They sprang, bounding, soaring away over the hills.

We descended slowly toward the gullies. The ducks remained invisible below the hill. Down through the first gully I saw the black muddy water. The Springer spaniel went on, walking at heel.

I thought of all my prairie hunting years. We haven't a chance to sneak these ducks. They must be worth a fortune in London to work this hard.

'Yank,' he said. 'Follow me down this gully.' He pointed up above, five hundred yards to the next gully that ran on opening into the lake. 'Paul, you lads go up there.'

'Are you going to toll them?' I asked.

'What?' said the old man.

'Come on,' I said. 'Decoy. You know what I mean.'

The old man smiled softly.

'We'll fool those Golden Eyes.'

I followed him and the springer toward the gully. The dog stopped, wagged his tail furiously.

'Heel,' whispered the old man.

I tiptoed behind the old man. Damn, I cursed the gully. Full of limestone, small rocks, shale. The invisible ducks were perhaps twenty-five yards around to the left from where the gully opened onto the shoreline. They must hear the falling shale under our feet.

Halfway down the old man stopped. He turned, motioned me to lie down.

I sank down slowly, squatting. I put my left hand down on the limestone and lowered myself without a sound. I lay on my side, my face hidden behind a few scrawny blades of grass.

The old man knelt down and whispered in the dog's ear. They ambled slowly down toward the water. I pressed the side of my face into the limestone. I froze my eyeballs. The spaniel nonchalantly glanced over his shoulder at us. The old man lay above me, about ten feet away. Suddenly the dog trotted straight to the water.

He stood on the edge of the muddy shore. He seemed to shrug faintly.

This could be a lovely shoot. The dog lapped water. Suddenly his head lifted, his eyes rigid, staring. The birds must be coming toward him along the shore. The tip of his little pink tongue protruded over the front of his lips.

Then suddenly I knew it was all going to happen in the flash of seconds. Crouching, I smelled again the cold smell of so many autumn Dakota prairie pot holes, the dry earth and grass, the gray sky.

The ducks came into view, moving across the mirror smooth water, softly gliding, paddling. They stared at the dog with innocent eyes.

I thought suddenly of ballistics and range. Twenty-five yards! Fair to jump shoot now. The ducks floated closer. I could hardly hold my breath.

A puff of breeze shivered the grass along the shore. I sprang up. The birds rose into the breeze, wings flashing, as though hurled suddenly from the smooth surface. For a fraction of a second they were outlined against the sky.

They started to swing, to turn down wind. I fired and the gun jarred against my shoulder. In that same second a pair of wings folded into a ball of feathers.

I swung back overhead and missed and reloaded. The air beyond was full of gunfire and the sky was full of birds. I fired. A wing dropped, the birds fluttered down.

I jacked in more shells. For the first time I realized I was shooting an American pump gun. Where in hell did they get it?

I ran toward the shore. Flocks slanted against the sky, wheeling and crying. The water mirrored the birds. They mounted, scattering. Their wings beat above my head. What a fine old moment!

I tried to count the flocks, ten, nine, six, broken about the sky. Suddenly, as if he had popped out of the ground I became aware that the old man had been shooting all the time above me. Now he was firing again, swinging right, the flock whistling down wind. I fired into the sound of their wings and the crash of the old man's gun. They passed over us, necks stretched forward as if seeking more speed from their wings. They were out of range.

But the old man still had his head down on the gun stock and he was swinging at a double, the far shot first, catching him slowly on the climb, then folding the rear duck. The old man lowered his gun.

'Bloody good,' he said. 'Bloody good.'

Another hour passed. The flocks returned. At the end of three hours there were three gunny sacks full of ducks. Alfie and I leaned back against them. The old man, smoking a pipe, glassed the moors.

Phillips came over the hill.

'Good lads,' he said, looking at the sacks. 'Let's go.'

I picked up one sack and we trudged up the hill.

'What about the grouse?' I asked Phillips. He looked at his watch.

'Not time,' he said quickly. 'We'll be back tomorrow.'

Just behind us a voice shouted: 'Drop your guns!'

I spun around, dropping the sack. About a hundred yards away, a man stood on the crest of a hill, pointing a rifle at us.

Alfie fired and the old man kneeling behind the sack fired.

I heard the rifle crash and the whistle of the bullet.

'Shoot!' Phillips screamed. 'Shoot.'

Hell, it was a hundred yards. No bloody fear of hitting him at that range. Might scare him off before we get plugged.

I lifted the shotgun, raised the sights over the man's head and fired twice, high over him.

The second shot knocked him down. I stared dully at the hill, the gun in my hand.

'Christ,' I heard my voice saying, 'I hit him.' I stared stupidly at my hand.

'Run!' Phillips shouted. 'Run.'

I started to run.

'The bloody birds!' Phillips bellowed. 'Get the—'

'Get the goddamn birds yourself!' I said and ran toward the car. I saw Phillips pick up a sack of birds. I got to the car first, and jumped into the back seat.

Alfie and Phillips came up with two sacks of birds. The old man was gone.

'You killed him!' Phillips shouted.

'At a hundred yards with number six shot? Bullshit!' I yelled.

'Bloody hell, let's get outa here,' cried Alfie.

Alfie pushed his sack into the front seat. 'Half a mo'.' He shouted at Phillips who was grinding the car into gear, skidding, fish tailing across the grass.

251

Chapter 26

At first I didn't hear the air raid sirens. I lay on the apartment bed, thinking of the drive down from Yorkshire.

In the car Phillips' cold voice: 'You're for it, lad. You can't run about shooting civilians.'

'He's only nicked,' I said. 'A hundred yards—'

'Stay in Beryl's flat. Don't get gatey. I'll bring you the newspapers.'

'Who's that old man?' I asked.

'Don't worry about him,' said Phillips. 'Mum's the word. Beside, he don't know you.'

Outside Beryl's flat now a lorry halted in the street. Then I heard an aircraft overhead. It was low and diving, whining, snarling engines filling the darkness.

The lorry started up. Then I heard a siren screaming. It seemed to pass out of the realm of sound. There was no whistling sound before the first bomb fell. I stood up swaying in the dark, sipping the glass of whiskey, listening, wondering why Beryl wasn't home from rehearsals.

Then I knew I was drunk. I took the

first step. I heard the second bomb, the heavy rush of air, the sound of more diving engines. I stumbled against the wall. The walls and windows reverberated in the explosion. Then I was running. I fell twice on the stairs and cursed.

I had the front door open when I heard the high, thin whistling of another bomb falling.

I froze. Then I was running. I fell twice and cursed and heard, high and thin, the terrifying sound of more bombs falling. Suddenly the street rose in a mound, a dark shape against the lighter sky. I fell into a thick darkness smelling of a wet basement.

I lay on the wet earth. Somebody's old backyard bomb shelter, I thought.

I listened. Another bomb fell and the ground shook, tearing into the wet darkness.

From somewhere in the murk a brick spun across the air and struck me across the legs. Then I heard more dirt and bricks splashing down into the water inside the air raid shelter.

I lay still and waited. Then out of the explosions silence rose like a substance. I could feel it all around me. No sound at all. Not even the far faint dying of Jerry engines.

I raised my head and looked at the other

entrance of the air raid shelter. I stood up and took three steps toward the entrance and stumbled over something soft.

I leaned down. Moonlight came through windy clouds, and the light struck down through the open door. I looked down at a woman, lying on her back, her arms back flung above her head.

In the moonlight her face was quite clear. Her eyes, little blue globes, reflected moonlight, the pupils frozen in shock.

I began to feel sick. There was a small blue hole in the center of her forehead.

It was Beryl.

I knelt down and braced myself with one knee in the water. 'Beryl,' I heard my voice, 'Beryl.'

'Jesus Christ,' I remember saying. I went toward the open door of the shelter. I just made it, my mouth full of vomit.

I leaned against the side of the air raid shelter. The street was full of smoke. Down the street fire rose from a house. Then the sound came down across the sky again. I started to run. Feet ran past in the street. Then into the silence came a monstrous roar and blast, shaking the ground, knocking me down.

I rose on one knee and saw the windows in the house across the street had vanished and the door hanging, bashed in. I realized I was in front of Beryl's house in the mews.

The doorway was blocked.

I heard another bomb coming. I kicked at the bashed-in door. Out in the street somebody screamed, then abruptly stopped. I stood for an instant in the hall.

I heard another bomb coming. At the end of the hall, where the wall was blown out, the open rectangle framed the sky, full of searchlight beams and flak bursts.

Get back to the shelter, I thought. What the hell are you doing here? Then I knew I was sober. I started to run. I couldn't remember vomiting, but I felt better. The ground shuddered with reverberations.

A flare lit the sky. In the glare of the flare I saw that Beryl's body was gone. Then the light of the flare went out suddenly, like a blown candle. I stood in the darkness. I couldn't move.

How had she died? Had she been machine gunned? The bullet hole looked too small. Where had her body gone? She had warned me. But about what? What had she feared?

Maybe somebody thought I knew something she knew. But what did she know?

I started to run. An ambulance and fire truck roared past. I went in through the ruined door, and upstairs. The lights were knocked out.

I rummaged in the bedroom closet, feeling for my clothes and kit bag. My uniform was in the bottom of the bag. I felt in the bag for the pad of furlough slips.

I slung the kit bag over my shoulders. There was only one place to go and go fast. Out and away.

I went down the stairs carefully. I stopped for a moment. The thing to do was to change into uniform, get to a service club where there was light, and fill out a furlough pass so I could get a room cheap in a service club.

Jesus, what was I going to do then? I had about a hundred pounds, but how long would that money last?

Chapter 27

The next morning it was raining and foggy in London. I had a room on the third floor of the Washington Club on Curzon Street. After breakfast I lay on the bed and read the morning paper. Fifteen aircraft missing after a raid on Dortmund. I studied each page carefully. London casualties had not been determined during the air raid. 'Fifty or more feared killed.' Then the two column head on the next page hit me.

GAME KEEPER SLAIN

I read the subhead: *Police search for Poachers.*

I stared at the headline. The hair prickled along the back of my neck. Jesus, I had shot him. But he had been one hundred yards away. At least that far. And I had aimed way over him, perhaps ten feet high. How the hell do you kill a man at that distance with a shotgun by aiming high? Of course, there was a drop at that range. But the bird shot wouldn't kill that far away. It didn't make sense, but the newspaper story was real.

I looked at my watch. The pubs would be open soon. I had a pass and I had polished the buttons on my uniform. I couldn't afford a hotel room for long, so I had to use the phony pass to get into this club. I needed a drink. I needed it badly.

The bar was jammed at Shepherd's in Shepherd Market. There was always a gang of RAF there with a mixture of Mayfair types and film stars. I couldn't get to the bar at first. There were two Highland Light Infantry Officers shoulder to shoulder and behind the rest of the people at the bar there was another row of drinkers. I tapped the Scottish Major on the shoulder.

'Pardon me,' I said. The Major turned his head. He was a big man with a waxed black mustache and an MC on his tunic.

'Yes?' he said.

'I can't get near the libation,' I said.

'Come in. Come in.' He stepped back and I bellied up against the bar and ordered a whiskey and water and a pint of mild and bitter. With a glass in each hand I stepped back and stood behind the two officers.

I drank the whiskey first. It burned. I drank it down fast. The quick shock brought me awake. What the hell had I been thinking, coming in here where I might meet somebody from the squadron?

But did it matter any longer? What if I did run into somebody from the squadron? I had left the squadron to keep from being killed. Now maybe the squadron was safer. Maybe even the Glass House was better than being alive in London.

I sipped the beer slowly. What if I did turn myself in? If I didn't, how long could I live on my money here in London? What sentence would I get? Six months in the Glass House. What made me feel it was dangerous in London? Somebody had killed Beryl. That was obvious. And I lived with Beryl. And she had been scared by something or somebody. So whatever or whoever it was might assume she had told me what frightened her. And the knowledge obviously was dangerous to

258

have. Somebody behind me said: 'Hello, Mack?'

I turned. It was an RAF Flight Lieutenant, but I didn't know him. He had a nice looking face, quite young, British, about my age. He smiled. His teeth were even and straight, very white. His features were just short of making him eligible for magazine modeling photographs for men's shirts or suits.

'How are you?' I said, pretending I knew him, trying to place his face.

'Ever see any of the gang?'

'Sure.'

'What happened to Dowman?' he asked.

'Gone for Burton.'

'John Baker.'

'Got the chop over Duisberg,' I said.

'Ruxton?'

'Essen,' I said.

The man smiled, lifted his glass, looked at me steadily, straight into my eyes as he sipped his pint. He lowered his glass. He was still smiling.

'You don't know me, do you, Mack?'

'To tell the truth—' I started to say.

'Thrisby, George Thrisby.'

I stared at him. I couldn't speak. This wasn't Thrisby. I hadn't seen Thrisby in nearly three years, not since we had flown Boulton Paul Defiants in defense of Cardiff, before we had converted on

259

to Whitley twin engine bombers. But this man was not Thrisby.

'Quit kidding,' I said. 'Where's Thrisby?'

He grinned. 'Right here. Me. Look.' He reached up and pulled down the top of his shirt collar. Under the shirt collar all the skin was dark as if he had washed his face and neck but he hadn't washed below his collar line.

He put one finger against his cheek, made a circle with the finger around his whole face.

'They made me a new one,' he said. 'Don't you remember?'

The trouble was I knew so many people who were dead or missing that I couldn't recall all of them. Just about all the first line regular bomber pilots from 1940 were dead or missing in action. I looked at him.

'Thrisby,' I heard myself say. Then I laughed. 'You're dead.'

Because I remembered.

'Christ,' I said. 'Didn't you prang one night at Stormy Downs? You burned up.'

'They made me a new face.'

'It's one hell of an improvement!'

He laughed.

'Right-oh!'

His teeth were his own, but his face was a complete transplant. Even his nose. They must have made him a new nose. His nose had been hawk-shaped before.

'Where did they get you the new eyebrows?'

'Off my legs,' he spoke in a bright, cheery voice.

'What're you up to?' I asked.

'Going back on ops.'

'Are you nuts?'

'I put in for it.' He smiled an embarrassed smile.

'You're crackers,' I said.

'Lancs.'

'You'll need a rocket to get away from those bloody night fighters.'

'What're you doing?' he said.

'Training Halifax gunners at operational training unit,' I lied. For the first time in weeks I felt a sudden twinge of guilt.

'I say. This calls for a celebration.' He lifted his empty glass.

'Or a wake. If you're going back on ops,' I said.

He shook his head.

'Drink up. Oy, Miss! Two mild and bitter, please.'

'You've got a fine face,' I said.

'I like it a lot.'

'Do you know what the casualty rate is on ops now?' He shook his head.

'I haven't the vaguest.'

'Nearly five percent.'

'Come on!'

'You'll find out,' I said, not wanting

to feel cowardly again, but the cowardly feeling was there in me again. I thought I had gotten rid of it. But it came back. I felt it stronger than ever as I stood looking at him, thinking of him having enough guts to go back on ops.

And that started me thinking about Joan. I wanted to see her so much. But if I saw her I would have to tell her everything that had happened. She would never forgive me for running out. I would have to turn myself in, if I wanted to see her first. It was the only way she would listen to me.

'I say, did you ever know a chap named Larry Stevens? Wireless op.'

'Sure. He's screened by now,' I said.

'He's dead.'

'Shot down?'

'Rum,' he said. 'He fell down the stairs in the Leicester Square underground toilet and broke his neck. It was in the newspaper.'

'You're kidding!'

'Didn't you see it?'

I couldn't speak. I stared at him.

'Broke his neck?' I heard my voice say. He shrugged.

'What a way to go. Killed accidentally in a toilet after a couple of tours of ops.'

'Are you sure it was an accident?'

'According to the paper. Drink up, Mack.'

Chapter 28

That afternoon I took the train to Dover. It was dusk when I got into town. I could smell the sea, and I walked along the street until I found a pub with bed and breakfast. I took my kit bag and went upstairs. There were only two bedrooms. I lay on the bed and looked at the ceiling and tried to make up what I would say to Joan when I saw her. When the bar opened I went downstairs. The bartender was a fat old man with a walrus mustache. He looked at my air gunner's wing.

'You're not from around here,' he said.

'No. Up north,' I told him and ordered a pint of mild and bitter.

'Don't see many gunners around here. Fighter boys.' He wiped the bar briskly. 'All fighter boys around here,' he said.

'I've a friend at Manston,' I wondered what he would say if I brought Joan back tomorrow and asked for a room. We would probably have to stay in Dover or go up to London if she could get away.

Manston was a pretty field with grass runways. I had seen it before, but I did not want to think about that time now.

I wanted only to think about Joan and the beautiful green runways and the sun sparkling on the Strait of Dover beyond the Manston cliffs. I thought about calling her but I still didn't know what to say for sure. A couple of sailors came in and drank beer and played darts. I bet a couple bob with them on darts, won one game and lost the other. I felt sleepy but when I went upstairs I couldn't sleep. I lay in the dark with my eyes closed, feeling confused, wondering what they would do to me when I turned myself in. Probably a year or more in the Glass House. Suddenly I slept.

It was sunny and clear in the morning when I came out after breakfast to catch the bus to Manston. A squadron of Spitfires came over low, their engines snarling as they went into a lovely climbing turn toward the sun and the sea, headed for a sweep over France. The bus came and I got in back and looked out at the fields and the sea. There was a milky mist with the sun coming through it over the water. We passed some smashed houses. They ought to stop firing those coastal guns from Dover. This is what they get back, and it doesn't add up to anything.

The bus stopped outside the guard house at the field. I could see the rows of Nissen huts and the Spitfires parked on the sides of the field. The corporal in the guard house asked to see my pass. I told him I was here to see Joan. He gave me a quick look as if to say What the bloody hell is a Flight Sergeant doing with a WAAF section officer? He probably thought I had to salute to get in bed with her. I signed in and asked where headquarters were located.

'Third Street. Straight ahead. You can't miss it,' the corporal said.

I walked up the street. I did not feel like a lover coming back to his true love. I felt as I had in high school when I had dropped the winning pass at the homecoming game because I thought I had heard the footsteps of a tackler rushing up to blind side me. I felt cowardly, defeated.

Whitewashed stones marked the garden along the side of the headquarters Nissen hut. I went in and found a warrant officer sitting at a table just inside the door. Behind him was a long hall with doors on each side.

'I'd like to see Section Officer Joan DeMarney,' I told him.

He gave me a long steady look. His eyes said nothing, but the steadiness of his gaze seemed forced.

'One moment, please.' He rose and went back along the hall and opened the third

265

door on the left. The door remained
opened. I could hear his voice but I
couldn't understand what he was saying.
He was speaking to another man.

When the warrant officer returned he
said: 'Wing Commander Ardsley will see
you.' I went along the hall to the open
door.

A tall, black haired New Zealander
with a DSO and a DFC and bar said,
'Come in, flight. Come in.' His voice
was warm and friendly. I saluted him
and he gestured toward the chair in front
of the desk.

'Are you a relative of Miss DeMarney's?'
he asked. He kept watching me.

'No. An old friend.'

'Well,' he started to say, and looked
down at his hand on top the desk. He
drummed his index finger and then lifted
his head. He spoke softly: 'Miss DeMarney
was killed two weeks ago.'

At first I was bewildered. It was unreal.
But I knew it was unreal like all the
other deaths I had not seen, just faces
that vanished from the Mess suddenly.

'Dead?' I heard my voice say. I felt my
body shudder and shiver, and then that
stopped.

'A tip and run raid,' he said. 'One ME
early in the morning. Right down the side
of the runway. Two bombs.'

266

I stared at him.

'I'm sorry,' he said.

I stood up. I had to get out of here, get out of here, get away from here, get away from here fast. I felt myself about to give away completely. Then the sudden grief hit me and I wanted to laugh and cry at the same time.

I saluted and turned and ran down the hall. Outside the grief hit me. I leaned against the wall of the Nissen hut, shuddering and shivering. Had to get away. Get away. Get away. Move. Can't move. Had to go, had to go. Go. Go. Go. Go. Must go. Must go. Must go.

'Flight, try this. This will help,' the warrant officer was saying, holding out a glass of whiskey.

I pushed his hand away.

'I'm okay. No thanks. Nothing to drink. I'm okay.'

'You forgot your bag.'

'I'm okay.'

'Try it. Try it, flight.'

'I don't want any.'

'Do you want to lie down?'

'I'm okay,' I said, and picked up my kit.

I tried, all the way up on the train to Yorkshire, not to think about Joan but what in hell else was there to think about.

I couldn't stop thinking about her when I had walked in on the warrant officer and that steady look he had given me, knowing even then something was wrong, but not wanting to think it might be true. But was that really true? Hadn't I always thought Joan was invincible, just as I had thought I was when I first started combat flying? Somebody else dies, never you, nor your true love. But they had been considerate at the Spitfire squadron. Well, why not? They'd had plenty of practice since 1940, with the way their next of kin rate soared day by day. I thought about seeing her. About going to her folks. It was too late to see her. But would I want to see her dead? I didn't even want to know how she had died. I couldn't stand the thought of her being in pain, nor the sight of her mangled body. I hoped just a small bomb fragment had gone through her heart. I prayed and prayed she had died instantly. I began to weep. Somebody opened the train compartment door.

'Go away,' I said. 'Get out of here.' I could not look up. The door slammed, and I was alone again, hearing the shuddering and catch of my breath, the click, click of the train wheels. Christ, this wonderful girl! To be killed by a flick of fate.

I didn't sleep all that night. I was

awake at dawn when the train pulled into the station at York. Out on the platform all the people looked cold and heartless.

I went out into the sunny street. It was a beautiful day. The high sky shimmered, blue, vivid as glass. Walking up the street to the station hotel, I started to feel tired. I got a room at the hotel and went upstairs and lay down on the bed. In a few minutes I was asleep. I woke at noon and had a bath and went downstairs to the bar and had bottle of pale ale.

I felt a little better before I remembered there was a long gloomy future ahead of me—and that I would have to start the future today or tomorrow. I wanted to be with Joan and thought of calling her parents. But as I sat there it seemed Joan was in this room, in the City of York, in the streets of York where we had walked so often on leave, where we had first made love in the park after an air raid. She was more real here than in whatever cemetery she was lying. I looked out the street along the cobblestones to the DeGrey Rooms where we had danced, and would never dance again. The thought of dancing with her made me feel like crying again. She was like all the dead young men from the squadron whose bones lay turning slowly on the bottom of the North Sea, all those cocky beer drinking types who had written their names on the basement mirror in Betty's Bar in Coney Street, with their tunic buttons shining and their caps and hats raked, swanking their flying wings and good ribbons, their arms around each other's shoulders, roaring songs... 'Roll me over...in the clover...'

She had their attitude of gallantry born out of facing death with a laugh and smile and song between nights of combat. Hurrah for the dead already. Here's to the next man who dies. Her attitude and manner was the same as the fliers. I would never see her again. But why did it have to be her? Why did she have to be on the field at just that moment in time? Why hadn't I gone to her before? Why hadn't I turned myself in before? Maybe it never would have happened. Was this what I got for desertion? There was nothing I could do now, but go back to flying, but they wouldn't let me. It would be the Glass House for sure...well, that was settled. I would go to the aerodrome this afternoon. Let the whole thing start.

'Mack Norton,' said a voice at his shoulder. 'What the bloody hell are you doing here?'

I turned. It was Bob Folkes, the bomb aimer for our old crew.

'Having a beer,' I said.

Chapter 29

When the guard came for me three days later I walked straight out of my cell. The Sergeant Major leading the guards gave the orders and I stepped between the two guards and we marched outside across the parade square to the Wing Commander's office. The Sergeant Major knocked on the door, gave us marching orders and in we went. The Wing Commander was talking to a man in civvy street clothes. They quit and looked up as the Sergeant bawled out directives. The guards and the Sergeant turned about and stomped out, closing the door.

The civilian wore one of those London businessmen suits, black sharkskin, white shirt, with a silver tie flecked with miniature lions. His bowler hat and umbrella lay on the table against the wall.

'Have a good leave, Norton? Stand easy,' said the Wing Commander.

He pointed at a chair, turned his head a little.

'Mr Barrington. Flight Sergeant Norton.'

What the hell. I was up on a court

martial. They sounded as if they were going to serve tea. Mr Barrington put out his hand and smiled. I shook his hand and sat down.

'Mr Barrington is with air ministry.' Barrington looked at me frog-eyed. 'Did you have a good time in London?' he said.

'Quite,' I said.

Barrington lit a cigarette and blew a cloud of smoke over his shoulder. 'You've been gone a good bit. Mind telling us what you did?'

I looked at the Wing Commander. His hand lay on the desk, holding a pipe. He had an RAF gold crested ring.

'Go on,' he said.

'I should testify against myself for a court martial without it being a court martial?'

'That's up to you.'

'I thought I was on charge.'

'You may well be,' said the Wing Commander. 'But it's obvious that what you tell us here won't incriminate you any more than you are now.'

Well, I thought, here goes the biggest line shoot of the war.

'I won a lot of money in a crap game. That's all I needed. And I had a package of leave passes, so I just kept filling out passes and moving around London from one hotel to another. Sometimes a service club.'

'Where did you get the passes?'

I told them. They glanced at each other for an instant.

The Wing Commander leaned forward and looked at me hard across the desk. 'Why did you turn yourself in?'

'I felt shitty.'

'What do you mean? Betrayed your comrades?'

'That and another person.'

They both looked suddenly interested. Their eyes faintly brightened. I told them about Joan. Somehow they seemed disappointed in my story. They sat back. The Wing Commander stood up and they went out into the hall and closed the door. They were gone only a few minutes.

'You know about the Glass House?' he said.

I nodded.

'You know what you could get for desertion.'

I looked at him.

'Well, I'll tell you, Norton. The rest of the war. Hard labor. The guards would make your life miserable. You'll be stripped of all rank. You'll do everything on the double in the Glass House, including going to the bathroom. They'll break you physically and mentally. Desertion is the worst charge on which to enter the Glass House.'

'Come on,' I said. 'Why are you telling me this? Get on with the court martial.'

The Wing Commander didn't say anything. He rose and turned his back and walked over to the window. He went on speaking with his back turned to me.

'You're a very experienced air gunner, Mack. There aren't many of you around with so much experience.'

'Sure,' I said. 'The rest are dead.'

'That's exactly my point. We can use you, Mack.' He turned around. 'This is a special mission. If you make it back, the past will be forgotten.'

'I didn't finish that last tour. What about that?'

'We'll scrub it. You'll be posted to an operational training unit to teach new aircrews.'

'What are the odds on getting back?'

'With your experience, fair.'

'I don't fly the kite, you know.'

'The pilot will be experienced, too. Three tours of ops.'

'Who?'

'Some of your old crew.'

'Hell, they won't fly with me.'

'Yes, they will.'

'How's that?'

He didn't say anything so I said, 'I saw

Bob Folkes in York. He knows the whole story.'

The Wing Commander shook his head.

'We've cleared that up. You were on a special mission in London for air intelligence.'

'Do you expect them to believe that?'

'Some of them.'

'Like who?'

'That's the point. We want you to fly with them to find out which one of the crew *doesn't* believe it.'

'What the hell is this all about?'

'Will you fly the mission?'

'What is it?'

'All I can tell you now is that it is low level. And if you tell anybody what I'm going to tell you now, you'll be in that Glass House the rest of your life.' He stopped talking and they both looked at me.

I looked at them my eyes perfectly blank. There was no sound in the room. Somewhere Halifax engines were warming up. Did I want to go to prison for a couple of years? The funny thing was that in that moment I suddenly no longer felt afraid. Cowardly for having let her die. Cowardly for not having seen her sooner. But no longer afraid. I could not understand it. But I felt now again as I had felt when first went into combat. I wouldn't die. It couldn't happen to me. And that's the way a lot of fliers felt after they were off combat long enough. Well, I had been off long enough. They couldn't kill Mack Norton. No way. I wasn't afraid at all again of flying missions.

'Well,' I said. 'Tell me the rest. I'm with you.'

'The Luftwaffe fighter force has five divisions. Lower Elbe. One near Arnheim. Metz. Dobertiz near Berlin. One to deal with raids from the south at Schleissheim near Munich. All of these air control centers have direct lines to the radar stations. Freya radar stations operate on the long 240 cm waves. Wurzburgs radar stations operate on 53 cm. Fighter control centers are helpless if these radar stations are jammed. We finally have a jamming system that will render their radar station echo points into an indecipherable jumble of echo points. Their radar screens will appear to be covered with a mass of giant insects.'

'Not only will the air controllers be blind but the flak batteries also,' said Barrington. 'They simply won't be able to tell on their radar screen which echo points are bombers so they won't be able to vector night fighters and flak onto you.'

'While the main bomber stream goes over head, jamming, your special squadron will be coming in low.'

'Then the bomber stream will actually carry the jamming device? It won't come from England?' I said.

'Right.'

'What is it?'

'You'll know in briefing, before the raid.'

The jamming system the British had kept secret for sixteen months, I later learned, was a simple device called Window, strips of silver paper. At minute intervals, each bomber crew would be dumping out this chaff. Fluttering apart, these bundles of silver strips would sink slowly to the earth in the form of a huge echo-reflecting cloud. The Luftwaffe air controllers of the night fighters would have to depend completely in darkness on their observer corps. Window was cut to exactly the wave-length of the radar stations. Behind this radar smoke-screen we would hide, moving in to attack, while the Luftwaffe not knowing our target would not commit its fighter force.

'One thing,' said the Wing Commander. 'Let us know if any member of the crew persists in asking you what you were doing working for air force intelligence.'

'What *was* I doing?'

'Just let us know. That's all, Mack.'

Chapter 30

It was a week later.

'How do you feel about it, Bob?' I asked Bob Folkes. He had looked scared all week.

'Any idea where we are going?' he asked.

'Not the foggiest.'

'Well, cheers,' Bob lifted his glass. 'I'm going to buy a new rabbit's foot. That black stocking I copped off a virgin at midnight has about run out of magic. We're going to need something new.'

'Ah, it's a piece of cake,' Billy Jaynes said.

'We'll be so bloody low, not even the light flak will swing fast enough to hit us,' said Jaynes.

'Sure,' I said. 'Remember the way we got out of Lorient through all those bloody ships.'

'Lorient,' Bob said. 'That was a piece of cake.'

It was Saturday night and we were downstairs in Betty's Bar in the City of York, Bob Folkes, Billy Jaynes, Eddy Maisen and I. There were some American fliers sitting at the next table. We were all boozing it up.

'Where do you get that crap?' An American captain said. 'What do you mean, Lorient's a piece of cake? You Limey bastards, flying around in the dark so the Germans can't see you to shoot at you. Where do you get that crap?'

'Let's go over to the DeGrey Rooms. What time is it?' I said.

'Piece of cake!' The American captain went on yelling. 'Since when did you Limeys ever raid Lorient in daylight? Flying around at night for three years, I'd like to get you in a Fortress during the day. If you ever saw a Focke-Wulf before sundown, you'd die of fright.'

'Right-oh,' Bob said. 'And let me know when you're going to raid Germany. You can't win the war dropping your load of Frenchmen.'

We got up and left. We were sore but we didn't want to get into a scrap at this point.

A few nights later I was in the Mess lounge with Ian Cuddington, our new pilot. 'Good weather tomorrow,' I said. 'We'll get in plenty of time.'

'Right,' Cuddington said. I didn't know what he was thinking about, but it wasn't like him not to be interested in good flying weather on this program.

'How'd the engines sound today?' Cuddingham asked me.

'Okay.'

'How was my flying?'

'Why are you asking me?'

'I want to know.'

'You're off,' I said. 'A little off.'

'I never felt like this before.'

'Forget it,' I said.

'I never used to.'

'What's the trouble?'

'I don't know.'

'Come on. How's your love life?'

'Fine,' he said quickly.

'Maybe you ought to take a couple days off. Go see her.'

'That isn't it.'

'You better eat something,' I said.

'I don't feel like it,' he said.

The rest of the week he wasn't sharp flying. He missed a couple trees too close for comfort.

Monday night, the light went on in my room and Cuddington was standing there under the light bulb suspended on a cord from the ceiling.

'Morning already?' I said.

'I can't sleep.'

'Look,' I said. 'It's another target, that's all. They must've picked you because you're one of the best low-level pilots in the air force and you've gone in this low before and they need you again because they figure you're the only guy who can do it right. What the hell is eating you? I've got to get some sleep.'

'I can't sleep,' he said. 'I never thought about surviving before. I started thinking about it lately. I don't know why. I shouldn't. I never did before. Thinking about coming out alive. And getting married. Settling down. But I hate the bastard Jerries. When the hell will the war stop?'

'Have a drink, old boy.' I reached for the bottle on the table and poured him a drink in the empty glass. I held the other.

'Cheers,' I said. We clinked the two glasses together.

I drank and he drank. He didn't say anything and I didn't say anything. We just sat there and drank in silence.

I poured myself another drink and poured him one. He sipped it slowly. I put water in mine. I offered to get him water, but he shook his head and held his hand over his glass.

'Listen,' he said. 'I don't want to be a hero any more. I'm scared shitless.'

'We'll make it.'

'I might as well tell you,' he said. 'About Helene. Two years we've been going together. I keep putting off marriage. Who wants to make widows? Now she wants to get married before this last do.'

'Last do?'

'This bloody well could be our last do.'

'Ah,' I said. 'It's a piece of cake.'

'Bloody balls up.'

He poured himself another drink.

'Take it easy,' I said. He lay back on the bed, set his glass on his stomach and looked at the ceiling. He didn't move. He lay there, looking up at the ceiling. I poured some more whiskey into his glass. I poured myself another drink. The bottle was almost empty, but it hadn't helped. Tomorrow was right here in the room. After a while, Cuddington sat up and looked at me.

'Do you know what's really going to happen on this mission?'

'Little bit.'

'Bloody hell you do. Did they tell you we're in a bomber stream?' I didn't say anything. I just looked at him.

'Well, we're not,' he said. 'We're all alone. Nobody can get to this target in daylight. It's right at the end of the lake. I've seen the maps. It's heavy water.'

'You're drunk.'

'Not the lake.'

'What the hell are you talking about?'

'Give me another drink,' he said.

'Pour it yourself.'

'Up your arse, Norton. I'll just do that.'
He reached and poured himself a drink.
'Jerries are working on making an atom
bomb.'

'What the hell is that?'

'Go sick. Get off this op. We aren't
coming back,' he said.

'Why don't you go sleep it off?' I said.

'Right. Right-oh.' He stood up very
carefully and walked stiffly to the door.
Before he left, he turned back to me. 'We
aren't coming back,' he said.

Chapter 31

About five o'clock that afternoon I went
into the bar. Cuddington was there
drinking a pint.

'All set?' I said.

Cuddington smiled and nodded.

'Everything okay?' I asked.

'Wizard,' Cuddington said. His face
looked different. His cheeks were pink
but his eyes were merry and bright, and
innocent looking. He looked quite sober.
I couldn't believe it.

Cuddington grinned and winked at me.

'Piece of cake,' he said. We stood at the
bar drinking beer.

'I really had my head up arse and locked this morning,' Cuddington said.

'Forget it.'

'I wish you would.'

We drank some more.

'How much did I tell you?' Cuddington asked. He started drawing a wet ring on the top of the bar with his forefinger.

The bartender picked up our glasses.

'Two pints,' Cuddington told him. The bartender went away.

'Something about heavy water,' I said. I thought about what Baker and Barrington had told me. Well, nobody had asked me anything yet about the operation, nor about my so-called work with RAF Intelligence.

'Fine,' Cuddington said. 'Fine.'

'I don't know anything,' I said.

'Fine. Drink up.'

We finished our drinks. Cuddington leaned on the bar, staring at the wall behind the bar. 'This is one target Jerry doesn't want hit.'

'We've got great cover,' I said.

'Window?'

I nodded.

'Oh, so they told you. Well, you're right.' His voice became bright and cheery again. 'We couldn't ask for anything more. See you at briefing.'

He walked away.

When I got back to my room they were

all there, just like in the old days, sitting on my bed, Bob Folkes, Billy Jaynes, Eddy Maisen. It reminded me of that night when we had sat together to vote whether we would abort to Sweden. Their faces looked the same.

We seemed to sit there half awake, staring at each other out of a dead time. The Nissen hut in its blue gloom from the blackout bulb, the night outside dead quiet. The small room seemed to stretch into infinity. The figures on the bed looked distant. I closed my eyes, and for a second shut out the dead.

'What in hell is buggering you lads?' I asked.

'Where are we going?' a voice asked. I opened my eyes.

'Who said that?' I asked.

The three faces stared at me.

'I don't know from shit,' I said. 'Not a pherkin thing more than you do. You'll find out at briefing just like me.'

'What's this shit about you working for RAF Intelligence?' Eddy Maisen asked.

'Pherkin truth,' I said. 'I was propping up civilian morale. Very rough do. They put gongs all over me. I had to go from bar to bar at night in Piccadilly and when the civvies asked me how we were doing I had to keep saying, "We're giving Jerry hell." Damn near killed me. Had to drink twenty pints a night.'

'Up your arse,' Billy Jaynes said. 'You deserted.'

'What makes you so sure?' I said.

'Working for intelligence? Sounds like bullshit.'

'Maybe it is,' I grinned. 'And they forgave me. They needed good troops.' Somebody laughed.

I looked at them, thinking about the years of our service lives; they were like long sleepless nights between two repetitive nightmares. The Nissen hut felt like a cave and we were all here as primitive men. And suddenly I heard again the sound of the train wheels clicking over the rails going down to Dover, the train wheels saying the quick and the dead, the quick and the dead.

After they left I lay in the darkness, thinking of Joan. And wondering why Bob Folkes was the only one of the old crew who hadn't asked me what I thought the target was going to be.

I dozed for a while and then it was time to go for briefing. It was dark outside. The operations map was covered.

Wing Commander Baker bustled in like a cheery vicar.

'Well, gentlemen,' he said. 'You are expected to destroy the hard water plant at Werschmeel.' He spoke with studied dramatic simplicity. 'It must be destroyed. They are planning to build an atomic bomb. I won't go into the scientific explanation, but two atom bombs could wipe out London.'

He nodded to the Intelligence officer who handed target photographs to Cuddington and Dowman, our new navigator. Then he pinned a small-scale map of the target area on the wall. He was out of pins so held up one corner with his finger. The objective was a long low building with a smoke stack and tower, facing an open field. There were both heavy and light flak guns in the open field and beyond. It was rolling open country all around.

Baker wagged a finger at the Meteorological officer. The weather was favorable...

'Jesus,' Maisen whispered. 'What the hell do they think we are. Pulling this alone... Never do it...'

Now in my mind I saw the raid, thousand pound high explosive bombs tossed low level at this small target. It would need at least twenty-four thousand pounds of heavy explosive bombs to do this job. And low-level fighter bombers suppressing the flak.

'You will be under the bomber stream,' Baker said. 'Very little risk of interception.' Then he explained how Window was to

287

be used to confuse both the radar and night fighters. 'Approach the target at one thousand feet. Start your dive two minutes from target. Drop delayed action HE at two hundred feet. Then go out across the flats to the hills about five miles due south. Do not bomb if the target is not sighted. Accuracy is the prime consideration.'

Nobody said a word. I wanted to tell Baker that with that much flak around we couldn't possibly hit that small target. The pilot would be too busy jinking. We would be a prize package at that height to gunners. The whole thing smelled. Why not a massive raid on such a small target? This was pin-point bombing. Sure, we had practiced it over the North Sea and in the Norfolk Broads and we hadn't been much good at it. We didn't have the right kind of bomb sight for pin-point bombing.

We stared at Baker and his face got redder and redder.

'Two Mosquitos will mark the target for you. H hour for heavy bombers on Hamburg north of you is 2025; TOT for your mark, 2016 hours or H hours minus 8 minutes. Set course 1832 hours, flying time to target, 0137.4 hours, 369 nautical miles. Primary Blind markers and flares to go down at H hour minus 10, Cross the North Sea to the Frisians at 15,000 feet, then into Heligoland Bay, crossing enemy coast at 53½ degrees north, using a narrow corridor minus flak, and then go south to the target, reducing height.'

I looked at the small scale map and the photographs of the target. Something was fishy. Why doesn't somebody say something, but I couldn't seem to feel excited, only detached and indifferent, not even nervous or expectant, yet curious why only one kite was making the attack. It was all what it had been again and again and again: H hour, TOT's heights, temperatures, winds, speeds, etcetera and etcetera, magnetic and compass courses, tracks, ground speeds, etcetera.

The Meteorological officer stood up again and gave the weather profile in detail: anticyclonic conditions and light winds, the target area clear, except for some slight fog mixed with some industrial haze, a warm front giving complete alto-stratus cover coming up from the southwest. Remote possibility of North Sea stratus at a thousand feet if the temperatures were suitable.

The phone rang and we all sat up waiting and somebody whispered: 'Scrub! Scrub!'

Baker put the phone down and smiled. 'That was met. Target conditions totally clear. Oh, yes, German colors of the day, red, red, green. Time check! Exactly

1803.15 hours. Good luck chaps.'

I looked at my hands. They were quite steady. I walked closely beside Cuddingtoon as we left the room. I turned my head for a moment, and still felt Cuddington near me, but when I turned around he was gone. I still felt as if somebody, something was standing beside me. It must have been old Death himself, waiting for my time to come up.

'Good luck, Norton,' Baker said as I went out. We climbed into the truck and went rolling around the perimeter track to flights across the aerodrome.

S Sugar stood up in the darkness, rearing high on its big undercarriage, like a prehistoric winged monster. I climbed in the side door and walked carefully along the fuselage, passing the long racks of machine gun cartridges, 11,000 thousand rounds, on metal conveyor belts along the side of the fuselage. I opened the doors of the rear gun turret, and climbed in and sat down. I checked the illuminated ring and bead sight, the cocking toggles on each gun. It was a Bolton-Paul electrically operated turret, with a gun stick like a joy stick in the metal table beneath my elbows. The firing button for the four guns was on top the stick. I could move the guns and turret with one hand.

'Eighteen-oh-nine hours,' the navigator

said. Eight minutes to take off. Outside I could hear the put-putting of the little engine on the starter accumulator. One by one, the engines coughed.

Contact: the port outer engine glooped, stuttered and then fired, then the port inner, then the starboard engines. A gentle vibration shook the turret as Cuddington opened up each engine to 2000 revolutions and made checks and then ran the revolutions up to 3000. The aircraft trembled against the chocks.

The Halifax started to roll slowly and smoothly onto the perimeter track.

'All set, chaps?' Cuddington asked as we turned onto the runway. I couldn't see the green light from the control tower but I could sense Cuddington easing the throttles forward, the engines beating triumphantly, the exhaust stubs from Billy Jaynes' mid-upper turret would be glowing white and blue and yellow like furious flowers. Suddenly airborne; up undercarriage and we swung in a slow shallow turn to port. Soon the lighted runway became an inch long. Darkness swallowed the land.

'Eighteen thirty-one hours,' the navigator said.

'Okay,' Cuddington said, taking the Halifax into a turn to bring her across the aerodrome.

'Compass course oh-eight three degrees,' the navigator said.

I felt Cuddington steadying the aircraft. We were now dead on course. It seemed no time at all before I saw the Fresian Islands on the starboard beam.

'Jerry is jamming,' said the navigator. 'Gee Box is fading.' It would be dead reckoning now all the way. There was heavy flak all along the coast here. But in a couple of minutes we crossed the German coast. It was quiet and dark and dead below, but somewhere the guns were waiting.

It was still quiet and dark below when the navigator said: 'We are entering the target area.'

The Mosquito raid controller must be making contact with the Flare Force Lancasters of the main bomber stream; for to the north, far down in the darkness, I saw the markers flowering below, turning night into day. Behind us, spears of light probed the sky, the empty darkness blossoming into fire. We were in a shallow dive now. I heard Folkes say the bombs were fused.

The first round balls of flak were a couple hundred feet below but right on for course and speed, in boxes of five; round balls of smoke centered with orange. The puff-balls drifted away. The flak battery corrected its error. A box of seven balls of smoke burst just beyond the tail at our flight level. Jesus, I thought, they'll nail us with the next burst.

Chapter 32

'Backdeck Controller. To S Sugar. Come in! Markers down? Do you read?' the Mosquito pilot called.

I could not see the markers up ahead, but I felt the aircraft slow as the bomb doors opened. I felt the balance of the aircraft change.

'Marker! I read!' Cuddington called.

I felt the Halifax turning and diving. He was trying to keep the speed down. Then I could see the ground. Suddenly I felt the aircraft lift and heard Bob Folkes: 'Bombs gone!'

Then we sped over the glowing patch of the markers in the darkness. We climbed fast to port.

'Good show, S Sugar!' The Mosquito controller-marker pilot called. 'Bang on!'

I looked back at the glowing stain on the dark ground widening.

Then far to the north I saw the bombs falling on Hamburg, stick after stick of bombs ripping up through the darkness, great roses of brilliant red. There would be white photo flashes stabbing down into that darkness. The bowl of light hollowed out of the darkness seethed like volcanic crater. Then the searchlights came on, conning the tiny silver bombers like fireflies. In con after con of searchlights there were exploding masses. Bomber after bomber was being shot down. What had happened to Window? Why were the searchlight batteries able to coordinate? Flak was bursting in all the cons of searchlight. Christ, I thought, the heavy bombers are getting butchered! Has Window failed?

'Let's get the hell out of here,' said Bob Folkes.

I felt sick, mouth filled with saliva. I tried to swallow it. I unsnapped my oxygen mask and spat on the turret floor.

'ETA base is twenty-one-thirty-six,' said Jock Shearer.

I watched the dull glow of the Hamburg fire. I wondered how many children and women were dying. Payment for London, the Baedeker raids on the Cathedral towns? The sins of Hitler revisited. Women and babies burning for the bastard.

'Is IFF on?' Cuddington asked.

'Yes,' Shearer said. 'Right at the coast. Base now Twenty-one-thirty-five.'

Jesus, I wondered, would there be any

German night fighter intruders waiting near base to nail us on return? I hoped Cuddington would change radio frequency.

I heard him calling base: 'Pocklington S for Sugar to Pocklington Control: are you receiving me? Over?'

'Pocklington S Sugar, receiving you loud and clear. The apples are sweet. The apples are sweet. Over.'

Bring on the spam and eggs, I thought, thank God, home again.

Then I saw the night fighter. At first I thought it was a Wellington bomber.

'Dive port!' I yelled to Cuddington. 'Dive port!'

There were two German fighters out there, one on our tail and one at eight o'clock. They were preparing to attack simultaneously so that if we turned inside the pursuit curve of one, we would be a sitting duck for the night fighter on the port side.

Why in hell doesn't Cuddington dive and turn?

Blue balls of fire flashed, suspended in the darkness. The fighter slid away. He was underneath.

'Call him out!' I shouted at the top turret gunner. 'Where is he? Call out the goddamn fighter position!'

Then out of line of thick darkness, the fighter's wing, blue balls of fire flashed again. Twin threads of fire whizzed under the turret. Glass burst across my face. The cold air whipped in. I crouched forward, searching for the fighter. My heart was pounding. Then the fighter was there, suspended, across the darkness, hanging on his propellors, big-nosed, long and round, fish-like. JU-88. Icy wind burned across my eyes. Press down on the firing button.

My guns hammered. The turret shuddered. The red illuminated circle of the ring sight jiggled. The turret smelled of cordite. Brass cartridge links rattled off the inside of the turret around my boots.

Suddenly the big black round-snouted fish jerked orange pennants of fire out of its nose.

The JU-88 slid away whirling fiery fragments.

I felt pressure against my back. I swiveled the turret. Starlight tilted. I peered around the edge of the turret. The port outer engine was on fire, just little tongues red nibbling out at the cowling.

'Port outer's on fire,' I shouted.

'Hang on,' said Cuddington. 'Feathering port outer.'

'Watch for the other fighter,' I said. 'Jaynes!' No answer.

I gave the guns a trial burst. Nothing happened. I pulled the cocking toggles on each gun to eject linkage. Still the guns would not fire. I lifted the lid on top of each gun. I kept my eyes up, sky searching, feeling in the dark for metal cartridge links that might be jamming the guns. All clear.

But the guns would not fire. The cartridge belt was not being fed into the guns. The belts of cartridges were stored in long racks just inside the fuselage behind my turret, and the conveyor belts were electrically operated to feed the belts up into the guns. Only one thing to do. See if the electric system had been hit or the conveyor system jammed. In my right boot I carried a hunting knife, and in my left boot, a small flashlight.

'Fire out,' Cuddington called.

'Jaynes,' I said. 'Keep an eye open for another fighter. I gotta check the conveyor belts. Guns won't fire.'

Jaynes did not answer. I pulled out the flashlight. I popped the ratchets on the turret door and stuck my elbows against the two little doors. As they opened I rolled out backwards onto the fuselage floor, righted myself, and on hands and knees crawled toward the conveyor belts.

The aircraft was steady now. Where was that fighter?

I stood up and shone the light beam on the conveyor belts. I ran the beam along

297

the wall checking each box of ammo. Everything seemed in order. Except the last box. It was blown right out of the wall. It jammed the whole system.

I turned to go back to the turret as the beam of my flashlight went across the dark floor and passed over a pair of flying boots. I lifted the light beam.

Suddenly my balls were in my throat and my heart was ice cold.

There was Billy Jaynes, looking straight at me. His helmet was off and he was pointing a black automatic at my chest. He was smiling.

His lips moved. The automatic lifted.

For Chrissake, I thought as I dived for his legs. I missed and as I hit the floor I heard the automatic fire. It struck the fuselage near my head. I slid around on my stomach. I could see him sticking up in the darkness. I got his ankle and jerked and the gun went off again. But he was down. The gun made a little flame in the dark, but I knew where his face was then. I swung in the darkness and missed and fell down. I landed on top of him. I caught his arm by the wrist. I couldn't see it, but knew he still had the gun. He hit me twice on the side of the face with his left hand but I had his right hand back pretty well. I kept on pushing and he kicked out with both legs trying to throw me off. I punched his face solid with my left and felt his head flop. The gun went off again. I couldn't see the flame. He must have shot a hole in the ceiling.

I bent his arm way back until I heard the automatic clatter on the floor. I reached for my knife in my boot and he kicked me off and turned over. While I was getting my knife out I heard him crawling around on the floor looking for his gun.

Just then the night fighter found us again. There was an explosion and a cannon shell went through the fuselage just above us. A hole as big as my head appeared in the side of the fuselage. I could see right where Jaynes was. There was a little moonlight and some starlight coming in through the cannon shell hole. It was big as a ship's port hole.

I got the knife out and slipped once as the aircraft bounced skidding. I got my left arm around his throat. He had the gun. I could see it. I rolled off him and pulled him over on top of me. He was sticking the gun over his shoulder when I cut his throat. I let go and he flopped away like a fish.

The aircraft was mushing, stalling. I sprang toward the turret. The machine lurched, dived. The angle was increasing. I was on my knees feeling along the inside of the turret for my parachute.

Damn it, the parachute had tumbled onto the floor of the cockpit. Only then I saw it was there not because I hadn't stowed it right, but because another cannon shell had struck the turret. If I had been in it, I would have been blown to bits. All the glass was shot out of one side. I reached for the parachute, leaning down into the turret and the parachute popped up in the air and over my head. For an instant I panicked...

Don't panic, Mack. Take your time.

The parachute tumbled down my back into the fuselage, and bounced off the wall. I could hear it but couldn't see it. I lay on my stomach and wiggled along the floor, feeling with hands and legs, like a four legged crab. I couldn't find it.

Now in panic again I wondered what we would plough into.

I lay there, listening in the dark for the sound of chute. There was nothing I could do.

Our father.

No, God, it's too late.

Then the machine lurched again and the parachute pack struck my arm and I caught it. I held it, felt for the buckles, rolling over on my back. I found the buckles, snapped it on.

I don't remember getting into the turret, nor rotating the turret until the open doors

300

faced out into the darkness and wind. I knew we were still falling. The machine felt pilotless...one two buckle shoe...three four open door.

I rolled out backwards, my fingers curled around the ripcord.

Chapter 33

I was falling. I couldn't find the ripcord. My right hand found it, and pulled. The parachute billowed out and opened and the straps jerked hard between my legs and it felt good.

The silence seemed enormous. I felt the wind blowing across my face and hair and I lifted my hand and brushed the hair away from my eyes. I looked down through the darkness but I couldn't see the ground.

Then I looked to my right and as I looked my hand felt for the knife in my boot which was gone. Not more than twenty-five yards away, parachuting down at the same time and at the same height, was another man. And I knew when I saw his flying jacket and boots it could only be one of the German night fighter fliers.

I knew I had hit his machine. He should have tried to bail out, but obviously they had tried to climb with a damaged machine and finally saw it was impossible.

The German was looking over at me. He was a big man, his hands uplifted, grasping the cords. We watched each other. Well, he was a prisoner of war in enemy country. He couldn't be foolish enough to think he could escape. But if we landed near each other, what the hell might he try to do. If he were a die-hard Nazi, he'd be apt to try anything. I would stay away from him.

Then I saw the ground. We would be down in a few seconds. There were cows in one corner. Then I saw the pond. It was right underneath me. I couldn't miss it. I was dropping fast. I jerked the cords, but the parachute wouldn't spill. Then the fear was inside me again. Could it be deeper than a pond, filled with mud? I could sink and sink and sink.

I went straight through the water and hit the bottom of the pond.

My legs sank into the mud and my head went under, and then I came up and I was standing in water up to my neck. The parachute covered my head and I was all tangled up in it and I could not see anything. I tried to move and my feet stuck and I got very scared. I started fighting the parachute, tearing at it with both hands. Then I realized I was under the water again. I opened my eyes and saw the bubbles in the water. The bubbles were above me. Christ, I was drowning.

Then I heard a splash and another body knocked against me and then the man stood over me and reached down for my neck with both hands. God, he's going to strangle me, steal my uniform and try to get to an aerodrome on the coast and steal an airplane. Then there were hands under my shoulders lifting me up, squeezing my arms.

I relaxed my body and heard the man splashing through the water, puffing and out of breath. Then I realized he was dragging me out of the water. I wondered if I were really dead, and I was seeing this all through my dead eyes. Then he knelt down. He searched my pockets, taking my money and identification card. He took off my watch. I did not move. It was nice lying like this. Maybe I was dead. He pulled off my boots. Then my trousers and tunic and boots. Then he disrobed, throwing his flying jacket and boots and trousers on the ground. He's mad, crackers, nuts. He must hope to walk into an RAF airfield, commandeer an aircraft before it's light.

'Take it easy,' I said. He jumped. He looked scared. He started to run, looking back at me over his shoulder. He went on running, vanishing into the darkness. I wanted his clothes. They were wet but the night air is cold. I pulled on his trousers and flight jacket. He had beautiful flying boots. Everything he wore was a size too large.

But I did not want to move after I was dressed. The hell with it. I would lie right here on the grass and sleep until it was light. Then I would know where I am. No more wandering around in the dark. I lay down by the fence.

I woke smelling violets and primroses. At first I didn't know where I was. I looked around heard myself say, 'Oh, my God,' because suddenly I did know where I was, about ten miles from the aerodrome. I had been here before. I felt my arms and legs to see if I were dreaming. It seemed incredible. I was alive, and Mary Wayne's house was about a mile away. This would shake her. The same bugger knocking on the door again, asking to use the phone. To hell with the phone. I didn't care if I never got back to the aerodrome.

Jesus, so Jaynes had tried to shoot me. But why? And his face. Now I remembered his face. That night in the adjutant's office when I was stealing a pad of leave passes.

That was Jaynes. Jaynes had been in that office. What the hell was he doing hiding in the adjutant's office? He was the bloke who had belted me on the head and left me knocked out in adjutant's office. It was a lot of balls. I couldn't figure it out. All cocked up.

It was not quite dawn. The starless eastern morning sky was red along the horizon, but behind me the night was still there, a single morning star fading high overhead into the rising morning light.

I found the road. I had told Mary Wayne I would come back and I had never come back, and now I was going back. It was dirt road. A truck passed. The backend was open. Italian prisoners of war dangled their legs over the edge of the truck and waved. I waved back.

As I walked I started to think about the operation. There was something fishy about it. Sending us alone to attack that valuable target. And Window? What had happened to Window? It was suppose to break up the night fighter radar coordination with ground stations. But I had seen at least fifteen bombers shot down in flames over the target. Something was screwy. It didn't add up.

The air felt thick and warm. The fields were a vivid green. I knew I would see her house soon. There would be the wall around the garden, the smell of roses. The sun was rising slowly and there was a cold front blowing cumulonimbus. The western sky flickered, far faint. Lightning from an approaching storm. I watched it come nearer. Flashes varied in intensity. It seemed to remain where it was. I went on. Eddies of dust swirled across the road.

Then I thought I heard whispering, but it was only the wind, even though the storm was still far away. It seemed strange that I smelled the roses before I saw the garden wall. I passed through the garden door. It was cold in the garden. I could hear the wind beyond the wall. Somewhere a church bell rolled. The wind seemed to rip the slow strokes of the bell out of the church tower across the land and garden walls, so when I heard the tolling it seemed to come back to me as an echo from far away.

I crossed the garden and touched the door of the house. Would she be here? The door opened.

I entered the hall and saw the empty living room and dining room on each side of the hall. I mounted the stairs and crossed the second floor hall. It was dark in the hall. Blackout curtains. I looked into the bedroom. The bed was empty.

I heard a quick sound. Soft arms encircled my neck. I felt my head being drawn down into feather-soft hair, into the sweetness of her, the silken folds of her nightgown.

'Mary—' I said.

'I saw you in the lane—' she started.

I turned.

'I was afraid you were dead,' she said. 'You never came back. Everybody I know is dead.'

'It must have frightened you.'

'I thought it was a dream,' she said.

Her hands came down upon my shoulders. I put my arms around her waist.

'It was a mistake,' I said. 'I told you I would come back. I never called. But I'm here.'

She braced her body against me and her legs came slowly forward. I felt pleasure drawn through me like a cord. A promise. A message. A treasure. Running through me.

'I'm so happy you came back,' she said.

Her body turned. I felt the life of her body in my hands, the lines of her flesh. She slipped away and turned on a light over the bed. She wore a pale yellow silk nightgown. It was long and old-fashioned. She sat down in a chair on the other side of the bed.

'This was my honeymoon nightgown,' she said. 'He is dead.'

'What happened?'

'I don't know. A telegram came.'

She rose, turning, plucked a rose from

the vase on the bureau.

'Come here,' she said, turning toward the mirror. She put the rose down the top of her nightgown. She drew back her shoulders, let them drop. The rose fell down through her gown. I picked it up.

I heard the rain slash suddenly against the window, the faraway barrage of thunder.

'Here,' I said, I drew the rose down between her breasts. She put her hands over her breasts, holding the flower in. Then she turned toward the bed. Lying on her back she held the flower to her lips.

Her gentle breasts curved smoothly, and she stretched both arms toward me.

'Take your talisman,' she handed me the flower. 'You need luck. You have brought me luck, I feel, just coming here again. You helped me before. Perhaps I can help you now.'

'You helped me then.'

She held up the rose. I reached for it, and her right arm drew the rose down upon her breasts.

'Come down here and get it.' She flung petals at me. Her eyes seemed to lie in wait. She sprang up, kneeling on the bed.

I hugged her with affection. She kissed my forehead and said, 'We're fools. I have a capacity for folly. I need you.'

308

For a fraction of a second she lay there. She looked a long way off, her body and face going out of focus, so again I thought it was a dream. Then suddenly her legs split, and her breasts exploded with beauty, fully blossomed. In the dark I smelled the rose again, heard the storm outside. I closed my eyes, saw lightning flickering in the darkness. Her long hair and soft body enchanted.

We soared in a long flight of infinity to stars and moon and back again, in which I found individuality realized by the remoteness of the room.

'You're lovely,' she said.

'Are you happy?'

'What happened to her?' she said.

I didn't answer.

'There must have been a girl. You never came back.'

'She's dead.'

'You're lovely, Mack. Were you in love? Could you be again?' she asked.

'I don't know.'

'You've been scared for so long you don't know any other feeling?'

'Maybe.'

'Were you happy just now?'

'Peaceful.'

'Not happy? Like being in love for the first time?'

'No,' I said. 'I don't think I can ever

feel that way again.'

But in a moment again like a blazing trail of falling stars a sense of creation flashed between us.

'God,' she said. 'I loved you for a moment. You could wring me dry right now and nothing but pure pleasure would run out of me. I feel warm and fresh as a towel in the sun. Mack, I'm so happy you came back again.'

We lay there kissing.

'What a wonderful gift from the night,' she said.

'Courtesy of the Luftwaffe.'

'Are you happy now?' she asked.

'For a moment it was like having everything in the world I wanted again.'

'Me, too. What are you thinking of?'

'Nothing.'

'Mack?'

'Yes.'

'Why are you worrying now?'

'I'm not.'

'What is it?'

'I was wondering how long it would last...our being like this. Everything's unreal, the war, death...you...me.'

'Why can't you live in the moment?'

'I don't know,' I said.

Her arm dropped away from me and she lay back. I did not know what to say and for an instant I had the terrible feeling I was going to weep again as I had after Joan's death. I looked at Mary's head, remembering Joan. Her eyes were closed as Joan's had closed, smiling in dreamy content after pleasure.

I looked at my watch, and listened to the continuous rain. I closed my eyes. There must be time for sleep, and I felt myself falling faster and faster under the water I had never seen, far, far down, wondering before I slept at the link here that bound me back to Joan. But had I ever really known Joan? Wasn't she, too, an enigma, sleeping fast in eternal dreams, like Mary, like myself?

Chapter 34

Barrington's voice was cold and angry. We sat alone in Baker's office, staring at each other across the desk.

'You dodo,' he said.

'How the hell was I supposed to know? You didn't tell me.'

'You killed him.'

'What the hell was I supposed to do. Kiss him? He was going to kill me.'

'We've been watching him for weeks.'

'What for?'

'Billy Jaynes' father was a member of Mosley's Black Shirts for years. The boy was raised on admiring Hitler.'

'A British kid like that?'

'You better read some history.'

'Screw you,' I said. 'I've had enough English history right here the last couple of years.'

'When did Dickson ask everybody to vote on whether you should defect to Sweden?'

'I told you.'

'Right. Well, Jaynes was the lad who voted against landing in Sweden.'

'You say he was transmitting information to the Germans. How?'

'That's what we don't know.'

'Have you watched him?'

'Of course. He never contacts anybody. But somehow he does.'

'How do you know?'

'Have you any idea how many bombers we lost last night?'

'I saw a bunch of them getting pranged.'

'Too bloody many. Somebody tipped the target to the Germans.'

'I thought Window would jam them up.'

'We had the hell shot out of us over the target.'

He drew in his bottom lip, angrily tapped a pencil on the table.

'What happened?' I asked.

'We want to find out. They had fighters operating at random. Right in the bomber stream. How did they know where the bomber stream would be if Window was jamming the radar? They were waiting for us. Their night fighters didn't work with the radar sites. They were waiting for us right over the target.'

'Why did you send us on a phony mission?'

'Phony?' he said.

'Come on,' I said.

'We had to take chances with Jaynes. To see if he could send a signal on the main target and your target.'

'Heavy water—' I began.

'No, that was only a supply depot you hit. We put you under the bomber stream, figuring you'd be safe. But they let the night fighters roam wherever they wanted to go. We wanted to see how Jaynes would handle notifying them of such a target and if he would go on the mission. He must have known he would be committing suicide if he told them his lone target. So he never told them. But he signaled them the main target.'

'Beats the hell out of me.'

'They'll be looking for another contact,' Barrington said.

Christ, I thought, could it be me? Was

there some tie up between Jaynes and my getting shot at in London? Had they wanted to kill me because I had seen Jaynes that night in the adjutant's office? Had he been looking for secret operational papers? But if they had wanted to kill me, then why hadn't they? Why had they stopped trying? How did they know I was at Beryl's? Had I been followed on the train or picked up in London? How had they managed to locate me in London? Well, if we could manage to have somebody planted in the Luftwaffe in Germany who transmitted to us each day, the Luftwaffe flare colors of the day, no reason why they couldn't have some agents planted in the RAF. The casualty rate indicated something was goofed up. Somebody had their hand in our pants.

'Did anybody contact you when you were in London?'

'No,' I lied. 'Like I said. I just knocked around from service club to service club until I ran out of dough.'

I was scared now. I couldn't tell Barrington. His eyes kept following my eyes. I could feel them on my face. I looked straight at him. His eyes were sort of too steady. Almost like a guy getting drunk.

I couldn't tell Barrington about Charles Seymour or Beryl shot dead during an air raid. All Seymour had to do was call in Paul Phillips and I would be up on a murder charge. Somewhere there was a tie up between Phillips and Seymour and maybe Jaynes. But I couldn't tell this to Barrington.

The problem was how could I flush out Seymour without flushing myself down the tube to prison. There was only one thing to do. Keep my mouth shut. And keep looking over my shoulder.

Wing Commander Baker came in. 'Well,' he said to Barrington. 'Everything tidied up?'

'I want Norton off ops,' said Barrington.

'That was part of the deal,' I said.

'Oh, yes,' said Baker. 'Of course.'

'Do you have a job for him on the squadron?'

'Quite,' said Baker. 'How about instructing the sprog crews, Norton?'

'Aircraft recc?' I said. 'Night fighter tactics?'

'Right,' said Baker.

So I started the next day. There were four sprog crews on the squadron. None of them had flown operations yet. They were still converting into Halifaxes after flying Wellingtons at an operational training unit.

I hoped I would save a few lives. I wasn't sure. The gunners were bored. They had attended too many aircraft recognition classes. They were young and eager and doomed. They wanted to fight. They looked half asleep in class.

The odds were that only one out of those four crews would finish a tour of 30 ops.

But even as I taught in class, I kept wondering how I could flush out Seymour and gang, whatever their game was. And why did I keep feeling they had something to do with Billy Jaynes? I couldn't put my finger on this feeling. But it was there.

Chapter 35

I had a fine time the next few weeks. I would teach five days a week and with a weekend pass go over to Mary's house. The squadron was flying operations every third night and the losses were decreasing each week. Window was working and the German night fighter command was having problems. The losses continued to recede and the bomb plots on the targets were stronger and stronger. We were winning the night bomber war.

I started thinking of being invincible again, of wanting to go on a mission, but I knew it was only an illusion. It was better to be with Mary on weekends.

The war seemed far-off, almost as if I had never been in it. I started to feel like a civilian. Nine to five at the office.

One Saturday morning, about seven weeks after the attack on Hamburg, I was bicycling along the road to Mary's house. All I wanted was to see Mary. I wasn't thinking of anything else. I didn't hear the car coming along the road behind me and when it honked I moved over close to grass along the edge of the road and went on pedaling.

The car drove up along side of me and honked. I looked up at the driver. It was Charles Seymour. He waved and pointed at the side of the road.

He turned the car slowly toward me and I stopped pedaling and braked the bike. He parked the Daimler ahead of me and got out and came back. He was wearing a tan Harris tweed jacket and cavalry twill slacks, and looked as if he were going to a point-to-point race.

'How have you been, Mack?' He was smiling. He carried a pair of yellow gloves in one hand and he slapped them into the palm of his other hand.

'Fine.'

'You left London so suddenly.'

'I had to.'

'I suppose your leave ran out.'

'Cut out the crap, Seymour. You know why. Who killed Beryl?'

'I say. Tragic. I heard about it.'

'What do you want?'

'Phillips tells me you were in a bit of spot when you left.'

'So is Phillips.'

'You're rather lucky, you know.'

'I need all I can get. Get to the point.'

'I had no idea you were here.'

'Like hell. Beryl knew where I was stationed.'

I watched his face. It looked like the face of a happy, cheery British beef eater, pink-cheeked and jovial.

Suddenly his voice changed. It became hard and cold.

'Of course, I knew you were here. They hang chaps for murder in this country, Norton. And you could hang.'

'I'd hang you and Phillips, too.'

He laughed. 'You are absurd, Norton.'

My guts felt empty and hollow. He had me and he knew it. The courts would never believe what I told them. Phillips would lie through his teeth. I could never hook Phillips to Seymour. Phillips would say he met me through Beryl. Seymour would laugh in my face in court. But there was a game to be played. That's why Seymour was here. If I played his game I was hooked, and if I didn't, he had me by the short hairs with a murder rap. Well, so they had set me up for something. Or had they? Had the shooting of the gamekeeper been an accident or had it been arranged? My guts churned. You're damned lucky if you do, and damned if you don't.

'What the gimmick?' I said.

'What?'

'Gimmick. Angle.'

'I say.' He chortled. 'Yankee talk. You chaps can be delightful.' Then his eyes changed. He looked up at me from beneath half lowered eyelids.

'Jaynes is dead,' he said. 'You play along with us or we kill you or put you in jail.'

'Go ahead.'

'I want the name of the target for tonight and the names of all the cities to be attacked by your squadron from now on.'

'How?'

He opened his wallet and handed me a sheet of paper. On the sheet were thirty-five numbers. After each number was the name of a key target city in Germany and France.

'If you recall,' he said, 'Billy Jaynes has a garden outside of his Nissen hut. Around that garden are thirty-five white washed stones. Count from left to right. When you

319

get the name of the target tonight, pull out one stone corresponding to that number. One wrong selection and you know what will happen.'

'I can't tonight,' I said. 'I have a date. It would look fishy for me to be hanging around the squadron tonight. I have a two day pass.'

'The first operation after Sunday night then,' he said and turned and went to the car and drove away.

I looked at the list: Essen, 15. Dortmund, 11. Wurpettal, 9. Stetin, 12...

Who on the squadron would pass on the information after spotting the stone I would pull out? Christ, was there *another* spy on the squadron? And did he phone the number elsewhere?

There was only one way to play their game and come out alive. The first wrong number fed to them would bring a beef, the second a warning and the third, who knows? Who was their other contact who sent the information on? I'd never know until I fed them a curve.

Chapter 36

I knew there was operation on the next morning, but I didn't have to go to weather briefing in the morning since I wasn't flying anymore. When everybody came back from briefing I got hold of Peter Foster, little Englishman who looked fifteen years old and was nineteen. He had done one tour of missions on Hampdens as a wireless operator.

He was digging a slab of white margarine, the color of lard, out of a bowl.

'What is the weather?'

'Duff,' he said.

'Where?'

'The whole bloody continent is open.'

'I thought you said it was bad.'

'It is. Every target on the continent is open.' Duff meant bad, so he meant it was bad weather because it was good weather for bombing.

'What's the target?' I asked. Peter shrugged. He didn't know. Sometimes you could guess the target at morning weather briefings, but the Met officer never told us until final briefing.

So I stooged around the rest of the

day, played some rugby just before dinner which the RAF served at noon. I still had not looked at Jaynes' garden, so I walked over to the Nissen hut. I counted the stones. Each stone about two inches in diameter, round and smooth, and there was exactly the number I had on my list.

Target briefing was at 1500 hundred house. I bicycled past the briefing room when the crews came out. The lorries were waiting to take them out to flights where the bombers were waiting. The crews were stuffing maps into cases, knives into the tops of their boots, lugging the chutes over their shoulders. I rolled up to Peter. He looked worried.

'Let's go, Peter,' somebody called.

'What's the bloody gen?' I asked.

'Nuremberg.'

I whistled softly. Nuremberg was a hell of a deep penetration raid. Long, long way down to southern Germany and back to England.

'Well, it's better than Munich.'

'See you at breakfast,' he said.

I never saw him again. The night fighters got him coming home.

I walked slowly back toward the garden. I stood there a long time, perhaps fifteen minutes. A peaceful ripple of wind passed through the trees behind the garden. Shadows of small clouds glided across the leaves. It had been a beautiful day. High in the sky clouds islands swam across the immeasurable distances of blue. Soon the clouds would be turning black, their edges curling pink, the horizon blood red for a while over the darkening earth, and then rising into the darkness, the squadron would go out against the first evening stars.

I counted the stones. Stone number eleven. Nuremberg. If it checked, I was sending people to their death.

But how was this information passed? Christ, it was my ass or theirs. There were three thousand fliers going tonight to attack Nuremberg. If the night fighters knew where the bomber stream was going, they would be ready and the bombers would get chopped up. I was filled with dread and remorse. I didn't want to die or go to jail. But I didn't want my friends to die. Jesus, Jesus, just this once, let me see if Seymour is lying. Give them the right target. Give them the wrong target next time and take the consequences. Come on, Norton, you're bull shitting yourself. You know Seymour isn't kidding. He'll kill you or betray you the first time you double cross him.

I knelt down and moved the Nuremberg stone faintly out of line, about halfway out from the row of stones.

I walked over to the woods. From a screen of trees I could see the garden. Whoever passed I could see. But there was nobody there. I sat there two hours. There were bushes between the trees. Maybe I had been seen entering the woods. But from where? The sun started to die. The darkness rose from the ground, swallowing the last light of the day, the black sky steadily arching overhead as if a monstrous hand were slowly drawing down.

I sat inside the darkness and waited. Far-faint now I heard the squadron going out toward the Cromer light on the Norfolk beaches, climbing steadily toward the North Sea.

There was no sound. The last truck was parked. The Nissen huts were shrouded in darkness.

Then came the sound. At first I thought it was a branch blowing in the wind. Then the sound came again. The air was still. Somebody was walking on hard packed earth path around the Nissen hut.

The beam of a flashlight made a target of light on the wall of the Nissen hut, moved down over the garden, ran along the row of stones quickly and went out.

I got up and sprinted.

The light swung around and hit me square in the eyes. There was no sound, but I heard the bullet zing past and sock into the tree behind me. I dived, lay flat on the ground, and rolled over.

The flashlight beam cut across the blackness and I heard another bullet zing past. Somebody with a silencer. There was no place to go except back in the woods. I would have to make a run for it. If he got the light on me I was finished.

I took a quick look at the light beam coming toward me and whirled running, keeping low, running zig-zag in a crouch. When I hit the brush I busted straight through it. The brush was knee high and I ran full speed, dodging among trees.

I stopped, listened. I could hear the man crashing through the bush. He had turned off the flashlight. I listened again. He was about fifty yards west of me. He kept going west, and after a while there was no sound.

I looked at my watch and waited, listening. I stood there for half an hour, and then walked east. I came out of the woods at the far end of the runway. The field was dark. It would be seven hours before the squadron would return from Nuremberg.

Not smart to return to my barracks. Best thing would be to circle the field, come in from the other side, pick up a bike. There would be lots of bikes parked beside the briefing room.

In an hour I could walk to Mary's house, rather than risk going into the barracks area before light.

I went across the open fields for about two miles. I knew the way to the road, but I checked the North Star anyway, just to make sure. There was a lot of cloud. I didn't feel so badly when I saw all that cloud. It meant the night fighters wouldn't find it so easy to pick up the bombers. Bullshit. If the target information went through from England there would be a roaming fighter operation right over the target, the sky full of blood red and white and yellow chandelier flares, the fighters going right into the flak, the whole bloody sky bright as daylight in the flares. There wouldn't be any vectored fighters off radar except on the bombers going home.

When I got to Mary's house she opened the door and shivered.

'Brr!'

'Meant to call.'

'Come in.'

'I'm off ops.'

'Thank God!'

'I can't stay all night.'

'Come in. Come in.'

She shut the door.

'Mack, what's the matter?'

'Nothing.'

'Yes, there is.'

I told her the story, the part I had not told Barrington.

'You must tell Barrington,' she said.

'And get up the pipe on a murder charge?'

'He'll believe you.'

'Like hell. I just want to stay here until morning.'

I kissed her and she pressed herself hard against me. I walked her into the living room and sat down on the davenport and put my arm around her.

'Not here,' she said. We went upstairs and undressed. When we were in bed she said, 'You have to tell him.'

'I'm not going to jail.'

'Are you sure you shot him?'

'He fell over. It was in the newspapers.'

'What else can you do?'

'Give them the wrong target. I'll pull the wrong stone and they'll come after me. Then I'll nail the guy on the squadron who's sending the information.'

'They'll kill you.'

'They can try.'

I kissed her and felt her hand touch me and I rolled over close against her.

'Do you really love me, Mack?'

'Yes.'

'Do you think of her when we make love?'

'Do you think of him?'

'Go home, Yankee.'

'Don't you like American style?'

'What is American style?'

'What you're doing.'

'Oh-no. This is very English, darling.'

'We invented it.'

'Oh-no. Veddy English. Ah, Mack. That's it. Oh, you darling.'

'Easy.'

'I don't want to. Oh, yes. Right there. Oh, yes. Are American girls different?'

'They think it's a commodity.'

'What do you mean?'

'They keep it on a string.'

'You're crackers. Mack, was she better for you than me?'

'Don't be silly.'

'Don't you lie. Don't you—Ah, Mack. There. Oh, there.'

'You're wonderful.'

'I'm second hand goods.'

'Not to me.'

'Oh, Mack. Go on. Don't stop. Go on. There. There. There.'

'I love you so much, Mary.'

'Go to sleep now, I'll wake you up.'

'I have to be in just before sunrise. The squadron will be coming in then.'

'Go to sleep. Don't worry. I'll wake you in time.'

Chapter 37

I could see the thin light of the morning at the bottom of the sky. The west was all dark and full of stars. Then from faraway in the pink and violet eastern dawn sky I heard the faint drone of Halifax engines. I looked at my watch. It was time they were home.

The air was chilly and across the moors a faint mist blew. I opened the door of the Mess. Inside it was silent. The debriefing officers sat at the long tables. I could feel the silence in the room.

They were all listening for the engines. Pencils and combat report sheets lay on the tables in front of them. A WAAF with a tired face stood beside the piano, her eyes lifted to the far sound.

Soon one bomber roared overhead. It was low. I waited to hear the engines change to course pitch as the machine turned into the down wind leg of the landing pattern. The engines snarled, fading. Maybe another squadron. Then another Halifax passed and went on and another and another. The intelligence officers sipped their white mugs of tea and stared at the walls.

I went over to the control tower. The Wing Commander had the tower microphone in his hand. He was trying to talk down the pilot of P for Peter whose landing gear hydraulic system was riddled by cannon shells.

The Wing Commander said: 'Everybody urinate in the can, and pour it into the system and see if you can pump the under carriage down.'

'We've pissed ourselves dry,' said the pilot. 'All the piss runs out the holes. We're bailing out.'

'How much petrol do you have?'

'Half hour.'

'Stooge around and belly land her when you're about empty.'

'Sir.' The pilot panted a little. Then: 'Yes, sir.'

We listened to the engines fading away to the east, to orbit clearly in the light side of the sky against the home coming machines. We waited and waited. Soon the sky was silent. I went outside. It was dawn. The sun was up drying the grass. The sky was empty, and all the fliers who were coming home had come home. We were missing seven crews. P for Peter had nearly run out of gas and belly landed at Middleton St George.

Shit, I thought, I killed them. They're

all dead. Christ.

I went down to my room. The bastards. There must be some way to get them. Only one way. Give them the wrong target and have them come for me. Make them show their hand. I lay on the bed and thought how to do it without risking my ass. There was no other way. Give them the wrong target. Make them show their hand. Come for my throat.

But at noon when I went to lunch at the Mess there was some better news. Three crews were back in England. Two had gone down in the drink off the Cromer light. The third kite had crashed landed with two wounded at Marston Moor.

It meant only one thing. The squadron wouldn't operate for a couple of days. Maybe a week. But I was wrong. That afternoon the Wing Commander called up the new crews, five new crews who were practising circuits and bumps and told them to do a four hour cross country that night because they would be on ops the next night or the night after.

I called Mary and told her.

'It's rotten,' she said. 'They won't make it through four ops.'

'Did you hear B.B.C?'

'Forty-one bombers missing,' she said.

I was leaning against the wall in the Mess. I didn't say anything. I thought about the B.B.C announcement of the raid. They had lied about casualties. They always lied. The Germans lied. Everybody lied.

I looked around the Mess. There was a gang around the piano singing. 'Roll Me Over, Lay Me Down and Do It Again.' There were others playing shove ha'penny and skittles. Some fliers were reading *News of The World* or leaning against the bar drinking mild and bitter. Nobody could hear me. She ought to know the truth. No, that wasn't fair. But why not? No, it might frighten her, make her feel I could get knocked off. Because I knew the real casualty figures. I had talked to a WAAF who worked in the intelligence office and she had taken it for granted that now as a regular staff instructor I already knew the true casualty figure.

'What a crusher,' I had said.

'An absolute balls up.' She talked like this then; she was some Lord's daughter, the last of the Mayfair pre-war debutantes. She felt she was manly and sophisticated.

'God, four percent,' I said.

'Four percent?' She looked at me. 'More like twenty.'

'I saw the teletype from headquarters. Twenty percent. They sent five hundred aircraft.'

'Jesus, that's a hundred bombers.'

332

'Maybe I shouldn't have told you.'

'I wasn't listening. Maybe he said twenty.'

'Don't say I said so.'

'Forget it.'

Now I put my lips against the mouthpiece of the telephone and whispered to Mary: 'Some of us are lucky.'

'Will you be coming over tonight?'

'I think I better.'

'What time?'

'Right after tea.'

I hung up and went looking for the bartender.

He was in the kitchen. 'Terry,' I said. 'Did anyone come into the Mess alone after take off last night?'

'Aye, there was a bit of a crowd.'

'Anybody use the phone?'

'I hardly noticed. What's up?'

'Nothing much.'

He shook his head.

'Bloody spies they must have around here. It's like Jerry knows what target we're going to prang.'

I looked at him and smiled.

'The place is crawling with spies.'

'Bloody likely, mate.'

The squadron stood down for another night. Then the next morning at weather briefing the crews were told to prepare for an attack on Cologne. That would be about a 4 hour and 20 minute mission. Take off at 1800. They would be coming home shortly after 10 p.m.

I went to the briefing to learn what the diversionary targets would be. Those were the city names I would need. The ribbons across the big wall map showed the diversionary raids: Flensburg, south of Kiel, and some mine laying in the Skattegat, where the German Navy trained, between Sweden and the east shore of Denmark.

After briefing I walked back to Jaynes' garden, and counted the stones. Number twelve represented Flensburg. I wanted only one number. If I pulled two stones it would look like diversionary raids or feints before strikes on a primary target.

I pulled stone number twelve, and walked past stone number six which was Cologne. My mouth was very dry. My legs felt stiff in the thighs. I didn't think my hands were shaking, but I didn't look at them in case somebody was watching with field glasses. I walked slowly over to my Nissen hut and went into my room and sat down on the bed. My legs felt dead, especially my thigh muscles, and sitting there, the muscles started to flutter. I pulled out my kit bag from under the cot and dug out the Webley. It was still loaded. I put the box cartridges in my trouser pocket and the Webley pistol inside my tunic, under my arm pit where I could hold it tight and it wouldn't bulge too much.

I wasn't going near the stones. I wanted to watch the telephone in the Mess. The trouble was there was a telephone box on the road about half a mile from the Mess.

There was still the smell of Spam and eggs from operational tea in the dining room. Regular tea was welsh rarebit and tea.

I went in the lounge and sat down and read the *Daily Mirror,* keeping the wall phone in sight.

I was there half an hour. It would be dark soon. Nobody used the telephone. I was still sitting there when I heard the first engine burst into life and start to revv. It wasn't long until the squadron was off and high over the field, setting course.

Good luck, lads. Good luck. God, don't let the fighters be at Cologne. Let them get sucked off to Flensburg. Oh, there would be some, but the diversionary raids would lead a lot of them north across the sea to Denmark, and they wouldn't get back in time to attack the bombers at Cologne.

I waited in the Mess. I didn't go outside until I heard the first machine returning.

By ten-thirty the whole squadron was home.

'Piece of cake...bloody awful flak...and searchlights...no bloody fighters in the searchlight...piece of cake...' said the voices at briefing.

I rode my bike back to my room, keeping away from the shadows of buildings. There was half a moon shining and some clouds. I pedaled fast when the moon slid behind cloud.

I shut the door to my room and doused the light and lay on the bed and held the Webley in both hands. I drew back the blackout curtain so that just enough moonlight came in to silhouette anybody opening the door. The door was unlocked.

I lay there, starting to sweat under my arms, my mouth dry and my stomach hollow. I felt more scared than during an attack. There was nothing to do but lie there.

I must have fallen asleep. Somebody was knocking on the door. There were other rooms along the corridor. If they were going to kill me, they wouldn't come like this. Or would they? Would it be an accident? Poison? Had they discovered yet they had been double crossed? Would a murderer knock on your door? Who could tell?

'What do you want?'

'Phone in the Mess.'

The voice in the hall sounded familiar.

'Who is it?'

'Mary, she said.'

'No, you.'

'Me. Bert.'

'Thanks, Bert. I was half asleep. Thanks a lot.'

Bert was the bartender. But I wasn't taking any chances. I opened the window. The bottom of the window sill was waist high.

I stuck my head out and looked right and left. The moor stretched flat out, away and treeless. The moon was shining and all was clear. I climbed over the sill and stood there on the ground outside and listened. My bike was on the side of the hut. I tiptoed over the grass and peeked around the corner. All clear. I jumped on the bike.

I rode fast to the Mess. What the hell was she calling me for at this time of night?

The telephone receiver dangled on the cord. I picked it up.

'Hello, Mary?'

'Oh, Mack. I thought you were coming over.'

'I told you. Not tonight.'

'Anything doing?'

'No. It's kind of late, isn't it?'

'Won't you come over, please?'

There was something odd about her voice. I couldn't place it. It sounded natural, yet there was something odd about it. Or was it just having her call this time of night? Maybe she was right. If nothing happened so far, perhaps nothing was going to happen. Why not go over? That might even draw somebody after me. Was this really Mary's voice? Was this a trick?

'Mary, where's my home?'

I had often told her about home.

'Fargo, North Dakota,' she said.

Still her voice sounded odd, strange. I couldn't be sure.

'What river runs near Fargo?'

There was a long pause and then the words rushed over the phone: 'Red... Red... Red... Red... Red...'

Hell, she knew the river. What kind of a mental block did she have all of a sudden?

'Red River,' she said. 'Please come over. I'm terribly lonely tonight. I don't know why.'

'Sure, I'll be right over.'

I hung up, but I stood there a couple of minutes. What was there about her voice that didn't seem normal?

I was halfway out the Mess door when it hit me...'Red...Red...Red...' Or was I dreaming? Did she know that in flying parlance that meant go around again, don't land, get away from the field, go around again?

Jesus, were they holding her to decoy me and then kill us both? Come on. Come on. You're dreaming. But I stood there frightened in a vision of two bloody-headed people, lying in a ditch on the moors, Mary and I. My heart pounded. For a long moment I couldn't move with the knowledge of what might happen.

Then I went straight out the door, running, the Webley out, in my hand, and I was on the bike pedaling crazily, my guts hard and knotted with anger.

The bastards. The bastards. I'd kill them if they touched her.

Chapter 38

But going fast along the road in the dark the anger changed to fear. Looking ahead in the dark, with the moon shining on the road at random intervals, I felt things were going to get worse. I did not know why I felt this just as I never knew why I felt some raids were going to be easy and some rough. Maybe my right guesses were only coincidental, but most of the time I was right even when I was scared.

Now I was ashamed of fear, but there was nothing else to do but to buck on. I tried to generate anger because I knew the fear was based on the fact that what I was getting into maybe could mean my ass, and this thought made me feel miserably ashamed for not thinking of Mary.

Where the anger had given me confidence, the fear filled my guts now with a cold hollow, slimy emptiness, and I felt my thighs getting stiff and my body heavy and my heart pounding.

So I pedaled faster. I knew I was panting. But I couldn't hear it. All I heard was a roaring in my ears that made me feel sick.

I tried to listen to the night sounds, but there was only the whirring of bike wheels. I slowed and stopped, and listened. There was no sound. Silent air. No breeze. Stars cold and frozen.

I started pedaling fast. The road curved in the moonlight and I sped down a hill. In the hollow road there was a cold, ghostly mist. I felt my hand trembling and I gripped the handle bars tighter. The gun butt dug into my palm.

When I was about half way to Mary's house I knew I would pass a high embankment on my right with a wheat field on my left. There were trees along the crest of the embankment.

I was looking up at the embankment. The moon was sailing in and out of clouds, and now it lit up the trees on the embankment.

'Christ,' I thought, 'You're a bloody coward!' I had never used that word about myself before. I had always avoided actually saying it. I had always felt it would hurt too much to tell myself this truth. I was afraid.

But suddenly in saying it I felt better. I was no longer scared. I heard my own breathing again.

But then I smelled something. I still say I smelled something. I had hunted since I was nine years old; deer, antelope, prairie chickens, sharptailed grouse, pheasants, ducks, geese, with the Sioux Indians in North and South Dakota, the Cheyenne River Sioux, the Hunkpapa Sioux of Chief Sitting Bull, the Mnikawanga Sioux of Chief Spotted Eagle.

They told me how their grandfathers could smell the enemy in ambush. I believe them now.

I could smell enemy. Ambush.

A breeze was blowing across the road and the grass in the ditch along the wheat field rippled gently in the wind.

The next thing I heard the *car-ra-wong!*

of a rifle and a second crashing shot, and
turning the bike toward the ditch heard
another blasting explosion from the line
of dark trees and felt the slam of a slug
bite into the front wheel fork of the bike,
and another crash that ripped the air apart
behind my head.

I felt myself flying through the air, and
then I fell flat on my face, still running.
Without stopping I flung myself down
with froth hot as blood in my mouth. I
wanted to get up and run but I crawled
another frozen three feet into the wheat
and lay there.

The gun fired again and I heard it
whunk into the dirt. I screamed and
moaned. It was an old Indian trick. Make
the ambusher think the bullet struck home.

I moaned again and stopped and lay
still, feeling sick at my stomach.

I knew the shooter was watching like a
hunter. I grunted like an animal blood-
choked.

I waited and waited listening. I turned
my head, looked up, but the wheat was
too bright and the sky was cloudless.

My crotch was wet with sweat and my
whole body narrowed with hate.

I longed to find the courage to sit up
and look over the top of the wheat at
the dark line of trees across the road.
I was frozen. But as I lay there I felt

my left hand dig into the earth, like a maddened claw, crunching the soft earth, and it went on doing it until I felt my whole being, fear and sick guts and hate, hardening into fury to rush the sonofabitch.

I felt crazy rage in me for one final charge.

My head jerked up for a fraction of a second.

I saw the man now. He was coming down the cut-bank onto the road, facing me, carrying a rifle. I lifted the Webley, wondering how far he was.

Range, range, I thought, shit, I didn't know anything about pistol range. They issued you the Webley and that was it. Good luck, chaps.

He looked big, silhouetted in the moonlight on the slant of cut-bank. Big shoulders. Body like a beer barrel.

How far? How far?

I raised the Webley. He looked goddamn cool coming across the road. He moved his head right and left, looking, looking.

My balls felt under my chin. Come on, you gutless wonder, I thought. There'll never be another now. Quit stalling. Shoot.

The man was halfway across the road. The clouds were sliding back toward the moon. I reached up with my right hand, and stuck the Webley pistol out over the top of the wheat. I didn't have much time to sight.

His gun flamed in the dark. But I shot straight into his figure before it was dark again on the road. I saw him slump before the moon was gone. I put another two shot burst into the dark, lower, where he had been.

Christ, where was he? I started to crawl through the wheat. I got to the edge of the wheat. I listened. No sound. Was he faking it? He had slumped as if he were truly hit.

I waited a few minutes, then stuck my head out of the wheat and held my breath.

The figure lay still in the middle of the road. The rifle lay beyond his reach. There wasn't any doubt about his having been hit. He was lying face down.

I walked slowly toward him. He moved a little. He was alive. His face was still down. He started crawling, keeping his face down. He hadn't heard me. He was crawling toward his rifle. He knew where it was. I circled around behind him.

'You son of a bitch,' I said and kicked him in the hip. He screamed and rolled over on his back and moaned and flung his hands over his face.

All the cold fear was gone now from

around my heart. Shoot him, I said to myself, but knew I mustn't. I knelt beside him and pulled his hands away from his face.

Jesus!

It was an aircraft mechanic from our squadron. He was a boy. I did not know his name. But I knew his face.

I put the muzzle of the Webley on his skull between his eyes.

'What's happening at her house?' I said. 'Hurry up or I'll blow your head off.'

'They have her,' he said. 'If I don't show up, they'll take her, and if you don't do what you've been told to do, they'll kill her.'

'I'll kill you. Who are you? All you people. What are you up to?'

'I didn't shoot at you for myself. It was for our organization.'

'What organization?'

'Are you going to kill me?' the boy asked.

'I'll let the government do that, but if you don't talk now, I'll kill you.'

'I think you have.'

'Where are you hit?'

He pointed at his stomach. Then I saw the stain just to the right of his belly button. Well, he could move, so his spine was okay.

'Don't move and you won't bleed so

much. What's our organization?' I put the muzzle against his eyeball.

'Revolutionaries. My father was with Mosley. When Germany wins we will do away with all the Churchills, all the phony politicians. All British imperialism. All the dukes and duchesses. The millions who are asked to die for imperialism. There will be no more dole. No breadlines. Hitler gave new life to the common people. He will bring it to this country.'

'Hitler's a gangster,' I said.

'You don't know how rotten these people are. I love England, but Hitler will free us from this upper class tyranny.'

'You silly son of a bitch,' I said, and stepped past him and picked up the rifle, a .303 Lee-Enfield. I went back and rolled him over and felt in his pockets and jerked out two cartridge clips in his tunic pocket while he babbled on about the revolution Hitler would support in England. Somebody had suckered him, the poor Limey bastard. You couldn't blame him, living on the dole all those years, his dad going for the Fascist crap Mosley had preached. But why hadn't Barrington or the Establishment brains had a line on boys like this and their fathers? How had they remained concealed? Maybe Barrington had the answers.

I got my hands under his armpits and

dragged him, moaning and heavy, off the road, and lay him in the weeds in the ditch beside the wheat field.

'Don't let me die,' he said. He had a monkey face, but there was a nice look to it because he was so young.

'You won't die unless they kill me. Then nobody will come back to get you. So long.'

I tried the bike. It worked. I couldn't believe it. I thought the bullet had gone through the front fork and destroyed it. There was only a neat hole right through the fork and a missing spoke. It was the shock and impact of the bullet which had knocked me off.

I jammed the rifle under my left arm and I rested the barrel on the handlebars and stuck the Webley in my back pocket.

Four rifle cartridges in a clip and the Webley was loaded. That made for some fire power. They would be in the house, waiting for their assassin to bring them the good word. The moon was high now and the trees were dark along both sides of the road.

Chapter 39

I had one leg over the garden wall and I hoisted myself up and lay down while I studied the house. There was a light in an upstairs window and one downstairs, but no car in front. I had left the bike in a field about half a block from the house.

I wished I had a drink. I laid the Lee-Enfield flat on top of the wall. The moors were dark all around the house, and the moon was sliding in and out of cloud again. My chest felt cold.

Then I heard her scream. And just as suddenly the scream was cut off.

I studied the windows again. Nobody there unless there was a head below the sill in one of the dark rooms. No time to consider that. I grabbed the rifle, dropped down into the garden and crouched down, watching the house.

Nobody fired at me. I lay down in the garden and squirmed over the flowers out onto the grass. It was dark now. The moon was gone.

I crawled along on my belly and knees and elbows, across a stone walk, over more grass. I was right under the first floor window. It would be the kitchen. Where would they be keeping her? Their car must be in the garage. I untied my shoes and took them off. I wriggled over to the back door. There was a single cement step. I got my butt up on it, and keeping low, reached up for the door handle. I tightened my grip and turned. The knob turned.

The door opened on a short hall off the kitchen. Two steps up the hall and into the kitchen. Why would there be a light in the kitchen unless somebody was there?

I heard radio music, very low. I slid inside. The step creaked faintly. I stopped and waited. No sound in the kitchen. I pushed down hard and got one foot on the first step, holding the rifle high with my right hand so the butt wouldn't strike the step.

I heard a scraping sound in the kitchen and stopped. The noise stopped. Then I had both feet on the hall floor. It was six feet to the kitchen entrance. I tiptoed and came in quickly, the gun up and under my armpit.

Mary was tied to a chair, hands behind her back, ankles tied, her wrists tied behind the chair and a gag in her mouth. Her eyes rolled white and wild. I held up one hand and gestured toward the ground floor ahead and up above. She nodded toward the living room.

349

I went across the kitchen floor softly as an Indian. I looked out through the entrance into the living room. The man was across the room with his back turned toward me. He was alone, looking out the front window. The room was dark. The man was seated on the floor so just part of his head showed over the top of the window sill, but he could see the front lawn and anybody coming through the front gate.

Why wasn't there somebody watching the back way? Then I heard footsteps crossing the floor overhead. The head in the window was outlined clearly. I waited to see if the man upstairs would come down.

There was only one way, flush him out upstairs by shooting down here. Then nail the upstairs man when he came down.

I aimed carefully below the outline of the head. The gun made a tremendous explosion in the closed room. Before the head vanished, I worked the rifle bolt.

I crouched low and waited. Footsteps started down the stairs and stopped half way. The body slumped on the floor. I listened. There was no sound now. I crept into the living room and lay on my stomach. The stairway was on the other side of the room. The moon came out from behind clouds and shone into

350

the room. A pool of light lay in a circle at the foot of the stairs. I held my breath and listened.

Was there an entrance into the kitchen behind me? I didn't remember seeing another door or stairway. I listened and the stairs creaked a little. He was there.

The man was sneaking downstairs. I could hear him on the staircase. He would have to show himself to find me. What kind of a gun did he have? I hoped it wasn't an automatic weapon like a Sten gun. He could spray the room. I lay flat on the floor, the rifle on the floor and the Webley in my right hand. I would have to flush him out and reveal myself.

I lefted the Lee-Enfield and fired into the staircase wall that concealed him. He sprang up. I saw him against the moonlight. He fired an automatic weapon over me, a short burst. His head and shoulders were above the staircase wall. I shot twice at his chest. He fell down the stairs and flopped out on the living room floor.

I didn't move. He didn't move. I lay there waiting for him to move. He didn't make any sound. I started to get up and the room exploded and a hot shocking blow hit me in the guts. The sonofabitch by the window wasn't dead. I sat down suddenly. I had been shot before. It always felt as if somebody had hit me with a hammer.

I still had the Webley in my right hand. I cursed him and shot at him twice. I could see his gun flashes and heard the bullets socking into the wall behind me. He was down for good. I crawled over to him, but not before I shot him twice. I flipped him over. It was Paul Phillips. 'You son of a bitch,' I said. 'I thought you were dead.' He sure acted dead now. He wasn't breathing.

I felt my side. Right in the old guts. Well, if that's all it was, a guy could spare a few feet of gut. But the bleeding was bad now. I put my hand over the hole. It was a little hole and my whole side was wet. I felt in back. It hadn't gone through.

I crawled over toward the kitchen door. I felt weaker than hell as I crawled through the doorway. I got over to the kitchen table and felt as if I were going to faint but I was surprised to find I had enough strength to reach up for the drawer handle on the kitchen table. I pulled the drawer open and I think I fainted for a couple of minutes.

I woke, lying face down on the kitchen floor under the open kitchen table drawer. I felt nauseated as I reached up inside the drawer, but I found it, fumbling around in the drawer. It was only a kitchen knife.

Maybe it would be enough. Screwed, I thought, I'm screwed. There was blood all over the floor. Well, maybe better this way than a lot of internal bleeding.

I got on my hands and knees and crawled over to the chair where Mary was. Then feeling faint and weak again, I got around behind her, and kneeling, hacked at the rope around her wrists.

I hacked and held my breath, knowing it wouldn't stop the bleeding. I felt myself sagging from side to side. I had never felt so sick. I hacked at the rope and Mary screamed and I got hold of her arms with my left hand and held on and sliced until the knife went through the rope around her wrists.

Then my head ballooned and I passed out.

Chapter 40

'You fool,' Barrington said. 'You almost killed Seymour.'

'That was the idea,' I said.

'Barrington sat beside my hospital bed. 'We need him.'

'Thanks a lot,' I said.

'You'll be all right. Why didn't you

tell us about London? Seymour and Company?'

'And get sent up for murder?'

'They framed you nicely,' Barrington smiled. 'You didn't kill that game keeper. They set you up. They shot him from behind. You were much too far away.'

'They had me by the balls. Who is Seymour? What is he?'

'Well, strangely enough, we thought we had dossiers on all of Mosley's Fascists, but we didn't. There was an entire underground, recruited to operate during the war. They never showed at any of the demonstrations before the war. Seymour was the controller. They had all classes, rich, poor, anybody who was bitter and felt he was superior. Divided into cells. Just like the Commies. Only Seymour knew the head of each cell.'

'Where did I hit him?'

'You almost killed him. Lung.'

'Will you hang him?' I asked.

'Not likely,' he said. 'He's going to make a fine double agent. We've made him a deal. He works for us and feeds whatever false information we want him to send.'

'How was it sent? Who was telephoned about the stones so Jerry knew our targets?'

'Little pub in York. Bartender came over here twenty five years ago. Good papers.'

'But what are the Germans going to

think when Seymour says he can't get the name of the targets through anymore?'

'Oh, he has another wireless in London. He's already told them in Germany that his contacts in the RAF have been caught and cut off. He won't start sending anything for a month. Told them he's laying low.'

'Are they going to believe it?'

'It's worth a try.'

'Who's our chap in Germany who radios the German colors of the day to us?'

'He's gone. They caught him.'

'Why did they try to kill me in London?'

'Jaynes told them you had spotted him the night you were in headquarters office stealing some passes. He thought his cover was blown. When he told them you were around asking questions about who had voted against the defecting to Sweden when he had told you he had voted to defect, he figured after you deserted you might have told the other members of the crew that somebody was lying about the vote, so they started killing off members of the crew to keep Jaynes covered.'

'Lots of accidents.'

'They were all "accidents". But what scared Jaynes about his cover was your seeing him in the orderly room that night.'

'I didn't know at first who it was.'

'Then nothing happened, so they figured you hadn't really seen him or didn't care or didn't know why he was there. It was pure luck Seymour ran into you on the train. He was trying to get Jaynes to find out more about the navigation Gee Box because it was a new device. That's why he was up in York.'

'What about Peter Dickson's uncle? Rodger Belton?'

'Just an eccentric old recluse.'

'Beryl?'

'They used her but never told her anything. Seymour kept giving her good parts in shows. She delivered messages for them. Then she started putting two and two together. I don't think she ever really had Seymour figured out, but she was getting suspicious. So they killed her.'

'Jesus Christ,' I said. 'The sons of bitches. How long am I going to be in here?'

'They only removed a foot of your intestine. You'll be fit in three weeks. What are your plans?' Barrington asked.

'I wish I knew.'

They took the stitches out two weeks later and I was walking slowly when Mary came to the hospital and we strolled in the Norfolk woods. Then suddenly it was a year later: a new war. Or it felt that way. I was posted to the Squadron as gunnery officer. We were married and lived in

Mary's house. It was spring again and we were sitting out in the garden.

'Do you want to go home after the war?' she asked. The air was almost summery under the beech trees.

'I don't know.'

'Would I have to become an American citizen?'

'That would be up to you,' I said.

I looked up through the beech leaves, thinking of time. The high sky shimmered. 'I used to be young,' I thought. Now I was twenty-six. I wondered if I would get used to work and children and a home, and nine to five at the office.

The next afternoon I went to Squadron briefing. All the faces were new, boy faces in blue battle dress. They eyed me strangely.

I sat there, looking at them, the rows of new faces. To me they were unreal. It seemed that long ago in a dream I had sat as they were sitting, busy with their maps and pencils.

After briefing I went out to the Control Tower to watch take off, the big, black Halifaxes lined up, their engines idling, at the mouth of the runway, waiting for the green flare from the tower. I looked out at the trees along the edge of the field, the leaves stirring against the evening sky.

'I am not dead,' I thought, staring

up at the sky, the trees, the aeroplanes taxiing into line, and then I saw the first one speeding broadsides to us, moving fast, then sky between the ground and the machine. I watched them all go off, lonely, puny vanishing specks against the rising darkness.

Now in the attic at home back in the States, the blue uniform, sprayed every spring with moth-killer, a little dusty, unpressed, looks ancient in this age of speed and steel helmeted jet pilots. The goggles and dust covered leather flying helmet on the attic closet hook beside the uniform look like museum pieces.

Mary tells me I ought to jog more or cut down on beer and play more tennis in the summer. But tonight I sit on the porch steps and sprinkle the lawn. It's nice to sit here waggling the hose feeling the pleasant lift of a second martini. But some evenings when the air is a green sea and there is a feeling of no time, only that moment of suspension just before the light rushes into the emerald green of twilight, then in that moment I wonder again. The feeling of guilt is there in me again after all those years, the guilt that will never go away completely, and I am alone with my thoughts of those who died when I ran away. The elms along the street stir in the wind and they say, 'You—you are not dead.' Were we all only figures in a masque?

When I think like this, alone, after a while a great calmness comes over me. The trees loom like silent apparitions, somehow speaking to me in the wind of time, until a stillness within the night seems to hold suddenly an old and unattainable happiness and the trees say, they say, 'You—you are forgiven. You are forgiven.'

But even if this dream were to become a reality, it is too late, because I know the thoughts of that dead time of betrayal will always bring a melancholy that make the summer night almost unbearable for an instant.

I snap on the porch light and go inside.

This Large Print Book for the Partially sighted, who cannot read normal print, is published under the auspices of

THE ULVERSCROFT FOUNDATION

THE ULVERSCROFT FOUNDATION

. . . we hope that you have enjoyed this Large Print Book. Please think for a moment about those people who have worse eyesight problems than you . . . and are unable to even read or enjoy Large Print, without great difficulty.

You can help them by sending a donation, large or small to:

**The Ulverscroft Foundation,
1, The Green, Bradgate Road,
Anstey, Leicestershire, LE7 7FU,
England.**
or request a copy of our brochure for more details.

The Foundation will use all your help to assist those people who are handicapped by various sight problems and need special attention.

Thank you very much for your help.

Other MAGNA Mystery Titles
In Large Print

ANN GRANGER
Say It With Poison

ROBERT BARNARD
A Fatal Attachment

PETER ROBINSON
A Necessary End

SARAH DUNANT
Birth Marks

ELLIS PETERS
A Nice Derangement Of Epitaphs

W. J. BURLEY
Wycliffe And The Dead Flautist

KEITH MILES
Double Eagle